OF ATTACK

ANGLE

ANGLE
OF
ATTACK

BY JOSEPH LANDON

DOUBLEDAY & COMPANY, INC., GARDEN CITY, N.Y., 1952

Library of Congress Catalog Card Number: 52–5535

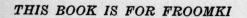

THIS BOOK IS FOR FROOMKI

*The incident upon which this book is based
is known to every man who flew Heavy Bombard-
ment in the European Theater during World War
II. By now it has taken on the nature of a
legend, for though each knows of it, none can
agree where or to whom it happened. As it
appears in this book it is a synthesis of many
impressions. The missions described in the
book are based on personal experience; only
the characters are invented. If they bear any
resemblance to any person, living or dead,
it is purely coincidental.* J.L.

ANGLE

OF ATTACK

1 The land beneath the Spur was held by the great estates and partitioned by long ranks of poplars into the classic checkerboard of orchard and farmland and vineyard. All through the spring and late into summer it had remained a region of blending semitones, pale with age and clay-colored, but now, as its fifth July of war ended, the earth quickened with growing things. In the gaunt orchards the slow-formed fruit flecked the trees with bits of brilliance. The vines in their harsh geometric rows were beginning to bend and promise grace as the grapes filled and colored. And the wind wheeling in from the Adriatic to ripple the grain fields revealed virginal green being transformed into richer gold.

From Cerignola the road curved south and east, threading its way in leisurely loops to Spinazzola, where it joined the main highway to Taranto and the sea. It was a dirt road, deep-rutted and cushioned with a layer of white talcum-like dust. Stone walls divided it from the quilted fields, and these walls were of the fields and very old. Bordering some stretches, they ran evenly, as high as a man's waist; along others they had crumbled away and gone back to the earth. Half a mile south of Cerignola, rising abruptly from the flatness of the landscape, a slaughterhouse stood in the elbow formed by a lane converging with this road. Built originally from a native stone of garish hue, the two-story building and the walls of its enclosing courtyard had weathered with the years until now its color was between pale pink and ivory.

Win Helman abandoned his strolling pace as he approached the slaughterhouse. A fetid odor penetrated his nostrils and he hesitated, arrested by the stink. Then, with sudden decision, he snatched off his cap and ran. Long-legged and graceful, he covered ground swiftly. At the end of fifty yards he came to a halt, stumbling on the road's uneven surface and gasping for air. He laughed aloud in self-derision. Avoiding the smell had not been the only reason for the sudden sprint. Primarily it had served him as a test to see how far he could run while holding his breath. Feeling foolish, he turned to see if he had been observed. From the direction of town a cloud of dust billowed toward him. He replaced his cap at its customarily rakish angle and waited.

Finally an army staff car came into sight from behind the slaughterhouse and picked up speed. As the car bore down on him, Win saw that the driver was an enlisted man, but by the time he had discovered that the passenger seated in the back wore the silver leaves of a lieutenant colonel, it was too late. He had already raised his right hand, thumb outstretched. The car came on without diminishing speed, and the colonel, mistaking the gesture, saluted smartly as it passed.

When the dust had settled, Win went over and sat down on the stone wall that bordered the road. He lit a cigarette and made himself comfortable, laughing aloud when he thought of what had just happened. It fitted perfectly with how good he felt. He decided not to move until he was offered a ride. There was no need for him to hurry back to the base. It was a fine day. The afternoon sun was well past its meridian, patterning the whole countryside in alternate bands of golden light and shadow. It was very quiet along the road. High up against the

Italian blue of the sky a B-24 droned along, slow-flying its engines, and the sound augmented his feeling of tranquillity, seeming more a pastoral, native thing than anything alien or mechanical. He felt far, far removed from the war.

Win glanced down at the new silver bar on his collar that glistened in startling contrast to the rest of his uniform and insignia. First Lt. Irwin Helman, he thought, grinning, and lazily his mind went back to the night that had just passed. It had been good, and it was still good now, when he thought about it. He had celebrated the promotion alone, celebrated the pride he felt, the pride he would have had to depreciate as was the custom had he stayed on the base and done his drinking in the officers' club. Instead, he had gone in to town, and he thought now of the men in the wine shop whom he had not known before that night, and of the amount of wine they had consumed together. He remembered how, much later, he had wandered out alone into the narrow cobbled side streets of the town and found that it had undergone a metamorphosis in the moonlight, making it unfamiliar and mysterious. And how, near the cathedral, he had seen the woman and had gone to help her, not even thinking it strange that it was well past midnight and that she looked as unconcerned as if she were returning from market in broad noon. He remembered how she smiled at him when he helped her carry the string baskets bulging with cheeses, walking beside her and thinking she was old and fat and respectable. And how he had changed his mind while following her up to her apartment, watching the abundant fruity swing of her haunches as she mounted the stairs in front of him. She had been neither old nor fat nor overly respectable. He had taken his clothes off first, and he remembered how she had looked at him. And how she had stood before him while she undressed and let down the great aromatic masses of her hair and got under the sheets beside him. He remembered her swelling bosom and her white, pillar-like thighs, and the flesh firm yet yielding. And her hunger—her frantic, incredible hunger.

And when he had wakened late in the morning, in that strange room, the first thing that had popped into his head was an essay he had read long ago, written by Benjamin Franklin and entitled something like, "Advice to a Young Man on Selecting a Mistress." And when he had gotten out of bed and seen his pressed uniform hanging across a chair, and then enjoyed the breakfast of fresh eggs and good warm bread and tomatoes and cheese, he had silently toasted the Old Man from Philadelphia.

Now, seated on the wall in the mellow sunshine, he felt indulged and contented. He flicked away his cigarette and stretched luxuriously. His eyes half closed against the sun, he was on the brink of drifting back into the daydream when an army six-by-six pulled up and the driver sang out: "Wan' a ride, Lieutenant?"

The 902nd Bomb Group (Heavy) was based six and a half miles south of Cerignola. The airstrip that serviced the group consisted of two parallel runways four thousand feet in length, one covered with steel matting and the other with blacktop. A perimeter track, elliptical in shape and dotted with enough revetments to accommodate sixty Consolidated B-24 type Liberator bombers, embraced the two runways. At the northern end stood Group Headquarters: administrative buildings, quarters for the group staff, and a big barnlike structure with a vaulted roof that was used as a briefing hall. The three squadrons that comprised the group lay outside the circumference of the ellipse, each clustered around its own nucleus of permanent buildings.

The 1240th Squadron, one of the three combat components of the group, was encamped adjacent to the road, its tent area sprawled in an irregular pattern to avoid the sodden green hollow that dipped away from the eastern end of the perimeter strip. The enlisted men lived on the side closest to the road, separated from the tents quartering their officers by the squadron mess hall. Except for the size of the tents, there was little difference between the two sections; the whole area bore the raw, unfinished look of a bivouac. The ingenious devices rigged up by the men in their attempts to create comfort and order failed to dispel the feeling of impermanence. Only the slit trenches, half filled with rubbish, recorded the tenure of the squadron. It was July of 1944, and for many months no strafing German planes had appeared over that section of Italy.

Win Helman jumped off the back of the truck while it was slowing for a stop. He shouted his thanks to the driver and started down into the squadron area, heading toward a tent distinguished from the rest by an imposing duralumin door. The door, reflecting the slanted sunlight like a mirror, stood propped open and he heard the men in the tent arguing. He stepped quietly into its hot half gloom and a voice roared: "*Attention!*"

As his eyes adjusted themselves to the whorls of floating dust and cigarette smoke that gleamed iridescent where bars of sunlight lanced through the canvas, Win saw that the six lounging figures were frozen where they lay. Nobody stood up. They were lying at attention, sitting at attention, and waist gunner Polletti was crouched at attention beside his cot.

"As you were, men," Win said gravely. "As you were. Sergeant Chicereno, give me General Order Number Three."

A dark chunky boy with black hair cut so short it looked like shadow began chanting: "Corporal of the Guard, Corporal of the Guard, I got to go take a——"

"Thank you, Sergeant. You win a cigar." Win extracted a bunch of cigars from his breast pocket and handed one to Chicereno. "And because everybody else was so much on the ball, everybody else gets one." Nodding solemnly to each in turn, he distributed the rest of the cigars.

Milbank, the engineer, made room on his cot and Win sat down beside him. It was silent in the tent while everybody lit up.

"That dentist's daughter up in Melfi have a baby?" Chicereno asked politely. "I was just wonderin', because if she did maybe we all better hand out some cigars."

Win ignored him. "What was all the yelling about?" he asked Milbank. "I could hear Chic up on the road."

The engineer chuckled. He was a tall, lean man with an Indian's high cheekbones and hawk nose. A thin scar bisected the left side of his face, beginning from the eye socket and disappearing into the hair behind his left ear. The lobe of that ear was missing.

"Chic's sayin' how he's gonna take off his uniform when he gets home and put on his blue chalkstripe," Milbank said in his soft drawl. "Twenty-seven inches in the knee and seventeen in the cuff. I say he'll be draped out like a New Orleans pimp."

"Well, that's better than them cardboard suits you wear in Tex-ass," Polletti said heatedly. "Ain't it, Win?"

"Leave me out of it, I don't want to be in the middle." He recognized the old argument, the old alignment of forces. Chicereno, Polletti, and Macchione, all from Pennsylvania, against Milbank. Reilly, the radio operator, who had worn overalls most of his life before entering the Army and now wore fatigues every chance he got was terribly interested in the whole new world being opened before him; he watched the debate like a tennis match.

"Ask Buck," Win said. "Don't ask me."

Buck Rogers moved his big, bulky body into a more comfortable position on his bunk and grunted. He was twenty-five years old and he looked like a slightly blurred image of the blond, taut young gods who appeared on Air Force recruiting posters. Rogers was superior to the whole discussion. The boys around Hollywood High in Los Angeles had long ago said the last word on the subject.

"Come on, Win," Reilly urged, his young face serious. "You're from New York. Is twenty-seven and seventeen too sharp?"

"Maybe Win gets his clothes up in Harlem," Rogers called out. "I hear all the latest New York styles are set up in jig town."

"Shut up, Buck." Reilly was annoyed at the interruption. "What do you say, Win?"

Win turned to face Rogers and a beam of violent sunlight struck the new bar on his collar, highlighting its brilliance. He hesitated, waiting to see if there would be any reaction. Macchione was on his feet instantly.

"That bar's silver," he said. "You made first."

Win nodded.

Macchione came toward him, his hand outstretched. He looked older than his twenty-seven years and it was primarily because he took himself so seriously, trying to achieve a kind of dignity, yet never sure whether he was succeeding. "Congratulations, Lieutenant," he said solemnly.

"Thanks, Gene," Win said, grasping Macchione's hand. Chicereno and Polletti crowded around, followed by Reilly, all of them grinning happily. Milbank stood up and put his hand on Win's arm. The new first lieutenant was embarrassed. This was one of the things he had been thinking about in connection with the promotion, one of the good things, and now that it was happening he was embarrassed.

"How do they promote navigators?" Chic asked. "How many times you got to get lost before they promote you to colonel?"

"Win never got us lost," Reilly said seriously.

"Aw shut up, you farmer."

"Well, I may be a farmer all right, but tell me one time he got us lost."

"O.K., O.K., forget it."

Win looked over at Rogers. The big gunner slowly unfolded himself and got up. Watching him, Win remembered when Rogers had first come to the crew in Tucson. He had told them immediately that he was a washed-out pilot, making a point of his bitterness. But the thing Win remembered best was how he had looked. Even then, five or six short months after his personal debacle, Rogers had no longer been quite thin, had begun to look blurred. The apparent outline of bone in cheek and chin and shoulder had softened. Watching him now, Win realized that the softening had ripened into grossness. The clean sculptured lines were obliterated.

Rogers lowered his eyes under Win's measuring gaze. He stood awkwardly in the middle of the tent, pushing his undershirt into his trousers. The other men were aware of his hesitation. He removed the cigar from between his teeth. "Nice going, Win," he said lamely.

"Thanks, Buck." Win smiled at them. There wasn't anything left to say. He started out of the tent. "I'll see you guys later," he called over his shoulder.

"Attention!" Chic screamed.

Win turned at the door. They were all rigid, their faces expressionless. Grinning, he raised his right hand with the fist clenched and middle finger extended. Then he turned smartly and left the tent.

The tent that Win shared with the other three officers of his crew was located upon the only surviving patch of grass in the whole squadron area. Standing on a slight rise, it was a little apart from the others, yet not too far from the generator that supplied electric power to the squadron. The tent itself was neat. The pyramidically sloped canvas sides were held rigid by taut guy lines. The short wooden walk that led up to the tent flap was symmetrical and in good repair. To one side, however, on the edge of the grass, there sprawled a huge, improvised reclining chair. It was really a caricature of a chair, a frame constructed of wood salvaged from engine crates that supported a seat and back of foam·rubber. The man who had built it had tailored its dimensions to accommodate his own formidable bulk. Zymbrowski had been his name and he had been the squadron's first commanding officer. Now he and his crew were dead, their airplane having exploded in the sky over Wiener Neustadt. The crew was pretty well forgotten, but the chair he had built and the grass he had cared for was part of a living memorial to the commanding officer.

Win walked past the chair, running his hand absent-mindedly over the foam-rubber back. He heard the men talking, Bane saying something about wishing he had an adz, and then the sound of hammering. He walked around the tent. Bane and Lange were crouched on their knees finishing the construction of a floor. Matthew Jones, the copilot, was sweeping up. They had built a square wooden frame matching the floor area of the tent and nailed flat boards of differing lengths and widths over it. But only three quarters of the frame had been covered with flooring. One quarter had not been touched and bare earth completed the square. Win recognized that the unfinished section corresponded to the corner of the tent where his cot stood, and suddenly the day's accumulated good feeling dropped away, leaving him· stripped and vulnerable. He watched them in silence. Jones saw him·first.

"Here's the wonder boy," the big copilot said. "Back just in time to miss all the work."

Albert Sidney Bane and Philip Lange, pilot and bombardier, looked up from their busy hammering. Illogically, Win was struck by how alike they seemed. Yet there was no real reason for this. They were roughly the same size, but there the similarity ended. Lange was very blond. His hair was like bleached straw and his complexion pink. He was twenty-nine years old, the oldest man on the crew, but he shaved only once a week.

Still he looked his age. It was because of his manner, the precise way he handled himself, as if he felt himself to be of great worth. And he kept himself immaculate. Even now, the green fatigues he•had been working in all day were spotless and uncreased. Bane, on the other hand, was twenty-four years old; a sandy-haired, serious-looking man who seemed sallow and a little faded beside the bombardier's brightness. He had a long straight nose and squint wrinkles around his light gray eyes that made him look perpetually harassed.

Examining them, Win realized that his reaction was similar to the one people had when they looked at couples who had been married for a long time. It made him smile in spite of himself.

"Who's the husband and who's the wife?" he asked.

They stared at him in surprise.

"What the hell are you talking about?" Lange asked petulantly. "You look sober."

"I'm sober all right." Win let himself down on his haunches. "What the hell was all the rush about? It's only July. You expecting it to snow?"

Matthew Jones came over and stood beside the pilot and bombardier. He had let down the top half of his fatigues and belted the sleeves around his middle, leaving him stripped to the waist. Standing almost two inches over six feet in height, his massive body was classical in its proportions. Win knew that Jones had been drunk, sodden-sick drunk, every night of the last two and a half months, yet his body had absorbed it all and remained in perfect condition. The only traces of deterioration appeared in his face, in the bloodshot eyes and flaccid skin. This, plus a nose that had been broken and badly set, and substantial but cosmetically unimaginative bridgework in the front of his mouth, made him reminiscent of a battered, carousing Roman gladiator. He moved with the same ponderous gait.

"You lazy bugger," he said, his accents a mixture of Tennessee drawl and the bad bridgework, "we tol' you we was goin' to start layin' the floor today. The geechees are comin' with the stone tomorrow."

"O.K., so you're started."

Matt grinned. "You bet we started. We not only started, we finished too."

"Then what are you bitching about? You want me to congratulate you?" Win turned to Bane. "That's my corner, isn't it, Al?"

"It sure is." Lange answered for the pilot. "Are you going to finish it up?"

"No, I like the grass."

"Come on, Win," Bane said. "You go on down to the line an' get you some more wood. We'll give you a hand."

"Like hell we will!" Matt broke in. "We been workin' since eight this mornin' and he ain' done nothin'. He didn' help us."

Win looked up at him and the big copilot grinned. His broken nose, the result of four years of football at the University of Tennessee, gave him a look of unmitigated ferocity. Bane and Lange were watching them now and Win remembered that lately, whenever he and Jones raised their voices at each other, everybody within hearing stopped what they were doing and listened. Looking up at the crooked go-to-hell grin, he knew that the copilot was aware of what was happening. Win stood up and took a cigarette from his breast pocket. He lit it carefully.

"Don't you worry about it, Matt," he said levelly. "I'm not asking you for any help. And I'm not building any floor either."

"Well, then you can sleep on the ground," Lange broke in angrily. "If you want to live like a pig it's all right with us."

"Thanks."

"Come on now, Win, don' be so hard-headed," Bane said mildly.

"Crap! You guys can lock yourselves in one of those stone cribs if you want, not me. I'm satisfied to stay in the tent."

"You can' do that," Bane said reasonably. "You know we are gonna take that tent and stretch it ovah the walls when they're built."

Win was silent. He was afraid that his hurt was becoming evident. The cigarette between his lips was bitter to the taste and he spat it out. Lately it always ended the same way, he thought angrily. Whatever he did he was in the wrong. Unless he went along completely, agreed to everything, there was the constant bickering. And today especially he had wanted everything to be pleasant and easy.

"Go on now, Win," Bane said patiently. "There's a whole heap of empty cases down on the line."

"Listen," he answered with deliberate harshness, for the urge to go along, the stirrings of retreat were beginning within him, "if you guys want the goddamned floor so bad, build it."

He turned on his heel and stalked away toward the officers' club.

Jesse, the sergeant who served as bartender, was setting out the galvanized iron tub with its melting cake of ice, ready to cool beer and cokes, when Win stomped into the club. It was after five o'clock and soon the before-dinner drinkers would be gathering, each with his own fifth of Old Crow or Old Granddad. These were the bourbon-and-water and bourbon-and-coke drinkers, the men who frugally husbanded their monthly ration of a fifth of stateside whisky, taking one drink a day before dinner and making the fifth last all month.

And they were allied, these planners, with the beer drinkers and the straight coke drinkers, for to cool the coke and beer required careful organization and thorough investigation of the wry economics of war. The plan finally devised ran true to character; it demanded self-denial as well as moderation.

There was an air force custom that every man returning from a mission received a shot of hundred-proof Old Overholt. But there was competition in the dispensation of stimulants to the returners from missions. Outside of the S-2 office, where inter- rogation was conducted, the Red Cross doughnut girls set up shop, dispensing smiles, doughnuts, and coffee in the winter- time, and smiles, doughnuts, and lemonade in the warmer months. So the planners, the beer drinkers, and the before- dinner bourbon-and-coke drinkers, the edge taken off their need by the ministrations of the Red Cross, passed up their shot of Old Overholt and instead poured it into a community bottle. For it happened that the first sergeant in charge of Cerignola's only ice-making plant was not only a before-dinner drinker, but an after-dinner drinker and a before-and-after breakfast drinker as well. And this same first sergeant took con- suming delight in the hundred-proof Old Overholt, all of which provided fertile ground for an agreement. In exchange for the accumulated after-mission shots he saw to it that ice was delivered to the squadron, the ice that was used nightly to cool the beer and coke. The arrangement was fair and just and it promoted better understanding between the ground echelon and the fliers.

There were in addition, of course, those officers who drank their whole monthly ration of American whisky the night it was issued. These men also drank the shots that were issued after every mission, sometimes even managing to convince those of their crews who shared in the community pooling to break faith. And for the rest of the month these drinkers drank the native gin and grapefruit juice or cherry brandy and grape- fruit juice. Quite often they even poached on the beer tub and finally the honor system had been modified so that every man scratched his initials on his can of beer before lowering it into the ice water. For beer, too, was scarce; the ration consisted of four beers or four cokes a week.

George Macy was seated at the poker table which stood in the far corner from the bar. The table was piled high with enlisted men's mail waiting to be censored before being mailed. Macy was working swiftly, with a kind of organized, controlled anger, signing his name and serial number on one envelope after another without as much as a glance at what was inside. He looked up without stopping his work as Win came toward him.

"A slip of the lip can sink a ship," Macy said seriously, in his low-pitched, soft voice. "And a guilty conscience needs no accuser. And congratulations."

"On what?"

"On being promoted. Welcome to the select fraternity of first lieutenants."

Win sat down across the table from him. "Thanks," he said absently. He had forgotten momentarily. The business of the promotion and all of the feeling connected with it was now submerged under the impact of his encounter with the other officers on his crew.

Macy went on working with the same sustained speed. Watching him, Win had a sudden intuitive feeling that Macy was the man with whom he could have celebrated. Macy would have understood. But Win knew too that he could not have extended the invitation, for he was unsure of how it would have been received. Macy was a strange man. Like sitting there alone, getting the mail out. Some of the letters had been lying on the poker table for a week or more, waiting to be censored before they could be sent out. So Macy did the job, not talking about it, not criticizing, just doing it in his angry but controlled way. He was angry all of the time, Win realized, like a man who carried violence bottled up within himself and was consequently under constant, rigid control. But still it showed, and set him apart, for it made one wonder what he was straining against, what it was he was keeping so carefully leashed. It was impossible for Macy to relax. Even when he was in repose it seemed that he was waiting for something to happen, marking time. He moved with the considered grace of a very powerful man and this somehow made him seem bigger than he really was. Actually, he was only a little over medium height, but his upper body, his shoulders, chest, and arms, were massively developed. His features were rugged. The hair clustered close to his head in tight curls, growing down into a deep widow's peak. His thick eyebrows almost met, and together with the triangle of hair on his forehead gave his face a watching, focused look.

"You want a drink?" Win asked finally, standing up.

Macy shook his head. "The bar's closed. Like on election day."

"How come?" Win looked over at Jesse and the bartender nodded.

"There's a big meeting over in the mess hall, Lieutenant. All flight personnel. You two ought to be over there right now."

Macy shrugged his shoulders without looking up, still signing letter after letter. Win shifted from foot to foot. Macy glanced up and smiled his slow sad smile at him.

"Grab a pen for a while," he said. "Then we'll go over together."

An enlisted man with a carbine cradled awkwardly in his arms was posted outside the mess hall. The squadron first sergeant stood beside him with a roster. He checked off Win's and Macy's names before allowing them to enter.

Inside it was low-ceilinged and cool. Before its conversion the mess hall had been a stable. Now the spacious whitewashed interior was divided into two sections by the exposed kitchen equipment. To the right there were two long tables and one short one arranged in a U. This was where the officers sat. The other two thirds of the room was filled with the enlisted men's tables. On the walls, all around the room, were painted fat red bombs. Each one was labeled for a target: *Gjurgjevac, Sarajevo, Athens, Belgrade, Ploesti, Vienna, Klagenfurt, Munich, Toulon, Friedrichshafen, Ferrara, Budapest* . . . The last bomb, *Wiener Neustadt,* was edged in black. It was the only one so marked. Underneath it was lettered the name Zymbrowski.

"Hey, Lieutenant!" a voice called and Win and Macy both turned toward the enlisted men.

"Not you, the *first* lieutenant!" the voice called again, and Win saw Chic and Polletti and Milbank and the rest of the gunners grinning at him. He waved to them and followed Macy over to find a seat in the officers' section.

Most of the chairs around the U-shaped table were taken. Win saw Lange and Bane sitting together listening to something Matt Jones was saying. In spite of himself a part of his mind registered that they had not saved him a seat. He sat down next to Macy and lit a cigarette. The screen door opened violently and the first sergeant came in and yelled: "Attention!"

The men rose and faced the door. Abbot came in followed by Captain Grover and Doc Parker, the flight surgeon.

"All present and accounted for, sir," the first sergeant said and saluted.

Abbot returned his salute and thanked him. The first sergeant executed a smart regular army about-face and went out. A wave of jeering laughter from the flight crews greeted this performance, but it died abruptly when the heavy wooden doors swung to with a crash, plunging the mess hall into semidarkness. The double doors had been open day and night since early April. Standing there in the gloom, the lighted cigarette cupped in his hand, Win remembered the enlisted man posted outside with the carbine in his arms. He turned to Macy but he was standing facing straight ahead and didn't notice. Just then the lights were switched on.

"Rest, sit down," Abbot said quietly. He stood without moving, his hands hanging naturally at his sides, waiting for the scraping of chairs on the stone floor to subside. There were major's insignia on his collar for the first time and already they looked old, as if he had worn them always. This same paradox, this old-young theme ran through his whole personality, through everything he did. He was only twenty-four years old yet looked ten years older. He had started getting bald when he was nineteen, the year he entered West Point, and now the whole top of his head was naked. All that remained of his reddish hair was a symmetrical band above the ears and around the back, not unlike a monk's tonsure. He was wearing G.I. khaki with epaulets sewed on. The uniform was faded almost white from its many washings. He was the only man in the room wearing a tie.

"Settle down now," Abbot said. "There are a couple of things I have to say to you that I didn't want you to see on the bulletin board or hear in the latrine. You're going to hear it all from me. That's the way it'll be from now on. When you hear it from me, it's official. If you hear it any place else—it's crap.

"First of all, I now officially command the squadron. Captain Grover is operations officer. The next thing is that the tour length is being changed . . ."

There was an instant reaction and Abbot raised his voice for the first time.

"The number of missions is being *lowered* from fifty to thirty-five. There will be no more double-credit missions. Everything will count the same. The tour will consist of a straight thirty-five trips over the target. And that goes for all the ones you've already flown. They all count for one. Captain Grover has the list of everybody's missions figured up the new way. After chow you all can go over to Operations and check your totals. Any questions?"

The hum of conversation started low, like a dynamo beginning to rotate. Then the men were talking out loud, not listening to one another, each one trying to put articulate sounds to his own confusion. They had prepared themselves for anger, but now that outlet had been short-circuited. Thirty-five *was* less than fifty. Still, they were suspicious. Even the most optimistic among them could not reconcile this seeming fact with previous experience. Here was the Army, gratuitously making things easier for them.

"Any questions?" Abbot asked again.

"Anything official on Zymbrowski?"

"What was that? I couldn't hear. Stand up when you ask a question," Abbot said, irritation seeping into his voice.

George Macy stood up. "I asked if anything official had come through on Zymbrowski."

The mess hall grew quiet. Abbot could feel them waiting for his answer and he knew he had been wrong to think that taking over the squadron would be routine. He had served as Zymbrowski's operations officer from the beginning, and thinking back, he remembered the many times he had thought of the squadron as his own. Zymbrowski had left him more than his share of the work and it had been easy to think of himself as its real leader. His eyes went to the black-edged bomb. *Big Ski, the man who farts and shakes the world,* he thought bitterly. An apt title and more than just a figure of speech. Looking around, Abbot could see how much Zymbrowski was reflected in the men: in their uncut hair and two- and three-day-old beards, in their carelessly rolled sleeves, in the low-cut Natal boots they wore (without socks, no doubt, for Zymbrowski had often said that socks, and the constant washing they required, were a waste of time).

"Major Zymbrowski has been officially listed as missing in action," Abbot said, and was surprised at how confident and matter-of-fact his voice sounded in his own ears. "There won't be anything further until a complete canvas of German P.O.W.

camps is finished. The Red Cross is on it now. Anything else?"

The silence held for a moment, then a bombardier named Brand got up.

"You mean Ploesti and Munich and places like that are gonna count only one from now on?"

"That's right," Abbot told him, glad to be off the subject of Zymbrowski. "Northern Italy, Yugoslavia, Hungary—everything counts for one—if you drop on the target. But we only have to fly thirty-five instead of fifty."

"And we lose all of our credited doubles?"

"No, we don't lose them, they count for one," Abbot said pleasantly. He watched Brand sit down slowly, his lips moving as he figured back. "The rest of you bombardiers got that straight—or you want to go get your computers?"

There was a splatter of nervous laughter that built and Abbot allowed himself a smile. He knew he was over the hump.

"O.K.," he said, "let's eat. And while you're all feeling so good, there's a mission in the morning. The crews flying'll be posted in Operations."

He turned away from the men, and followed by the flight surgeon and Captain Grover, made his way to the bend in the U which served as the head for both of the officers' tables.

Win calculated rapidly. He had thirty-seven missions the old way; thirteen doubles worth twenty-six, and eleven singles. He had had thirteen missions left to fly. Adding up his actual times over the target came to twenty-four, leaving only eleven the new way. Eleven the new way, thirteen the old—it didn't look bad at all. He turned to Macy. "How do you make out?"

"I get screwed the same as you," Macy said, smiling with his mouth but the rest of his face cold, "the same as everyone else."

"What d'you mean, screwed? I had thirteen left, now I only got eleven."

"That's how it looks—but figure it again."

Win stared at him. "You mean I made a mistake?"

Macy nodded.

One of the Italian boys who waited on the officers' tables put a plate down in front of Win. He saw that they had pork again, pork and dehydrated turnips, and he pushed the plate away from him. The whole corner of the table was listening to them by now. None of them were eating. Win felt a sudden stab of panic. Maybe he . . .

"Listen," he said, figuring out loud, "I had thirty-seven missions. That left thirteen to go. The thirty-seven made twenty-four trips over the target. That leaves——"

"You're forgetting something," Macy interrupted.

"What?"

"The joker. What they call the gimmick."

Now the whole U-shaped table was listening. The conversation, the questions and answers, echoed their own suspicions. For the Army suddenly to relent and allow them to go back home earlier, without exacting full payment, was more than they could accept. They all wanted to accept it, wanted it with yearning that was like pain, but it was illogical.

"What's eatin' you, Macy?" Captain Grover called from the head of the table where he sat between Abbot and the flight surgeon. "What're you bitching about now?"

"I'm not bitching, Captain," Macy answered, his deep voice loud for all to hear, "I'm just tryin' to show the boys how figures can lie."

"What in hell d'you mean by that?"

Grover was on his feet. He and Macy had come overseas together as members of Zymbrowski's crew. They still flew together on lead missions, Grover as Abbot's copilot and Macy as lead navigator. Both of them had been away on flak leave to Capri the week Zymbrowski had gone down.

Macy pointed to the wall behind Grover's head. "Turn around

and take a look," he said. "You can figure it out for yourself. Look at the last six targets: Vienna, Ploesti, Gleiwitz, Augsburg, Linz, and Wiener Neustadt. Do you by any chance notice any kind of a trend?"

Grover turned back to face down the table. "So what?" he asked.

"So they're all doubles, that's what. And that's probably how they'll be from now on."

Macy turned and without lowering his voice spoke directly to Win. "So you're getting screwed. You only got eleven left the new way instead of thirteen. But what if all eleven are doubles? Does it still look like a good deal?"

Win shook his head and Macy turned back toward the head of the table. The flight surgeon tugged at Grover's sleeve and he sat down. The men, following Macy's gaze, turned their attention to Abbot. The major went on with his methodical chewing. Not once during the entire exchange had he raised his head or given any indication of interest. Even Grover looked at him now. Abbot swallowed a bite, taking his time, and the expectant men saw his Adam's apple bob.

"You picking the targets now, Macy?" he said finally. "I always thought your job was to try to find the target and then try to find your way back."

Macy didn't answer. He looked down, saw his plate for the first time, hesitated, then sat down and began eating. Everybody switched their eyes to him but he continued eating, as if unaware that they were waiting for him to keep the discussion alive and somehow allay their uneasiness. It was silent around the U-shaped table. The flat authority in Abbot's voice had made an impression, and one by one the men looked away. But the silence held and the tension was unabated.

Win felt his impotency. He wanted an opening, an opportunity to ally himself with Macy against the others, but none came. And he could make none of his own. He pushed his plate farther from him and lit a cigarette. Beside him Macy ate stolidly, showing no sign of hurry. Finally he was finished and Win pushed his chair back from the table. Macy smiled and they stood up and left the mess hall together.

Outside the twilight was purpling into night and they walked slowly, eyes on the uneven ground. Without speaking they moved toward the operations hut. Inside the C.Q. sat alone behind the desk, eating his dinner from a mess kit. They went up to the bulletin board. Win saw that his crew was posted for the next morning's mission. They were leading Easy box. Abbot's name headed the list, flying squadron lead. Macy's name was right under his.

"Ass-end Charley again," Win said, more for something to say than because his crew's position in the formation worried him. He needed to talk to Macy, needed to explain away his failure to take sides against Grover and Abbot. His guilt was even more urgent because of his confusion. He didn't know what he should have said or done—only that he should not have sat silently by while Macy stood alone. "You want to check the mission totals?" he asked tentatively.

"Not now."

Win remembered the three cigars still in his breast pocket. They were the ones he had bought for Bane and Phil Lange and Matt Jones. He took two from his pocket and held them out.

"Here, have a couple of cigars."

"Thanks." Macy smiled and took one, sniffed it appreciatively, and put it carefully away. "I'll save it for briefing. Now I think I'll hit the sack. See you in the morning."

Win stood in the doorway. Men were beginning to come out of the mess hall. The enlisted men carried their mess kits to the G.I. cans filled with boiling water. Most of the officers were coming toward Operations. He looked at his watch and saw that it was almost eight o'clock. He started over toward the officers' club, then changed his mind and cut across to his tent.

Win flicked on the switch and the tent was illuminated by the bulb hanging from the center pole. It was pleasant inside, cool and smelling of sun-baked canvas. He went over to his cot and unzippered the mosquito netting so he could sit down. The low-hanging, unshaded bulb was still swaying, and the disproportionate shadows it cast swayed with it. A cicada blundered into the tent and then found its way unerringly to the light source. It bumped its head against the bulb, producing a dry feathery tapping. Win lay back on his cot and as he stretched became aware of how tired he was. He relaxed for a moment, enjoying the rare privacy, then rose and began his preparations for the morning's mission.

From the foot locker beside his cot he took a pair of brown oxfords. They were the same shoes he had worn the day he was inducted into the Army. Back in March he had gone thirty miles to Bari to have them resoled with leather fully three quarters of an inch thick. The same shoemaker had sold him a pair of leather laces two feet long. These were to be wrapped around and tied above his ankles so the shoes wouldn't come off if he had to parachute from the airplane. The thick soles were designed to absorb the many miles he would have to walk if he ever went down in Occupied Europe and avoided capture. It was all part of the plan he had formed in the first third of his tour. The regular high G.I. shoes would be a dead giveaway, he had reasoned. As part of the same plan he had had a thick red corduroy shirt sent to him from home. The pants he now laid out were a pair of regulation officer's pinks. He had worn them steadily since O.T.U. in Tucson and now they were so marred with grease and dirt as to be completely unrecognizable. He took two pairs of socks, one white wool and the other black silk, from the foot locker and stuffed them into the fleece-lined flying boots he would be wearing over his oxfords. In the side pocket of the pinks he put a six-inch-long spring button knife. In the watch pocket he placed the stolen dog tag and his four fifty-dollar bills. He laid out a suit of long winter underwear, checked his map and instrument case, and was finished. He undressed quickly, switched off the light and got into the sleeping bag that lay on his cot.

Lying there in the gentle darkness, Win went consciously to the familiar fantasy he had spent so many hours creating. But tonight something caught him up, held him, and he wondered if it was being faced with accepting the possibility of the waking dream becoming reality. And this held him. Not that he feared the ending of illusion. From its conception he had couched the fantasy in concrete terms, every expectation capable of practical fulfillment, its very life dependent upon eventual conversion to reality. He knew exactly what he would be wearing for the homecoming; he could see the pinks and battle jacket complete with bars and ribbons and wings. He knew how much the taxi fare from Grand Central Station to Brownsville would be. He could picture himself entering the tenement, smell (not imagine) its reek of too many people in not enough space. He could see (not picture) his mother and sister when they embraced, see how their eyes would look and how their lips would be shaped. He could move through the warmth of the first evening, pass through the first days spent among the family, gathering the emolument accruing to him from his new position. He could start the discovery of the city (the biggest city in the world) in which he had been born and lived all of his life until the war without ever knowing. He knew the restaurants (couldn't taste the food, how could he?) that he would go to for the first time, the plays he would see, the wonderful girls he would meet, the heretofore only fleetingly glimpsed parts of the city he would plumb—secure, always secure and unfailing in the ribbons and bars and wings. He could—but he couldn't, it was meaningless, the life-giving detail

lacking. And he tried again. *Only ten left after tomorrow's.*
OVER THE HUMP . . . But it was no good and he was thinking about Macy's smiling bitterness and the tour change and
what did it mean? Were they really goosing the odds, jacking
up the vigerage, cutting an extra round for the house? Would
they, just when he had a chance to beat it? And then he was
remembering back through the phases of feeling that had corresponded with his different stages of progress through the
tour. He thought how it had been at first, when they had
arrived at the group. How vague and unreal and completely undefined. FIFTY MISSIONS TO FLY. Then he had gone on his
first, and how separate it had been; how he had secretly scoffed
at the black puffs of smoke that had appeared, blossomed,
then drifted through the formation. And then the flash of red-
orange flame that had appeared in front of them right before
bombs away. He had ducked as it swept past them and then
looked to see if anyone had noticed his fear. When they had
landed he had asked the experienced man who had flown for
Bane that day, asked him casually if there had been rockets
shot up at the formation. And the man had looked at him
strangely and said rockets? no, that was Wagner blowing up
and no 'chutes, and Win had known then that some had died.
Then Chic had yelled to them to come see the two jagged
rips in the wing, the larger one fully eight inches in diameter.
Still, it had been disassociated, unreal, but someone *had* died,
and he remembered Wagner, a slow-spoken gaunt man who
wrote letters all the time. . . .

And how after six missions, when he had himself witnessed
the frigid butchery of fighter attack, what they had to go
through began to take on shape and substance, and he had
known then that he had to find some way to stop his mind or
go mad. FORTY-FOUR TO GO. It had seemed longer than all
of his life that had gone before. The end had been farther
away than imagination or hope could bridge, and he had or-

dered his mind, compartmented it to keep the limits undefined and vaguely in the future. He had refused to think of the end and had bent himself to think only of the day, of the individual mission, of how best to become hard and tempered and uncaring. But the hope, as much as he denied it, held it in abeyance, was there on the fringes of his consciousness. So he had laughed and said well, we'll be here the rest of our lives. And someone else had said that's right, one way or another, one way or another. . . .

Win heard voices and footsteps approaching the tent. He turned over to face the tent wall. Bane and Phil Lange came in. One of them switched on the light and he heard their voices change as they discovered him under the mosquito netting. He lay perfectly still.

"He asleep?" Bane asked softly.

"He ought to be. He was probably shacked up with some geechee pig all last night."

Bane giggled, and Win, his eyes closed, pictured Bane's face: the solemn expression, the deep-etched worry lines around the eyes, and the incongruous sound of the small-boy snicker. They didn't talk for a while and Win was able, from long intimacy, to follow the progress of their getting ready for bed. Lying there, feigning sleep, he began to doze. When he awoke it was dark in the tent.

"Phil," Al Bane called softly. "Phil, you still up?"

"Yes. What's the matter now?"

Bane sighed. "Ah keep thinkin', and Ah can't sleep. We're sure to make it by Christmas the new way, Ah think, then Ah remember what that Macy was sayin'. You reckon it might turn out the way he says?"

"It might."

"Yeah. He sure was right about the last few. They sure was bastards——"

Lange changed position irritably. "Everybody knows that, but that doesn't prove he's right. How the hell can he know what'll happen?"

"Ah guess he don'——"

"Then what's he bitching about? He isn't any different than anybody else around here. We all want to get finished and get out of this filthy hole. I want to get home, that's all I care about."

"Me too, but that ain't what Ah mean——"

"Look, Al, let's get some sleep."

Bane said nothing. Win had been sleeping on his right arm and it stung. He rolled over to a more comfortable position. The illuminated dial of his wrist watch showed after midnight. They would be getting up in a couple of hours, he thought sadly, and now he concentrated on getting to sleep.

A few minutes later he heard someone approaching the tent. The footsteps were loud and unsteady, and he knew it was Matt Jones. After much fumbling with the latch the door opened and Matt stumbled in. For a while he groped around for the light switch, talking to himself steadily but incoherently. Whenever he was drunk the copilot breathed through his mouth and the rasping intake of breath fuzzed his words. Finally he found the switch but nothing happened. The power had been shut off. With a sigh he lurched in the general direction of his cot and began undressing. It was the business of taking off his pants that gave Matt the most trouble. Instead of sitting down he would balance himself on one foot and try to pull the pants over his shoes. Then he would fall. Still mumbling to himself, without anger, he would pick himself up and repeat the operation. Sometimes it took as long as half an hour. At first, early in the tour, Win or Bane had gotten up to help. Now all three of them lay there, all awake, all listening, all trying to get back to sleep. Finally Matt grunted in satisfaction and crawled into his cot. Immediately he began to snore.

"Matt! Hey, Matt!" Lange called angrily. "Turn over!"

The snoring stopped and the big man heaved himself to his side. It grew quiet in the tent.

2 Win came awake and although it was not a violent sudden thing, the hang-over of fear was present. Lying still in his sweat-soaked sleeping bag he heard the C.Q. on the boards outside the next tent. The gross tremor of his shuddering was gone and he was cold. He knew that it was probably the noise that had brought him out of sleep, yet the other was there too. Then he remembered. It was the dream, the only recurring dream he ever had, the only one that always adhered to the same pattern.

There was only a minute before the C.Q. would be coming into the tent. He went back over it. He had never been able to pin down when it had started. Way back when he had been a little boy, when his father and mother had still lived together, he had dreamed it . . .

They were crossing the Brooklyn Bridge in the 1927 Buick. The driver's seat was fixed into the floor like an easy chair and he was sitting in the little drop seat beside it, the one that folded so people could get into the back. Just the two of them, his father and him. It was the year he was seven years old; somehow he remembered that. It was in the middle of winter, about five o'clock in the evening, and the polar twilight, hazy and ice-bearing, stained the air. They were high up on the tall narrow bridge. The cobbled roadway was a sheet of ice and the car slewed from side to side. They were driving on the inside, riding the trolley tracks, and every time the wheels came into contact with the glass-smooth rails the car lurched. Halfway across the bridge they were halted. A long line of horse-drawn wagons was being re-routed from the outside lane to theirs. They crawled along in low gear and finally he saw it up ahead, a wagon turned sideways and the huge white horse fallen in the traces. Then, magically, it was all very close and he saw the sweat-steaming beast's frenzy, its abortive efforts to rise, and the fear was transmitted whole into him. His father jammed the car into higher gear and swung into the now empty outside lane. The car skidded as it gathered traction and at that moment the horse, half up on his feet, had fallen again, the hoofs lashing out. As the car slid broadside to the barrier he saw the flailing hoofs and the river cold and far below him, and he was falling. Actually falling. His breath stopped. It was just a second and then he heard his father laugh and he realized that his agonized face was turned where it could be seen. His father asked him if he was scared and he shook his head no, and a second later he was laughing too. But inside him he was still falling.

That's how it ended; always the same. Even now, when it was somehow connected with flying, its pattern never varied. It's true that now the airplanes were in it, that the cold was not only the cold of winter in New York, but the cold of flying at twenty thousand feet as well. That the falling was falling from an airplane as well as falling from the bridge. But he never saw any airplanes in the dream, only the bridge and the river cold and far below. And so it had become his fear. He never dreamed of the flak, of the B-24 exploding, of twenty-millimeter shells tearing into him, of burning alive and smelling his own roasting flesh. The only thing he dreamed was the falling, straight down to the river cold and far below.

The C.Q.'s steps were on the boards outside their tent. Win heard the door unlatch and saw the searchlight's finger groping for the light bulb that hung suspended from the center pole. Then the light came on and the C.Q. was urging them to get up. Win looked at his watch and saw that it was three-thirty. "How's the weather?" he asked automatically.

"Fine." The C.Q. checked his list and started out. "Briefing at four-fifteen."

From long experience they kept out of each other's way, co-ordinating their movements to give each in turn the use of the water tap outside the tent. It was damp rather than cold, yet they all shivered as they dressed, not speaking except for periodic calls to the still inert Jones. Matt was on his back again and snoring fiercely. Every few minutes Bane shook him. The big man would open his eyes, blink, close them again, and the snoring would resume.

Phil Lange stooped down beside Matt's cot and put his mouth close to the copilot's ear. "Matt, get up! Briefing's in fifteen minutes. Come on, get up!"

There was no reaction, then Matt opened his eyes and stared blankly at the bombardier.

"Come on, it's getting late. Get up!"

The copilot grunted and turned his face to the tent wall.

"Goddammit, get up! This is the last time I call you."

Matt heaved himself out of his sleeping bag and dropped his legs to the floor. He tottered on the edge of the cot, stupid with sleep, his eyes unfocused. His tongue went helplessly over his parched lips. Bane laughed and Matt looked up at him, first uncomprehendingly, then reproachfully.

"Ah'm up," he said to Lange, who was still crouching near him. "There's no call for you-all to yell like that. Ah don' feel too good." Sighing, he got up and left the tent.

Win checked to see if he had everything, then followed the copilot outside. It was still night. A hundred yards away the brightly lit mess hall cast a circle of soft yellow light into the area. On the flight line the initial hesitant thunder of starting engines began and the ground moved beneath his feet. Soon their roar would fill the air all down the Boot from Foggia to Lecce. He paused to light the first cigarette of the morning and in the flare of his lighter he saw Matt standing huge and naked at the washstand that was improvised from a P-38 belly tank. The copilot was blowing lustily as he poured a helmet full of water over his head. Before Win extinguished the lighter he saw Matt drop the empty helmet and crouch to place his head directly below the tap. He heard his feral moan as the water gushed out full force. Win grimaced in wonderment. It had been this way every morning for the past two months. Once they had come out of the tent to find him lying naked in the mud under the tap, the tank emptied and Matt fallen back into sleep.

Win started over toward the mess hall. Groping his way in the darkness, he tripped and fell painfully to his knees. He cursed aloud as he struggled back to his feet. He had fallen over the raised wooden floor that they had built the day before, the floor for the stone hut that was to replace their tent, the three-quarters-finished floor that had provided him with graphic evidence of his exclusion. Shivering with anger now, he resumed his way through the darkness to the mess hall.

Briefing was in a high, windowless building that had been the estate's private winery. Its conversion had transformed it into a theater. There was a waist-high wooden stage at one end and rows of backless metal seats. In the middle aisle between the seats, where the estate's coat of arms was mosaicked into the cement floor, stood a slide projector. Over the stage, stretching the entire width of the arch, was hung a twelve-foot-square conic projection of the European continent. The group's rendezvous area was circled in blue, and thrusting up out of it into the body of Occupied Europe ran a line of red tape. The line ended at that day's target.

Win arrived with the first truckload of officers from the squadron. Entrance into the briefing hall was through a low tunnel-like door, and there was always a queue, for as each man ducked his head into the room, he turned, without straightening up, to see how far in the red line ran. Waiting outside, Win listened to the muttered curses and felt his stomach contract. Nothing ever prepares you for where the line goes, he thought. Even when the target was part of the muttering, and you heard it, you were shocked anew when you saw it for yourself. Like being told the ocean is cold and then feeling the first impact for yourself when you dove. Finally it was his turn and he ducked his head into the light and saw the red line reaching out deep into Rumania. Oh Christ no, not again, he thought, moving toward the stage to be sure. Maybe it'll be Brasov this time, or even Bucharest.

"Old faithful," someone said.

The line ended at Ploesti. Win looked down and saw that it was Macy who had spoken. He was sitting in the first row that was reserved for lead crews.

"Not again," Win said.

"Sure." Macy was smoking a cigar. He took a puff and arranged his face into solemn lines. "Oil, my boy," he said.

"Yeah, but how many times do we have to keep going back for it?"

Macy blew a smoke ring. "Very strategic material, oil."

"Shit! What's our altitude?"

"Twenty-one thousand."

"Well, I guess it could be worse."

"Gillespie predicts the flak will be heavy, intense, and accurate."

Win laughed bitterly. "And he ought to know. Wasn't he up there with Cain on the low-level job?"

Macy nodded judiciously. He blew another smoke ring and they both watched it get sucked away into the draft from the open door. "Very high-class cigar," Macy said, and smiled.

"I still got two left," Win told him. "We can smoke them after dinner tonight." He stood there, looking absently at the rapidly filling room. "Well, I'll see you later."

Bane and Lange had come in and he went over to sit with them. The room was almost full. The last unorganized minutes of the morning were slipping away, leaving time tight within the grip of the schedule. From now until they returned every minute was accounted for. The close-huddled men shifted about uneasily, but there was very little talk. Then the projectionist mounted the stage and lowered a white screen in front of the map. Major Warren Gillespie, the group S-2, jumped up on the stage. At exactly 0415 hours the lights went out. The major called for the first slide. The room grew hushed as an aerial photograph of the vast oil-producing installation appeared on the screen.

In a precise, carefully modulated voice, Gillespie described the general target area. Using a long wooden pointer, he indicated the differences between the actual refinery buildings and their camouflaged dummies. He traced the pattern of railroad and road, showing them how they could be used to positively identify essential units. He pointed out the specific landmarks that could not be disguised. Then he asked if there were any questions. There were none. In the darkness someone shifted nervously, scraping a metal seat on the cement floor and the nerve-wrenching screech sent its reaction around the room.

The next slide was a blown-up section of map representing the same area, showing the Initial Point and bomb run. When it had been on the screen for a few seconds and its message became plain, an angry muttering went up from the men. The I.P. was a railroad bridge spanning the Ialomita River twenty-three miles northwest of the target. Flying at one hundred and sixty miles per hour indicated air speed, it would take the bombers eight minutes to complete the bomb run. During those minutes there would be no way for them to escape their punishment, for they would be flying straight and level, never varying their altitude or direction. The hundreds of guns concentrated in the target area would have more than ample time to track them before they could release their bombs.

Gillespie stood motionless in the white beam of the projector, holding his pointer like a cane. Then, ignoring the angry rumble, in his ordinary tone of voice, he described the flak pattern in detail, outlining the area that the guns commanded, enumerating density and caliber. Finally he traced the direction of their sweeping, dipping turn after bombs away and marked the rally point where they were to regroup and set their course for the return home. Finished, still oblivious to the muttering that had grown in intensity throughout his lecture, he asked again for questions. The muttering faded, fell short of articulation, but he remained where he was, perfectly relaxed. When it had grown silent, he left the stage and switched on the lights.

"It's a double, sure enough," Bane said sadly. His solemn face with its boy's eyes surrounded by a web of sun-squint and worry lines was turned to Win.

"Yeah, and it looks like a bitch."

"That makes it seven doubles in a row."

"Well, what did you expect after they changed the tour," Win said irritably. "They'll probably be doubles from now on."

"You really think so?"

"Why not? This way they get two for the price of one." And then he saw how worried Bane's face looked and he was sorry. "Ah, maybe they won't be," he made amends. "Maybe they'll ease up. We got plenty of altitude for this one, anyway."

Bane sighed. "What d'you think, Phil?" he asked the bombardier.

"I don't. I'm not the one with the crystal ball. All I'm interested in is trying to hear the briefing."

"Excuse me," Win said and turned back to the stage.

Gillespie had given over his pointer to the group meteorologist, who was explaining the weather. A shy, scholarly-looking captain with an untidy mustache and G.I. steel-rimmed spectacles, his manner was diffident, at times apologetic. In a voice so faint that the men had to strain to hear it, he spoke of semi-permanent highs and continent-sized air masses funneling down from the Arctic. He predicted normal summer fair weather cumulus between six and eight thousand feet building to twelve thousand in the afternoon. There would be some cirrus over the target area, he said, but not more than two-tenths coverage. They could assume that bombing would be visual. Winds aloft as recorded in the flight plan were most probably accurate and could be relied upon due to the general stability of the current weather over Europe, he said, and stopped talking. With a bob of his head that just missed being a bow, he handed the pointer back to Gillespie and left the stage.

The navigation briefing came next and Win was busy recording the flight plan. The whole mission had been worked out in advance from meteorological data: the true course on each leg, winds at different altitudes, ground speeds, elapsed time for each leg, and E.T.A.s for each of the turn points. After leaving rendezvous, flying third position in the wing formation, the group would set a northeast course across the Adriatic, making landfall north of Dubrovnik. At that point they would alter course slightly for the leg across Yugoslavia, skirting the flak areas of Sarajevo and Belgrade, pointed directly toward Budapest, thus alerting that city. Thirty-five miles north of Belgrade, where the Tisa River forked with the Danube, they would swing east into Rumania. Here they would parallel the spine of the Transylvanian Alps, feinting toward Brasov.

Then, at the Rosul Pass, they would swing southeast in their last turn to the I.P. on the river above Ploesti.

After the flight plan had been read and recorded, the men co-ordinated their watches and briefing was finished. The men rose and pushed their way outside to the trucks that were waiting to take them to the bombers. It was 0500 hours. Start engine time was 0520.

The sun had not yet risen and the morning was windless, without movement. There was a pink glow in the eastern sky that spilled over the horizon and was reflected on the underside of the few puff clouds that hung motionless over the field. The dun-colored B-24 squatting toadlike on its tricycle landing gear was without life, without grace, even without strength; a thing of the earth, not of the upper air. Flying, its gear retracted and concealed within itself, the airplane had a kind of slow majesty, a kind of power through sheer bulk. On the ground it was a hulking machine of metal and plastic and rubber, its too narrow wing seeming insufficient for the support of its deep, boxlike fuselage, its four propellers completely inadequate for lifting its thirty-five tons from the runway.

The enlisted men of the crew were already at the revetment when the truck from briefing stopped to drop off the pilot, bombardier, and navigator. Milbank, the engineer, was high up on the wing, checking the gas caps. The other five were lying on the ground, smoking.

"We start engines in about ten minutes," Bane called to them. "You seen Matt yet?"

"He's taking the cure," Chicereno said. "He was here before us."

Lange called Macchione, who was the crew's armorer as well as ball gunner, and they disappeared into the open bomb bay to check the arming vanes on the bombs. Bane walked around the airplane to get in from the left side. He did this simply, as he did on every other mission morning, and none of them would ever have known that this was his fetish, if once, when they had already started engines and were waiting to taxi out, he hadn't suddenly unstrapped himself from his seat, let himself down to the ground through the bomb bay, and walked completely around the plane to re-enter it.

Win paused at the edge of the revetment to take a few last drags from his cigarette. He squatted down on his haunches and put his hand on Reilly's shoulder for support. The boy smiled shyly at him.

"How does it look, Win?" Polletti asked.

He turned so that he was facing all of them. They were ready to listen and he saw their willingness and their anxiety. Each was controlling it in his own way. Rogers was sprawled full length on the ground, his lips pursed, feigning boredom. Reilly wore a wooden, remote expression. Chicereno had a grin on his face that was more grimace than laughter. Only Polletti was frankly frowning. Win suddenly understood, with a sympathy he had never felt before, that they too had begun to think of the end of the tour; that they too had begun to hope for home in a conscious fashion, and he knew how this made each mission still to be faced infinitely more frightening.

"We been there before," he said finally. "They only got around three hundred guns."

"*Only!*"

He smiled. "Listen, we don't make any mistakes and we won't have any trouble. The same as all the times before. You got to keep your eyes open all the way. You got to keep those goddamned turrets turning all the time. You got to be sure and stay off the interphone on the bomb run. And, Chic, you got to keep Bane posted on how the formation is. Even if he forgets to ask you. We're leading Easy box and we got to keep everybody tucked in for our own good."

"The prayer meetin' all done?"

Win looked up and saw Jack Milbank crouched on the tip of the wing, grinning down on them.

"Yeah, we're all done, but that reminds me." He turned to Polletti. "If we get hit and Jack has to fix something, you got to cover both waist guns. Now let's go. We're starting engines in a couple of minutes."

Climbing up through the bomb bay, Win told Phil Lange that he would do his navigation from the flight deck, leaving the crowded nose compartment to the bombardier. Bane was in his seat, parachute on, finishing up his preliminary check list. Matt, slouched in the copilot's seat, was holding his oxygen mask to his face and breathing deeply. The therapeutic effects of oxygen on hang-overs had been discovered accidentally, but its potency had been widely circulated and now it was in constant use.

Win laid his chest pack, heated jacket, oxygen mask, and navigation equipment down under the radio table, lodging it securely. He put on his parachute harness, and then pulled himself up and out through the open escape hatch to perch on top of the fuselage. He leaned back against the plexiglass dome of the Martin turret and brought his legs up to stretch them out comfortably in front of him. Looking down through the glassed-in portion above the pilots' seats, he saw Matt take a last deep breath from the oxygen mask and then put it in his lap.

Win checked his watch and saw that there was a little over a minute left before start engines. During this fragment of time, as he sat drinking in the freshness of the morning, he indulged himself in the small routine that had become *his* fetish. This pre-mission regimen had no special sequence of rationale or fixed litany. Part of it he had already accomplished while talking to the gunners. His insistence on not making mistakes, on each man keying himself to a high pitch of efficiency, was one component. It was the method with which he tried, with a semblance of logic, to control the seemingly aimless and unreasoning fate that decided where in the formation exploding flak took its toll. The other part, and the main reason that he did not remain within the airplane, cramped in among the others on the flight deck, was to achieve the privacy he needed in order to offer his own personal vows.

The auxiliary power unit began its raucous clatter. The ground crew took their places, fire extinguishers ready. The number-three propeller kicked over, jerked, then disappeared into a glittering arc as the engine caught and roared, sending its vibration through the entire airframe. In rapid succession the other engines came to life. The chocks were removed from the wheels. On signal the B-24 inched out of its revetment and waddled onto the perimeter strip. From all over the field the bombers were taxiing to the foot of the runways. Win remained where he was, bracing himself against the bucking of the huge plane, until they were stopped in the long line waiting for take-off. As the B-24 in front aligned itself with the runway, its slip stream pelted him with loose earth and gravel.

"*I wish I come back,*" he said aloud and the words were snatched up in the thunder of engines. He said it simply, without particular emphasis, not to God and not entirely to himself, but to articulate a whole rush of need that he could not fill with reasoning. Then he lowered himself down onto the flight deck and slammed the hatch shut. For him this enclosing of himself in the airplane was the real beginning of the mission.

Minutes later, at 0540, their turn came. The bomber bumped onto the runway and swung around. Bane brought all four throttles forward to their stops. The big plane gathered momentum and eased its weight off its nose wheel. With his usual caution, Bane held the B-24 on the ground as long as possible, using the maximum of runway. Then they were airborne.

The group's rendezvous area centered on the mountain towns of Melfi and Lavello roughly eighteen miles southwest of the base. The B-24s rose from the runways at one-minute intervals and climbed away from the field in slow spirals. The other two groups of the wing had taken off earlier and were almost finished arraying themselves in formation. The forty-odd bombers of the lead group, formed in overlapping diamonds of seven airplanes each, had reached an altitude of eight thousand feet. Altitude and time were now the dominant factors. As the individual echelons circled for height, it was necessary that they ascend slowly, utilizing moderate power settings and proportionately conservative consumption of fuel. There was no opportunity for relaxation among the crews as the B-24s jockeyed for position. The sun had risen in a round red ball and the air was turbulent. The ever present danger of mid-air collision was enhanced by the constant circling.

At 0640 the lead group of the wing, having reached twelve thousand feet, left the rendezvous area. The other two groups followed in train. Climbing in a long, gently upward slope, they crossed the Adriatic, made their landfall, and started the long leg across Yugoslavia.

Win had been working steadily, and as they passed over the coast he was far enough ahead to relax. They were at sixteen thousand feet and most of the crew was already on oxygen. He had the nether half of the flight deck to himself. Up front, Bane and Jones were leaning back in their seats. The airplane was flying on automatic pilot and every few moments Bane leaned forward to make a minute adjustment. This was their last respite from tension. Crossing Yugoslavia their danger would increase steadily. Drawing ever closer to the borders of Hungary and Rumania, threatening Budapest, they would soon be within range of the German fighters stationed in the Lake Balaton area. Win sighed. From where he sat he could look out through the front windshield and see the massed phalanx of bombers that made up the group. Above his head the Martin turret turned unceasingly. The bottom half of the turret that supported Reilly by means of a bicycle-like seat and steel stirrups was suspended down into the area of the flight deck. One of the gunner's fleece-lined boots was not fastened all the way. Win reached over and pulled the zipper closed, but Reilly's headless, shoulderless torso did not interrupt its slow revolutions as the turret turned. Looking back at his log, Win saw that it was time to testfire the guns. He called Bane on the interphone, told him, then called each of the gunners in turn. A few moments later, as he was fitting his oxygen mask over his face, the lulling drone of the engines was obliterated by the hammering of ten fifty-caliber machine guns. The last quiet phase of the mission was over.

3

The group's thirty-seven bombers, arrayed in six tight boxes, were deep in Rumania. They had reached twenty-one thousand feet, their bombing altitude, flying through soft yellow sunlight and cloudless blue sky. Beneath them the valleys of the Transylvanian Alps were giving up their shadow as the sun mounted toward noon. Ahead of them lay Rosul Pass, where they would make the last turn before I.P. There was no longer any deception in the mission; they were committed for Ploesti, and in all of the bombers there was present that fearful, supercharged alertness that characterized the last hour before target.

Three thousand feet above the group, flying top cover, the escort of P-38s pirouetted gracefully, their normally bizarre silhouettes further distorted by the belly tanks they carried.

They saw the German fighters first.

Holding formation as the wedge of Messerschmitts converged slowly upon the B-24s below, the P-38s waited to see if the Germans really meant to attack. The escort commander was faced with a delicate decision. If he dropped his belly tanks and dove to the attack—and the Me-109s veered off without accepting combat—it would mean that the bombers would be forced to proceed the rest of the way unescorted, since the

P-38s did not have enough gas in their own tanks to take them all the way and back. He was trapped in the inflexible proportion of time and altitude. The closer the Germans came, the longer he waited as they gained height, the nearer he came to losing the advantage of being able to hurtle down on them from a superior altitude if they should have to be fought. As the Messerschmitts climbed closer another factor entered the proportion, one which made the escort commander's three-thousand-foot edge in altitude even more precious. There were forty Germans to his twenty-eight. His decision became automatic. Upon signal the P-38s dropped their encumbering belly tanks and dove to the attack. The Germans deployed themselves for combat. In a few short seconds the ordered echelons were splintered into the phantasmagoria of aerial combat.

The B-24s gathered themselves into tighter formation, huddling together for mutual protection. As the battle between the fighters slid swiftly astern, the crews in the bombers experienced the morally dirtying relief of knowing that other men were dying in their place. But their relief was short-lived. A few minutes later, as they were pivoting over the pass, they saw a formation of yellow-nosed Focke-Wulfe 190s rising to meet them, rapidly attaining sufficient altitude to attack.

The Germans didn't strike immediately. Instead, they throttled back until their speed was roughly the same as the bomber formation. Flying parallel to the B-24s, about fifteen hundred yards off to the side, they were well out of range of the first frantic bursts from the gunners. Then, magically, they split into two long queues and slid across the intervening sky. They hit the last flight of seven B-24s first. Two Focke-Wulfes attacked each bomber simultaneously, angling up under its belly, closing to within a hundred yards, then breaking off in opposite directions. When that pass was finished the next two fighters in the queues came up. If one of the Germans was destroyed, another took his place. The B-24s, each loaded with over two thousand gallons of high-octane gasoline, full racks of bombs, and thousands of rounds of ammunition, burned fiercely and exploded when hit.

Easy box was smashed in a matter of seconds. Men escaped from some of the bombers, their parachutes mushrooming out and lowering them to safety. In other planes men remained in the turrets, melting the barrels of their guns with furious bursts, until their planes exploded into bright balls of red-orange flame and sifted from the sky in dust. And although on almost every pass one of the Focke-Wulfes was hit, often mortally, others took their places and continued to press the attack. When Easy flight was finished, the queues moved on to the next box in the group.

The B-24 leading Easy flight was the last of its box to be hit. Three passes by three different pairs of Focke-Wulfes inflicted savage wounds on the plane and crew. Win, sitting at the radio table when the attack began, made his way forward and crouched down between the pilot's and copilot's seats. In the first pass the left outboard engine was hit and a fire started. Bane pressed the switch that released carbon dioxide into the burning engine and called the engineer forward to turn off the fuel selector valve. This was accomplished and the fire seemed to subside. But in the seconds that followed two more passes on the bomber ripped its vitals out. The bright tongues of flame reappeared and now seemed centered in the wing tip. The bomber fluttered and yawed all along its length as it was raked by exploding twenty-millimeter shells. Bane pressed the nose of the B-24 down into a steep dive. He called Lange to salvo the bomb load. There was no response. The interphone was dead. Bane began groping for the emergency bomb-release handle on the rear of the pilot's pedestal. Win recognized his intention. He grabbed the handle and yanked it up, paused momentarily to allow the bomb-bay doors to open, then pulled it up the rest of the way. Forty-five hundred pounds of high explosive spilled from the plane's belly, lightening it. Seven thousand feet above the ground Bane strained the bomber from its dive. As the plane shuddered and righted itself he saw that the fire had been fanned out. When he was holding a fairly level course he checked again to see how the men were. There was no communication with either the waist or nose compartment, or with any of the turrets. He snatched his oxygen mask off and turned to Win.

"Check the waist an' see how everybody is. Get Jack to check the nose."

Win divested himself of his entangling interphone and oxygen lines and started away. As he lowered himself into the bomb-bay well he saw Milbank examining the wiring under the flight deck. Win yelled at him to check the nose, then started across the catwalk over the open bomb bay.

At the same time Bane sighted the three Focke-Wulfes that had followed the B-24 down. They were flying above him and off to the side. For the first time since the attack he looked across at Matt Jones. What he saw only increased his feeling of helplessness. The copilot was lolling unconscious in his seat. Bane looked back up at the German fighters and saw the leader wag his wings and dip to the attack. It was then he realized that none of the bomber's guns were firing. More as a result of reflex than of thought, he pulled his throttles back and hit the button for emergency lowering of landing gear, the signal of surrender. For the next seconds he was totally immersed in keeping the wounded plane from going into a stall. When he was free to look up again he saw that the three fighters had arrayed themselves around him, one up ahead and one off each wing. The leader waggled his wings in a way that was clearly a direction that he be followed.

During this time Win had been picking his way carefully across the catwalk that spanned the open bomb bay. Underneath him the ground was rushing by, far below, yet close. He had to force his feet to move and he kept his eyes ahead so as not to look down, but still he was terribly conscious of the narrow, tricky catwalk that held him suspended in the air. As he was about to kick open the door leading into the waist, the airplane seemed to stop, as if it had hit a wall in mid-air, and he felt himself leave his feet. His whole being froze with horror. Clutching convulsively for a grip to keep himself from falling out of the airplane, he was thrown painfully into the waist, fetching up against the ball turret.

"What happened?" He had screamed without meaning to, out of pain and bewilderment. There was no answer and he lay inert, waiting for his muscles to stop twitching. The waist was in shambles. Exploding twenty-millimeter shells had opened gaping holes in the fuselage and the slip stream poured in with the force of rushing water. The deck where he now sprawled was aswim with hydraulic fluid from the cut lines. The oxygen equipment had been torn from the bulkheads and its yellow bulbs and tubes lay twisted in the pink fluid, like the entrails of some butchered elephantine creature.

Win raised himself cautiously and looked over the ball turret toward the tail. One of the waist-gun mountings was shattered and hung down at a crazy angle. Lying beneath it was a lump of meat, a thing with members and parts that he recognized as coverall-clad legs, an oxygen mask, fleece-lined boots. It was Polletti, his body cut almost completely in two. Shaking with hysteria, forcing his legs to keep him erect, Win checked Macchione in the ball turret, then edged his way back to see Chic in the tail. His examination was brief. Their white, fear-numbed faces nodded to him that they were all right.

His inspection tour completed, Win crawled back through the bomb bay on all fours. He met Milbank coming back out of the tunnel from the nose.

"Lange's hit," the engineer yelled.

"Bad?"

"I think so, in the legs or belly. He won't let me look. But Buck's O.K."

Win didn't answer him. He boosted himself up on the flight deck and made his way up to the pilots' seats. Bane was bent over his instruments and he pounded him on the back to get his attention.

"Polletti's dead," Win screamed into Bane's ear. "He got ripped right in two. And Phil's pretty bad. He wouldn't let Jack see."

The pilot raised his eyes to the escorting German fighters. Following his gaze, Win saw them for the first time and instantly divined what had happened, what had made the airplane seem to stop in mid-air.

"What'd you do?"

Bane didn't answer.

"You went and dropped the gear, you dirty sonofabitch. Didn't you? Didn't you?"

He was crying now, without effort, the tears streaming down his face.

"Dirty lousy bastards," he sobbed. "Just look at 'em, the lousy murderin' Nazi bastards . . ."

Bane kept his eyes averted. There was bitterness and shame in his face, and a naked irresoluteness. He was making a difficult transition, adjusting himself to the fact that he was now docilely obeying the men who a few short minutes ago had been trying to kill him.

Win turned away from him. To by-pass his agony he snatched up his charts and began searching the ground below, checking swiftly back and forth between map and terrain, but could identify nothing. He had not as yet oriented himself to the difference in scale, to the change in the size of objects and detail that had resulted from their fifteen-thousand-foot drop in altitude.

The pilot interrupted his search by tapping him on the shoulder. "Where they leadin' us?" he asked.

"I don't know. What difference does it make?"

Bane sighed. "You better check Matt," he said quietly. "Ah think somethin's the matter with him."

Win dropped his charts and reached around the copilot's seat to unfasten Matt's oxygen mask and helmet. As he pulled the helmet free, Matt's head rolled forward and he caught at it. When his fingers came in contact with the hair he snatched his hand away in revulsion. Beneath the hair, where he should have felt scalp, there was the viscidity of blood. As he stared at his soiled hand he felt nausea knot his stomach. Vomit roiled up into his throat and he tasted it bitter in his mouth before he regained control of himself.

"Look at him!" he shouted hysterically, pounding the pilot's shoulder. "He's bleeding like a pig."

Bane never raised his worried eyes from the instrument panel. "Ah think it'd be better to feather number three. Temperature's way up and oil pressure's droppin'," he said.

Unnoticed during the exchange, the copilot's body toppled forward in his seat and came to rest against the control column, depressing it and causing the nose of the B-24 to dip alarmingly. Bane wrestled desperately with the controls before righting the plane. Win held Matt's shoulders, keeping him back in his seat.

"Easy now. Easy," Bane said quietly, talking to the plane. "You got to watch that stuff." He jerked his chin in the direction of the escorting Germans. "Those buggers like to made a pass on us just then."

"I better get him out of your way. Reach over and release his belt."

The engineer came up on the flight deck while Win was tugging at Matt's big body. Taking in the situation instantly, Milbank came to help him. Together they finally got the copilot's body free and stretched it out on the flight deck. Win unsnapped a first-aid kit from the bulkhead and tore it open.

"We're sure a mess," Milbank said, a rueful smile on his face.

"How's Phil doing?"

"I got the bleedin' stopped, put the tourniquets on, and gave him some morphine. But I don' think he knew what was going on. He just lay there holdin' himself." He paused. "What we gonna do now?"

Win anchored the dressing on Jones's head. Then he turned furiously on the engineer. "How'n the hell do I know? What do you want to do? Maybe *you* got an idea, huh?"

Milbank shook his head, looking down at the knuckles of his clenched fist.

"Well, then get up in the copilot's seat. Bane probably needs you."

Crouched on his knees beside Matt's body, there was a moment of hiatus and Win felt for the first time the cumulative impact of what had happened since the attack. A tiny revolution was brewing within him. He had always been afraid on missions. But never before had he been able to translate his fear so completely into hatred. Seated among his maps and instruments and computations, it had always been quite impersonal for him. There had been no blood before. But now he could feel the blood all around him. Matt's blood and Phil's blood and Polletti's, cold and congealed by now on the deck of the waist, and it awakened in him a lust to strike back that he had never known before. After the blood this acquiescence to the killers was maddening. He looked out at the Focke-Wulfe flying off the wing. It was close enough for him to see the German's head under his canopy; close enough for him to see the patches on its dirty mud-colored fuselage; close enough for it to appear suddenly vulnerable, and his mind shied away from accepting it as the object to which they had surrendered. Without conscious ordering his fear and frustrated anger jelled into resolution. His features strained themselves into a cunning grin. He pulled away from the window and dropped flat on the flight deck. Suddenly it was of the utmost importance to him that he not be seen by the near-flying Germans. Crawling swiftly, keeping himself flat, he made his way up and wedged himself between the pilot's and copilot's seats.

"Listen, Al," he began as the pilot looked over at him, "let's not go in with them. Let's make a break for it."

Bane's gray eyes watched him uncomprehendingly.

"We can't do that," he said, shaking his head slowly. "We surrendered."

"So what? You want to follow them in and spend a couple of years in a prison camp? You think the war'll be over in a month? Like hell it will! We'll rot there for years."

He paused and dropped his voice into pleading. "We get out of this and we can be home in a couple of months, Al. We only got a few more to fly . . ."

Bane turned his eyes away and the navigator found himself addressing the side of his head. In the engine-throbbing silence he heard Milbank's voice, low but somehow positive.

"What? What you say?"

"I said," Milbank repeated for the two of them, for Bane had turned to listen again, "I said we could knock them off easy. Real easy. They're hanging out there like sitting ducks."

The pilot stared blankly at them.

"Listen, Al," Win began again. "Maybe you feel bad about breaking your word?"

Bane didn't answer.

"Jesus Christ, man!" Win exploded, "they followed us down to kill us, didn't they? They killed Polletti. He's layin' back there with his guts hanging out. Matt's bleeding like his head's split open. Phil's more than half dead. He won't even let you see where he's hurt. You think they'll take care of him down there? They won't care if he dies——"

"Poor Phil," Bane said softly.

"Poor all of us!"

Again, as if of their own volition, Bane's eyes strayed back to the instrument panel.

"Don't worry about altitude," Win said sharply. By now he was anticipating the pilot's thoughts. "We don't have to go back the way we came. We can come out over low ground all the way. Six thousand feet'll be all we'll need."

"Only got two engines."

"That's all we'll need. You could bring her in on one, Al."

"Ah don' know." Bane's face was pinched. His nostrils were white. His expression was peaked, like that of a cross, hungry little boy about to break into frustrated tears.

Win cleared his throat. He felt his control ebbing away. "What d'you say?" he asked, his voice tight.

"Ah cain't do it. We gave up."

"Like hell we did! You gave up, I didn't. You didn't ask anyone when you dropped the gear. How d'you know I gave up? How d'you know Chic gave up? or Macchione? or Rogers? or Phil? Did you ask them?"

"Now wait a minute. Ah'm the one flyin' this friggen airplane——"

"Sure, but we're ridin' with you." With effort he dropped his voice back to pleading. "Listen, Al, we got nothing to fight about. Let me go back and see how the boys feel about it. If they want to go in—O.K. But let's give them a chance to say."

"This ain't no goddamned votin' party. We'll be lettin' down in a couple of minutes."

"We got time. Let me ask them. What d'you say?"

Bane didn't answer.

Win started away, then stopped. He turned back to the engineer. Milbank smiled and nodded for him to go on. He turned and crawled swiftly toward the bomb bay. Halfway across the deck he stopped again. He remembered for the first time since the attack that Reilly was sitting up above him in the Martin turret. The lower half of the gunner's torso that was suspended into the area of the flight deck had become for him an inanimate part of the airplane. Without really noticing, he had lowered his head to avoid striking the steel stirrups that supported Reilly's legs every time he went down into the bomb bay. Now he reached out and plucked at the pantleg of the gunner's coveralls. There was no response. He pulled harder and Reilly's right foot came clear of the stirrup. Win crawled over and craned his neck to look up into the turret. He saw first the three clean holes drilled through the top of the plexiglass dome. Reilly's head was resting on his chest, facing straight down, and Win saw the wide-open eyes staring at him. He reached under the turret's saddle seat and pressed the release catch. The seat collapsed and Reilly slid to the deck, his body limber, lifeless. The bullets had entered at the base of the boy's neck and gone down and in. There were two lipstick red blotches on the sheepskin collar of his flying jacket, nothing more.

Crouched over him in an attitude akin to prayer, Win looked down at the dead boy's face. He felt none of the shock that he had experienced upon seeing Polletti. Instead, kneeling there, he was overcome with lassitude. He felt tired and beaten.

Somebody plucked at his boot. Turning, he saw Rogers standing in the bomb-bay well, fear marring his face, the dirt from his oxygen mask streaked by tears. His lips were moving but Win heard only a disjointed mumble. Irritation at Rogers's abjectness shocked him back into urgency and then into fury.

"God damn you!" he screamed, his voice out of control. "Who told you to get out of your turret? Get the hell back where you belong!"

"I can't, Win. Please——"

"I said get back!"

"I ain't gonna. I can't."

Win lunged forward to hit him in the face. The gunner ducked and he missed him, his momentum carrying him halfway down into the bomb-bay well, leaving him hanging head down. Rogers was crouched directly beneath him in the passage that led into the nose.

"I'm gonna kill you, you fat sonofabitch," Win ground out.

He let himself slide down into the well, then turned on Rogers, but by then all he saw was the gunner's wide rump retreating up the passage into the nose. He crawled after him. When he entered the nose compartment he saw Rogers standing at bay against the open doors of the nose turret. Instead of continuing after him, Win went over to the bombardier. Phil Lange was lying beneath the navigation table, his body curved into the fetal position, his legs drawn up and both hands clasped tight to his groin. Lange's straw-colored hair was plastered to his brow with sweat. His eyes were wide open, the pupils vastly dilated. Carefully Win checked the tourniquets on Lange's thighs and felt the bombardier's body tense as he touched him.

"How you feeling, Phil?" he asked. "You still got pain?"

Phil shook his head.

Win looked up at Rogers. "You loosen those tourniquets for a one-minute period. Do it about ten minutes from now. We'll be on our way home by then and I'll get up in your turret."

Rogers considered him dumbly.

"You understand what I said? Answer me."

"Home? You say we'll be on our way home?"

"Yeah. That is, if you got the guts of a pig. Now get back in that turret and do what you're told."

He had been pointing at Rogers to emphasize his words. Through the open doors of the nose turret he saw the Focke-Wulfe flying up ahead. He turned back to Lange.

"Phil, we're going to blast those bastards out of the sky. How d'you like that?"

"Kill them. Just kill them." The bombardier's voice was high and thin, but he didn't move. He lay there in that self-huddling curve, his hands clasped at his groin. "Don't ask me. Just kill them."

"O.K." Win turned to face Rogers. "Now you. Get back in that turret and move your sights up on that German bastard flying out there. When you get the word you open up—and you don't miss. You hear?"

"How'm I gonna get the word? My interphone's dead——"

"You'll know when. I'll start shooting and then you start too. And listen. When you're moving your guns up on him, do it real easy. Understand?"

Rogers stood there staring at him.

"Get up in there." Win took a step toward him. "You going?"

Rogers turned and lifted himself into the nose turret. Win slammed the doors shut behind him and turned and started out through the passage. He traversed the open bomb bay and lifted himself into the waist. His eyes averted, he picked his way back to the tail turret and hammered on the doors. They opened and Chicereno's head appeared.

"You want me to come out?" he asked eagerly.

"No."

"Jesus, Win. I can't do nothin' back here. Why do——"

Win put both of his hands on Chicereno's back. "Listen," he said confidently, "we're going to make a break for it. We'll knock those fighters off and come on home."

"You gone completely nuts?"

"It's all taken care of. All you got to do is say yes or no. There's no time to argue. Yes or no?"

"Polletti's dead, ain't he?"

Win nodded.

"Christ!"

"*Come on,* Chic, there's no time."

"What does everybody else say?"

"They all say yeah. You're the last one."

Chicereno blinked his eyes rapidly. "O.K., O.K., why not?"

"Great! You get back in there and just keep your eyes open. If any of them gets in range for you, blast 'em. Got it?"

"Sure." He swung around and reseated himself firmly. "Close my doors."

Win slammed two doors shut then turned and edged back to the ball turret. Macchione was sitting still, staring blankly at his hands. He had been trying to pray. He looked up slowly, without surprise, as the hatch of his turret opened. Win leaned down and in until his lips were almost touching the ball gunner's ear.

"Can you get your sights on one of 'em?"

"Huh?"

"Can you?"

"Why? We going to make a break for it, Win? Are we?"

Win grinned wolfishly. "Yeah, now don't be scared. It'll be easy, they're not expecting anything."

Macchione pulled his head away slightly. "How's Polletti feeling?"

"He's dead. Reilly too."

"Dead!"

"Yeah."

Now the gunner's lips began moving in prayer. His right hand came up out of his lap and Win saw that he was going to cross himself. He caught the hand and held it.

"Let's make them pay for it," he said savagely. "Just you follow orders. Milbank'll take the right waist gun. You cover him. After Milbank lets go a burst and the bastard starts falling away, let him have it. Let him have it for Polletti. O.K.?"

Macchione was silent for a moment and then he nodded. He moved his gun handles slightly and the turret began to inch to the right. Win patted him on the shoulder. He pulled his head out of the turret. Before he slammed the hatch shut he saw that the gunner's lips were moving steadily. Smiling to himself, he started back toward the flight deck, stumbling in his haste.

But when he reached the flight deck and perched himself at Bane's elbow, all of Win's exhilaration faded. The strained, sullen face that the pilot turned toward him was like a blow. The whole business had begun to take on a dreamlike quality. Crouched there in the brilliant sunlight of the pilot's compartment, the steady throbbing vibration of the plane's flight seemed reassuring. Only the trembling of his exhausted legs was real. And the frustration. As if through the wrong end of a telescope, he saw the Focke-Wulfe flying ahead of them waggle its wings and start a turn to the right. Its slip stream hit the slowly reacting bomber, causing it to buck and yaw. Bane turned away to co-ordinate his turn and the mood was broken.

"Can you see a field?" Bane asked quietly.

Milbank half rose from the copilot's seat to scan the ground. "Not yet."

"Good! Then we got time." Win was surprised to hear the confidence in his voice. "Soon as you're straight and level we'll do it."

"Do what?"

"Goddammit, Bane, you know what. They're all for it. Chic, Macchione, Rogers—all of them. Jack here too." He pointed to the engineer. "Ain't you?"

Milbank nodded his head but the pilot didn't see him.

"What Phil say?" Bane asked.

"He said kill them, that's what he said. And that's what we're gonna do." Win grasped the engineer's shoulder. "You take the right waist gun. Macchione'll cover you from the ball. Rogers takes care of the bastard up ahead and I'll take the Martin. Reilly's dead," he added.

Milbank started up instantly. Bane reached out and clutched Win's arm.

"What do you want now?" he demanded, jerking his arm away. Bane's face was etched with fear and doubt and he felt a rush of pity.

"What's the matter?" he asked in a lower voice.

"Give me a headin' for after."

Win calculated swiftly. His mind was wonderfully clear.

"Take a heading of about 225," he said. "Just hold her nice and steady and don't worry, boy. Everything's going t'be just fine."

Win pulled himself up into the Martin turret and settled himself in the seat. Two thin jets of cold air whistled through the bullet holes in the plexiglass, turning the sweat on the back of his neck to ice. He was facing almost straight back toward the tail of the bomber. By twisting his head he could see the escorting Focke-Wulfe. Its proximity came as a shock. It was no more than twenty-five yards away. He felt naked under the transparent plexiglass. Twisted around in the tight confines of the turret, his knee nudged the gun handles and the turret began to move. He froze in absolute panic, straining around to watch, positive the enemy pilot had seen him. The leather-helmeted head of the German didn't turn and Win felt as if he were a small boy sneaking past a sleeping man, trying to get by without waking the sleeper. Cautiously he reached up and pulled the charging handles, twice for each gun. The solid resistance of the spring mechanism and the metallic snap as the bolt threw new cartridges into the barrel filled him with confidence. He felt armed and powerful. His eyes on the sight reticle, fingers clawed on the trigger levers, he deflected the handles and the turret turned slowly, delicately, toward the fighter. The tail, then the fuselage of the Focke-Wulfe edged into the sight. Suddenly, with remarkable clarity, he saw the German pilot watching him. As if of their own volition, the guns began to fire. He heard his own voice screaming aloud, the words tearing from his dry throat, "*Short bursts*, you bas-

tard; SHORT BURSTS!" Pieces began to fly from the Focke-
Wulfe's wings and fuselage. The fighter reared straight up
like a lanced beast. He followed it up, hosing bullets, firing
high and watching himself miss. The fighter was turning slowly
on its back, beginning to slip away. Trying to correct his aim,
he overcompensated. The guns stopped firing. He mashed the
firing levers but nothing happened. Furiously he jerked the
control handles and the guns resumed their hammering. The
Focke-Wulfe, hanging almost motionless at an impossible
angle, was back in his sight. As the bullets tore into it, it began
to smoke and then to burn. A wing tip flew off and then part
of the propeller and then the canopy. He saw everything
clearly, in minutest detail. He saw the pilot struggling to get
out of the cockpit as the plane began to fall away. Trying to
follow it down, he stood up in the turret and smashed his head
painfully against the plexiglass dome. Helplessly he watched
the pilot work his way clear and then the fighter dissolved itself in an explosion of orange flame.

Win stopped firing. His ears were ringing from the din. His
body flushed with relief, personal relief, and then triumph.
Then the bigger thing welled up. They were still flying and
the other guns were silent! "We got them," he said in a loud
logical voice. "We're still flying; that means we got 'em." He
reached down and tripped his seat release to let himself down
out of the turret.

The flight deck was littered with spent shell casings. Reilly's
body was lying face down near the radio table and a number
of the brass tubes had come to rest on him. Win saw Milbank
come popping up out of the bomb-bay well, looking like a released jack-in-the-box, his face split in a delirious grin. Moving
forward, thinking to embrace him, Win stepped on the dead
Reilly's hand. He leaped aside, his stomach turning over, and
the joy within him died. Motioning for Milbank to follow, he
went up to the pilot's compartment.

Bane was fiddling with the command set when Win slipped into the copilot's seat. He grinned at the pilot. Bane nodded and held his hand up for silence. He motioned for Win to put on a headset. The navigator turned to Milbank.

"Jack, hand me my maps. Then you go back to the waist and tell Chic and Macchione to stick in their turrets until they're told to get out."

The engineer handed him maps, computer, and log, then started away.

"Wait a second," Win called. "After that you go on up in the nose. Check Phil's tourniquets, then get up in the nose turret yourself. Send Rogers back to handle the Martin. And remember, everybody keeps their eyes open and nobody leaves his guns until he's told. O.K.?"

Milbank grinned. "Roger, boss."

Win clamped his headset over his ears and busied himself with his maps. They were limping along at eight thousand feet over an area of rolling foothills completely devoid of any detail that could be used as a navigational aid. For long minutes he searched the ground, finding nothing. Then, as panic began taking control, he saw the twisting ribbon of river vague on the horizon. The Danube, he exulted, and clicked his interphone switch.

"Listen, Al, I'll have us pinpointed in another couple of minutes. How about taking a chance on picking up some escort now?"

Bane nodded.

Slowly the river advanced to meet them. As its detail grew clear he saw the huge right angle bend above Turnu-Severin off to their left. On the other side of the river was Yugoslavia and low country showing fifty miles ahead on the map. He turned his interphone switch to Command.

". . . Calling Priscilla. Bassoon 31, Bassoon three one calling

Priscilla," Bane's voice chanted monotonously. "Bassoon 31,
Bassoon three one calling Priscilla . . ."

In spite of the increasing tension, of the vulnerability he felt
from flying alone and crippled over a hostile area, Win smiled
at Bane's Florida drawl voicing the incongruous call signs.

". . . Bassoon three one calling Priscilla——"

"Bassoon 31, this is Priscilla. Bassoon 31, this is Priscilla one
one, Priscilla 11. Go ahead."

Bane's hand trembled on the mike switch. "Priscilla 11,
Roger. This is Bassoon 31. We're in trouble, flyin' on two engines. Can you give us escort?"

"Bassoon 31, Roger." The voice, obscured and disembodied
in the phones, was strong, confident, reassuring. "Where are
you, Bassoon?"

Win pressed the throat mike to his Adam's apple, speaking
slowly. "Priscilla 11, this is Bassoon 31. Our position is 44 degrees 50 minutes north, 22 degrees 18 minutes east. Flying at
8000 feet on a heading of 225 . . . 44 degrees 50 minutes——"

"Roger, Bassoon. I got it. We'll be right over."

The phones went silent. Win cocked the headset up off his
ears in time to hear Bane's long sigh of relief. He nodded happily and began to scan the sky. Everything was working out.
With a couple of fighters to escort them back to Italy all he
would have to concern himself with was avoiding flak. He
tried to control the rush of confidence he felt, telling himself
they were still a long way from home, but it was to no avail.
The pilot's compartment was bright with sun and he could feel
its warmth in his lap. He stretched his arms above his head
in a sensuous, exuberant gesture. The travail of the past minutes seemed a long time gone.

As time passed and the friendly fighters did not appear, they
searched the skies constantly. These next minutes were crucial.
The radio frequency on which they had contacted Priscilla was
monitored by the Germans. In giving their position to the

friendly fighters, they had at the same time given it to the enemy. Win had his headset back on, straining his ears. The worry that had faded a little from Bane's face returned.

"Bassoon three one." Priscilla's voice sounded in the phones. "Bassoon three one, this is Priscilla. We can't find you."

"Goddammit, git your head outa your ass!" Bane exploded. "We give you our exact position."

"Now listen, Bassoon——"

Win broke in, fighting to keep his voice level. "Listen, Priscilla, let me give you our position now. We're just crossing the Danube about fifteen miles north of the big Turnu-Severin bend. You know where that is?"

"Well sure." Priscilla was indignant. "Why didn't you say so in the first place?"

"O.K., now get this. Our heading is 225 degrees. Our gear is down and we only got two engines. So you better get here quick. The whole fucking Luftwaffe's probably listening."

"O.K., Bassoon. Don't wet your drawers, we'll be there in two minutes."

Win relaxed. Bane was leaning toward him, shaking the radio flimsy in his face.

"Stupid sonsabitches!" Bane's voice was high with fury. "You mighta known it, it's the Ninety-ninth. Stupid goddamned niggers . . ."

Win reached over and snatched the pilot's mike-switch plug out. "You gone nuts?" he screamed. "You're on the air. You want them to help us? They hear you talking like that——"

"Well, they better get here," Bane said, his voice thick with anger and disgust. "Black bastards flyin' airplanes——"

"They'll get here, just take it easy."

The three P-51s came wheeling down toward them from the north, silver and shining and beautiful in the sunlight. Win pounded Bane on the shoulder and he nodded morosely. The fighters approached them cautiously, sliding in sideways, keeping their noses pointed away from the bomber, taking no chances on nervous gunners failing to identify them. When they were close enough they arrayed themselves around the bomber, one off each wing, one above and behind them. The pilot flying off their right wing removed his oxygen mask and Win saw the smile of welcome on his dark face. He waved and the man waved back.

"Talk to them," he said harshly to Bane. "I got to get to work now."

It took the crippled bomber more than an hour to cross Yugoslavia and reach the Adriatic. While Bane babied the plane along at 145 miles per hour, Win worked incessantly, keeping their position pinpointed, seeking out low ground and avoiding all towns and rail lines. The P-51s swung about in constant patrol. When they were within sight of the sea, Bane put the plane into a long shallow descent, gathering speed. The P-51s stayed with them all the way across the Adriatic. When the coast of Italy was in sight they waggled their wings in farewell and zoomed off.

Over Italy, Win got out of the copilot's seat and sent Rogers back to summon the rest of the crew to the flight deck. One by one they came up. Macchione and Milbank carried Lange up and made him as comfortable as possible beside the still unconscious Jones. They moved Reilly's body under the radio table and covered him with flying jackets. His body had stiffened and one of his arms was crooked at a fantastic, painful angle. Their joy at being so close to safety was thus modulated by the prone bodies. None of them said anything about what they had gone through.

Milbank got up into the copilot's seat and the rest of the crew huddled at the foot of the pilot's compartment. Bane turned to them, his face solemn.

"We got to decide somethin'," he began in a strained, formal voice. "First off we are goin' to have a tough landing. The hydraulic system's shot and we ain' goin' to have hardly any brakes at all. An' Ah ain' sure the gear's in such good shape."

"I checked it," Milbank said quietly. "It looks O.K.."

"Well, that's good, but we still ain' got any brakes." Bane hesitated. "What Ah mean is that anybody that wants to bail out's got a right to say. Nobody's got to ride down that don' wan' to."

There was silence.

Macchione cleared his throat. "What about Jones and Lange? They can't bail out in no parachute, can they? Somebody's got to stay with the plane to get them down all right."

"That'll only take two men an' me. The rest of——"

"Shit on that!" Chicereno was embarrassed. He was blinking his eyes rapidly. "I'll stay."

Win felt the hot tears forming. "We'll all stay. After what we been through we all get out or none of us do. At least that's the way I feel about it."

There was an excited babble of agreement as they all spoke at once. Win waited for it to subside so he could go on. There was much more he wanted to say. For the past hour, from the time the Adriatic had appeared on the horizon, he had known that the air danger was over. But there had been no slackening of tension, for his mind had been free to project ahead to what would happen when they were back on the ground. A new apprehension had formed. It had been vague at first, but with the crossing of the sea and the coast of Italy beneath them, it had taken on definition and grown into fear. Now he saw the opportunity of dissolving it in this new feeling of oneness. He wanted to share it with the others, mesh it with their own misgivings, but he was unsure how to begin. Then Bane was talking again and the moment was lost.

"That's fine, men, jus' fine. Now here's what Ah was thinkin'. Everybody gets back in the waist except one man stays up here to hold Phil an' Matt. Those in the waist run back to the tail the minute we touch. That way we drag the skid. O.K.?"

"Listen, maybe we can lash a couple a 'chutes to the waist-gun mounts," Milbank suggested. "We swing 'em out the windows and pull the cords when we touch. If they open they'll slow us down. I heard a boy once say he seen it work."

"O.K., we'll try it, it can't hurt any."

"And we better shoot out some red flares."

"We'll do that in about a minute." Bane was dividing his attention between the controls and the men of the crew bunched behind him. "Everybody better take their places now. Ah'm goin' to come straight in without makin' a pattern."

The men rose to their feet. Milbank cocked the flare gun and put it in his lap. Bane set his throttles and then delicately depressed the control column. As the nose of the plane dipped they saw the field below and in front of them.

"Won't be long now!" Chicereno yelled. He turned to Macchione. "Come on, Gene, let's go back."

They started away and Win felt himself suddenly alone. Rogers had gone over to crouch between Phil and Matt. Both Bane and Milbank were facing straight ahead, intent on their approach to the runways.

"Altimeter set . . . crew to stations . . . auxiliary hydraulic pump on——" Milbank began chanting from the pre-landing check list.

"*Wait a second!*"

Chicereno and Macchione, about to let themselves down into the bomb-bay well, were arrested. Rogers looked up. Milbank turned to face him.

"What's a matter?"

Win had cried aloud as the empty void of panic flushed through him, but now he was unable to summon any further words. The men remained fixed, staring at him.

"What's a matter?" Milbank repeated.

Win shook his head. It was too late, he realized; too late yet too soon. Too soon because they were still completely focused on the immediate crisis of the landing, and too late because the moment was lost beyond retrieving.

"Nothing," he said. "Nothing's the matter. It can wait. I'll go back in the waist with Chic and Gene."

Macchione had covered all that remained of Polletti's torn body, but the deck of the waist was still slippery with blood and hydraulic fluid. Working swiftly, the three of them tied parachutes to the gun mounts and swung them out the windows into the slip stream. Then they went forward of the ball turret to wait.

Crouched together, they felt the rush of the plane's descent increase. As the B-24 tilted sickeningly and then righted itself, Win saw the ground from the waist windows. The rate at which it was welling up to meet them came as a shock, and he was transported back to the present, to the air-related danger that still remained. An arm brushed him and he looked over in time to see Macchione crossing himself. The gunner's lips were moving. Instead of contempt Win felt a beat of tenderness. At that moment Chicereno grabbed his arm, hurting him, and the bomber met the runway.

Together they rushed toward the tail. Win jerked the ring on the right parachute. Nothing happened. The plane swerved and he was thrown from his feet but managed to retain his grip on the metal ring of the rip cord. From where he lay he pulled again, savagely, and the white silk trailed out. Then he heard its angry *crack* as it filled with air. It seemed to him that the plane's momentum was undiminished. A moment later he heard another *crack* as the other parachute filled with air. The tail of the B-24 came down hard, jolting on its skid, throwing the men against each other. Now he felt the plane's rush definitely decrease. Bumping and grinding on the steel matting, the bomber came to a stop.

The three men ran and crawled to the waist windows. They stood looking out, yelling incoherently. Chicereno threw his arms around Macchione's neck and kissed him. Win watched them with a grin that was pain etched on his face. He raised his right hand to wipe his eyes and saw that he was still clutching the rip-cord handle. It took a conscious effort for him to open his fingers and let the metal ring drop to the deck.

4 Captain Grover guided the operations jeep along the perimeter strip. He had an unlit cigar clenched in his teeth and every few moments he changed its position, using his teeth and tongue to roll it from one corner of his mouth to the other. He faced straight ahead, his eyes carefully averted from Win and Al Bane, who sat beside him. The enlisted men of the crew were huddled on the back seat of the jeep. There wasn't enough room for all four of them side by side, and Chicereno was on Milbank's lap, his arm clasped tightly around the engineer's neck. Beside them Rogers crouched forward, his body stretched into an arc of unreleased tension. His face was a mask, the lips curled back in a mirthless grin, the dirt on his cheeks scored by dried tears. Macchione was crowded into the corner, yet he had managed to keep some space between him and the others. He sat bolt upright, his eyes brooding, his whole being turned inward.

Nobody spoke, and the silence was composed of two parts, one a corollary of the other. From the time their battered B-24 had ground to a halt at the end of the runway and they had found themselves no longer alone, the men of the crew had not spoken. Their silence had been transmitted first to the medics, who had swarmed aboard the plane to remove Matt and Phil to the waiting ambulances, and then to Henry Grover, who had come racing out in his jeep to transport them back to the squadron area. He had noticed it, and had not spoken, and the pattern had been set. And it had not been easy for him to refrain from questions, for the B-24 sliding wildly to the runway, the holes in its skin visible while still high in the air, the puny parachutes trailing from its waist windows had served to complete a picture for the men on the ground. Although they were the first home, the group had known for hours before their arrival that the mission had met with disaster. Still, it had been an incomplete, a theoretical kind of knowing based on the terse "bombs-away" message radioed back to the base by those elements of the formation that had reached the target. From the message it was known that there had been a fighter attack, and it was surmised that bombers had been lost. But only after they had seen the riddled B-24 careen crazily to a halt, only after the dead and wounded had been removed, only then was it really felt that men had died, and only then had the agony of their dying filtered down to those who remained on the ground. It was because of this that the crew was afforded that special, silent solicitude reserved for the bereaved.

Grover drove slowly along the uneven perimeter strip and it took a long time to get from the head of the runways to the squadron area. In the empty revetments the waiting ground crews stood watching them, following them with their eyes, and Win had the uncanny sensation that they were passing in review. He turned uneasily and looked straight into Rogers's eyes. Surprised, the gunner dropped his gaze and his face closed like a fist. Win felt the pre-landing panic again constrict his throat. He searched their faces, Chic's and Macchione's and Milbank's. None of them would look at him, and for a moment he was certain that it was more hatred than wariness that he saw in their eyes. Then, as if in answer to his unspoken appeal, Milbank smiled at him and he was no longer sure.

Seconds later Grover brought the jeep to a stop in front of the squadron S-2 office. The crew dismounted and filed in. The office was a stone hut, a twin to Operations, but inside it was different. It had an interior-decorated look; there was no bareness, no austerity. The whitewashed walls were covered with a colorful array of maps, posters, pictures, bomb-strike photos, souvenirs. There were silhouette charts of German and Italian fighters that were designed for aircraft recognition courses. An up-to-date battle map of Europe replete with colored pins hung from one wall. Small plastic models of Junkers 88s, of Messerschmitt 110s, of Heinkel 111s were suspended from the ceiling in attitudes of flight. Two desks arranged back to back stood near the door. Each was neat with clean blotter and covered typewriter. The desk facing the room had a name plate on it that was carved from a section of propeller. Lt. Sanford "Sonny" Ethridge was spelled out on it in gold leaf. The rest of the office was taken up by three long tables, each able to accommodate ten men. The ash trays on the tables were cut-down shell casings.

Sonny Ethridge had a fresh fifth of Old Overholt out and ready before the crew got seated. Grover remained standing near the door, visibly controlling his impatience. Ethridge, his young-collegiate face grave, took his place at the head of the table and busied himself filling in the top of the interrogation form. He made a point of not watching the fliers as they passed the bottle. There was only one shot glass and usually much horseplay accompanied the taking of the official drink. Now each crew member had his drink in silence. Even Bane, who never drank, raised the glass to his lips and emptied it, taking comfort from its raw strength.

Ethridge cleared his throat. "Well, how was it?"

The men were silent and Win looked at them. Now it would come. He prepared himself, waiting to see who would be first to seek absolution by putting the blame on him. But there was only silence and the men unwilling to look at each other. "We have to get the report," Ethridge said plaintively. "Come on, how many dead?"

The men fidgeted and finally Win could stand it no longer. Anything was better than not knowing. He turned on Bane.

"Go on, tell it!"

Bane was taken back by the force of Win's demand. He straightened up and faced Ethridge. "Two," he said. "Two dead an' two wounded."

"Who?"

"Polletti and Reilly dead."

"You know their full names and rank?"

"Yeah. Staff Sergeant Martin Polletti an' Walter Radford Reilly. He was a tech."

"And the wounded?"

Bane sighed. "Phil Lange and Matt Jones."

"How were they wounded?"

Bane stared at him. "They got hit," he said.

"I mean how bad?"

"How bad?" Finally Bane's calm was leaving him. "How bad you think? They took 'em to the hospital, both of 'em unconscious."

Ethridge flushed scarlet but recovered almost immediately. "O.K., then," he said briskly, "let's get the routine stuff down. I want take-off time, time on course—all of that, you know. Helman, you ready to begin?"

Win came to with a start. He had heard their voices, but not their words. The warm yellow sunlight streaming in through the open windows had hypnotized him. He looked at his watch. Although it was not yet three o'clock, it seemed wrong for the sun still to be shining. Only a few hours had passed. Only a few hours and Reilly was dead and Polletti was dead, cut in two by twenty-millimeter shells. Illusion and reality were fused for him. Here they were sitting at interrogation answering Sonny Ethridge's questions just as they had more than twenty times before. Nothing was different; nothing was changed. Everything was meshed together; the struggle and the routine, the agony and the ordinary.

His fears were unfounded and unshared. The taboo shattered, the unnatural deed done in the air, in that now unreal moment of panic and pain and anger with the dead and the bleeding all around them, had unhinged him. It was done, he told himself, done and finished and they were safe.

He shook himself like a dog emerging from water. Automatically he unzipped his map case and spread the log out on the table in front of him. It read like a graph of terror. His entries in the beginning; the time of take-off; the group's rendezvous and setting out on course; the compass headings and ground speeds he had computed while on the first long leg over the Adriatic; all of these were neatly and accurately noted. He had entered the precise latitude and longitude of their landfall, and the precise time. There was the exact time and position of their meeting with their escort. But at 1144 hours, the time the first German fighters had been sighted, the carefully kept log disintegrated into a barely legible scrawl.

He looked up with a vague feeling that he should apologize for his lack of neatness and then thought better of it. What would routine and neatness matter when what they had done became known? Was he really going crazy? Wasn't the room filled with the echo of his crewmates' uneasy silence? Didn't he have his own log lying there in front of him, a record in his own handwriting of the mission's carefully planned routine as it was obliterated by disorder? He sighed. It was the not knowing, the seesawing between dread and confidence that was so hard to take. He sighed again and began to read.

He spoke slowly, keeping his voice even and unemotional. In broad practiced strokes he took them through the first phases of the mission. His reportage was factual and detailed.

He commented on the formation, on the weather, on the accuracy of the meteorological data that was contained in the flight plan given them that morning at briefing. Once he called on Chicereno to corroborate an observation. In this fashion he brought them up to the time the first German fighters were spotted. Then he stopped to light a cigarette.

Ethridge broke in for the first time. "How many 109s were there?"

"About fifty, I'd say. What d'you think, Gene?"

Macchione took so long answering Win thought he was going to refuse to speak at all.

"At least fifty," he said finally. "I watched them come all the way up till the 38s hit 'em."

Ethridge turned to the pilot.

"Don' ask me. Ah couldn't say. Ah was too busy tryin' to keep Easy box tucked in."

Grover moved for the first time since entering the S-2 office. He picked up the bottle of Old Overholt and poured himself a drink. Then he put it down in front of Bane.

"Here, have what you want," he said.

Bane smiled his thanks and passed it to Milbank. The engineer poured himself a shot and started the bottle around again. Sonny Ethridge watched them, trying to hide his impatience. He waited until the bottle was back in front of Bane and then asked them to continue. Win looked around the table. By unspoken yet mutual agreement, they were waiting for him to tell it. It wasn't necessary, but he nodded to them.

He told it straight, speaking very slowly, doing his best to keep it within the framework of fact necessary to satisfy the interrogator. There were elements of it that he left unspoken, things that he felt were private to the crew and nobody else and it seemed that the men understood and responded, huddling toward him, intent on every word, every cadence. It was as if the passing of a few hours had caused the deed to grow dim for them and now they were struggling to recapture it. And the two men who had remained on the ground were equally caught up. Ethridge was staring at him, his lips parted, the pencil forgotten in his hand. Grover stood rigid with excitement. As he spoke, it all came back, it lived again, and Win saw it mirrored in their faces. In spite of the flatness with which he told it, in spite of the things he omitted, the essence of it became plain, and they all grasped it. Finally it was finished and he stopped talking. Then, for the first time, they heard the returning formations and became aware of the air-filling drone of engines. It was quite close now, yet none of them had noticed it until Win stopped talking.

Ethridge got up and went to the door. He opened it and scanned the sky. The returning formations were still far enough away so that the beating of their engines filled the air from all points of the compass at once.

"They won't be here for a half hour yet," he said vaguely. Then he faced Grover. "Jesus Christ, Hank, what are we going to do?"

"How the hell should I know? Do what you're supposed to do," Grover said angrily.

"Yeah, but what? I know I can't just send this thing through regular channels."

"Why not?"

"Why not! Because it's dynamite."

Grover shrugged. "Then go get Gillespie. Let him take the responsibility."

Ethridge snapped his fingers. "That's it."

He ran out of the office, then ran right back inside again and up to the table. "Listen, you guys stay right where you are. Don't you leave. I'll be right back. Have another drink," he added over his shoulder on his way out.

This time the door stayed shut and they heard the jeep start up and pull away, its tires screaming in protest.

"*Now we get it, now we really get it,*" Rogers said in a stran-
gled whisper, as if to himself, but in the strained silence they
all heard him, even Grover, who stood over in the corner looking out the window.

"Be quiet, Buck," Macchione said sternly. "Take it easy."

"Sure, sure, I'll take it easy."

Milbank pushed the bottle and shot glass in front of Rogers.
"Here, take yourself a drink, Buck."

Rogers was keyed fine with the tautness of hysteria. His
hand was too steady as he picked up the bottle and carefully
tipped it to the shot glass. Nothing happened.

"Take the cork out," Milbank said softly.

Rogers stared at him.

"You forgot to take the cork out."

"Sure, sure . . ."

Rogers straightened the bottle and withdrew the cork. His
hands, with their measured, wooden movements, seemed disconnected from the rest of his body. He tipped the bottle again,
too steeply this time, and the whisky slopped out on the table,
missing the glass by a wide margin. An emotional release
tripped deep within him and he let the bottle fall from his
hand. Dry, tearing sobs racked his whole body.

"Why'd it have to happen to me?" he cried. "Mother of God,
why'd it have to happen to me?"

Milbank moved with the speed of pure reflex. He snatched
up the bottle and righted it and leaned over to put his hand
on Rogers's heaving shoulder. "Come on, boy, come on now."

He put his other hand on Rogers's other shoulder and rocked
the sobbing gunner back and forth. Macchione got up from his
chair and went to stand behind him.

"Is he all right?" Grover asked, coming to the table.

Bane twisted around to face him. "He's O.K., Captain. He's
just kind a shook up."

Grover stopped, aware of his exclusion. He stood still, undecided about what to do. Finally he turned and went back to the window. Macchione handed Rogers a handkerchief and he blew his nose like an obedient child. His sobs died into hiccoughs and then stopped completely. It became quiet.

Minutes passed, ticked off by Rogers's still spasmodic intake of breath. Win sat staring at the door. He knew that he should be doing something to prepare himself for what was about to come, but the exhausted, empty silence of the room laved him, blunting his inner tension. Then he heard a jeep skid to a stop outside. Almost before the sound had died the door flew open and Major Gillespie came charging into the room with Sonny Ethridge trotting at his heels. The S-2 nodded to Grover and came up to the table, glancing briefly at the crew. By that time Ethridge was at his side.

"This is the crew," Ethridge said formally. "The pilot, Lieutenant Bane, the copilot——"

"You can introduce us later, Sonny. Where's the log?"

"Right here, sir."

Gillespie took the log and sat down at the head of the table. He bent to study it, disregarding everyone in the room. "This tells me nothing," he said finally without looking up.

"Yes, sir." Sonny Ethridge was ready. "Here's the interrogation form."

Gillespie placed it beside the log and compared the two. He traced his index finger from form to log. "Who's the navigator on this crew?" he asked, not raising his head, his finger still moving between the two papers.

"I am."

"How many missions you got, Lieutenant?"

Win kept his eyes fixed on the major's bent head. Gillespie's gray hair was exactly divided by a wide part that showed a stripe of pink scalp, and somehow this started the anger boiling up from deep within him. He hesitated, waiting for the head to be raised, but Gillespie didn't move.

"You mean the old way or the new way, Major?"

Now Gillespie looked up. "Oh, it's you, Helman." He lifted the log by one corner, as if it were a thing unclean, and threw it toward Win. It fell into the pool of spilled whisky. "It would seem to me you'd have learned to keep a log by now. I can't even read this."

He got up and paced up and down the length of the table, his hands thrust deep in his pockets. In the far corner of the room, beside Grover, he stopped and stood considering the crew members. Deliberately he turned his heavily fleshed, florid face on each man in turn, letting the tension build. Gillespie had a reputation for toughness that went beyond the group. Part of it was automatic, stemming from the World War I Observer's Wings and D.S.C. ribbon he wore pinned to his shirt. But the biggest part of the reputation was courage, constantly demonstrated. He was not required to fly combat, yet he flew at least twice each month, selecting only the most dangerous missions, the deepest penetrations. This did not endear him to the rest of the fringe flying personnel, the flight surgeons and squadron S-2 officers who were content to get their flying time in on hops to Rome and Naples, but it set him apart from them in the judgment of the combat crews. It made it possible for him to feel that the crew he now stood considering would be unable to categorize him as just another ground officer, and thus he took from them the only lever they had for erasing differences in rank.

"Well, suppose you tell me what happened," Gillespie demanded.

Now it begins, now we really get it, Win told himself in a kind of numb calm. It was very hard for him to keep his eyes from sliding away from Gillespie's face; he kept bending his head to stare down at his own hands lying tightly clenched in his lap. There was a deep unease in him, old and familiar yet unidentifiable. It had something to do with Gillespie's gray hair and authority and righteousness. Win felt himself flushing with a combination of shame and guilt.

"Tell me what the hell you thought you were doing up there." Gillespie was whipping himself to anger. "Did you all go crazy?"

"They were trying to kill us," Win said in a choked voice.

"Were they?" Gillespie snorted disgustedly. "Well, well, well, well, and what did you expect them to do—kiss you?"

Win shook his head, sliding his eyes around to glance at his crewmates. They were immobile.

"Maybe I ought to remind you that this is a war!" Gillespie yelled. "We're fighting *men*, goddammit, white men, and *we're* supposed to be men too, not guttersnipes. You think just because you get scared shitless, lose your nerve, you can hide behind the white flag and then stab people in the back? This isn't the Pacific, you know. We're not fighting Japs here!"

"They were trying to kill us," Win repeated stubbornly. "What's the difference?"

"The difference is that there are certain rules of warfare established between civilized people," Gillespie roared. "You're carrying the insignia of the United States Army Air Force up there, or doesn't that mean anything to you?"

"They followed us down to finish us off," Win said sullenly.

"They did, eh? And why'd you go down? Was it because you couldn't take it?"

"No, we had to——"

"Why? Was it your idea, Helman? The whole thing?"

The shift in focus, sudden as it came, still wasn't unexpected. It was the corollary of the shame. But now the shame became fear, real and cold, and Win felt his stomach turn over.

"So it was your idea, eh? You're the one who figured it all out."

Win shook his head.

"What's the matter, scared again?" Gillespie moved toward

the table. "You're the one with all the alibis—it must have been your idea."

"No, it wasn't——"

"It wasn't?" Gillespie cocked his head. He was sneering. "Then whose was it?"

The words echoed in silence.

"Who did it?" Gillespie turned to Bane and bent forward, thrusting his anger-congested face close to the pilot's. "I want to know who did it. Who shot those fighters down?"

Nobody answered.

"Speak up!"

"We all did," Bane whispered.

Win felt the almost inaudible words reverberate through him like the tolling of a huge gong and a fierce gladness thickened his throat. "That's right, we all did," he said loudly. "We voted!"

Still bent forward, Gillespie slowly rotated his head to look at Win. "You voted, eh?"

"Sure." Win looked around at the men of the crew. Now they all met his eyes and there was in it a tacit giving of consent, an acknowledgment that he had assumed a new position in the crew. Not that he was replacing or supplanting Bane. Rather it was the filling of a need that had never been filled before.

"Me and Milbank and Rogers did the shooting," he said finally.

"I got in a few bursts too."

"And who the hell are you?" Gillespie demanded.

"Macchione, sir."

Win pointed. "That's Sergeant Milbank, and that's Sergeant Rogers, our nose gunner."

"And I'm the ball, sir," Macchione said.

Gillespie straightened up and strode angrily around the table. "I guess you all feel pretty satisfied with yourselves."

"No, sir, we don'," Bane said. "We lost two of our boys an' two more are in the hospital right now."

"Well, this is a goddamned serious thing. And don't think for a minute that it isn't."

"Yes, sir," Bane said.

"Don't give me that 'yes, sir.' I suppose you didn't get their insignia, either. How about that, Helman? That's your job, isn't it?"

Grover had had enough. These men were in his squadron, one of his combat crews, and he wasn't going to allow any ground officer pushing them around, even if it was Gillespie. Fliers were fliers and all the rest were less than nothing to him. He strode past the S-2 to stand in front of Bane.

"Did you get all the pilots?" he demanded.

"What d'you mean?"

"I mean did you get the bastards? Did you kill them all?"

"Ah don' know." Bane looked at Win.

"Yeah," Win said positively, ahead of his doubts, "sure, they all blew up. There were no 'chutes."

"Well, O.K. then." Grover turned to Gillespie. He wasn't afraid of the S-2 or any other ground officer. He reached out and picked up the almost empty bottle, poured a drink, and handed it to him.

"What's all the worry about? Go ahead, have a drink. You think those sonsabitches are gonna know what happened to three of their fighters someplace over Europe? Like hell they will. They'll count 'em missing and hand out three more Iron Crosses."

"But what if those fighters were sighted following them down? What if they radioed in that they were bringing in a Twenty-four? What about that?"

"So they never got there. They were intercepted and shot down by our fighters," Win said levelly. "It could have happened."

"Sure it could have," Grover said.

"Maybe, maybe not." Gillespie held the shot glass up at eye level and changed his tone to sarcasm. "Did you by any chance get a position report on where you dropped your bombs?"

Win reached for his log. "You want latitude and longitude?"

"No—unless you're going to claim a target of opportunity."

Bane cut in. "We don' want to claim nothin'. We jus' dumped 'em."

"That's what I thought. Well, don't expect to get mission credit. And about this other thing—we'll see."

The major tilted his head back and tossed the hundred-proof rye into his mouth. "Cheers," he said, and started out.

The crew stood up. Win felt the wet clamminess of his palms. He reached back and wiped his hands on the seat of his pants and a sound long and low, composed of pain and fear, escaped him. They all spun around to look at him. He held his hand up. It was marred with dark red blood.

"You hurt?" Bane demanded.

Win shook his head. "No"—his voice was thin and out of control—"it must've just got on me. I guess it's Polletti's."

They filed out of the office. In front, the men gathered in a hesitant knot. Ethridge and Gillespie got into the S-2 jeep and drove off to Group. Still the men stood there, not knowing how to part. Grover was caught in it too. A formation of low-flying B-24s wheeled overhead and banked away to the south, headed for Spinazzola. Finally the gunners began drifting toward the enlisted men's section. There was a quiet sadness in their going. Win felt it as he stood looking after them, his bloody hand held rigidly away from his side.

"Hey! Wait a minute," he called impulsively.

They stopped and he saw how eager their faces were. "Maybe we can get a jeep and all go in to see Phil and Matt. You want to, Al?"

Bane considered it. "Ah think that'd be fine," he said. Although he hated to do it, he turned to Grover. "Captain, would there be any——"

"Sure, take it," Grover interrupted him. "I can use Abbot's. Just don't forget to pull the rotor when you park it in town."

"We'll be sure an' do that an' we thank you."

Grover nodded and walked away. Everyone was smiling. Bane looked at his watch. "Let's all meet back here in fifteen minutes. Is that O.K.?"

They nodded in unison.

"Can I drive?" Chicereno asked.

"Sure, but hurry up."

There were six groups stationed around Cerignola and the sky over the town was filled with returning bombers. They watched the formations circling to land, counting the feathered propellers and the planes that shot out red flares for an indication of how bad it had been for the others. On days when the Air Force really suffered the B-24s came home in uneven, tattered formations, in echelons of three and six and ten. Today most of the groups seemed intact. By the time Chicereno parked the jeep in front of the hospital they knew that the mission as a whole hadn't been too bad.

The base hospital had as its center the building that had served the town as a hospital before the war. Now this three-story château-like structure was embraced by two long lines of wood and tar-paper barracks. While Milbank lifted the jeep's hood and removed the rotor, Bane went into the main building to find out where Lange and Jones were. A few minutes later he came out and motioned for them to come on.

Bane led them down a long corridor. They walked in single file, conscious of the ringing clatter of their heels. At the end of the hall they came to a desk that blocked the entrance to a ward. There was a middle-aged nurse on duty. She looked up from the copy of Stars and Stripes she was reading, and they saw that her long-jawed, good-natured face was very tired.

"We come to see Lieutenant Lange and Lieutenant Jones," Bane told her.

She jerked her thumb over her shoulder, indicating the ward. "They're inside, but don't stay long. Lange just got a sedative."

Phil Lange lay in the second cot from the end. The sheet and blanket covering him had been drawn taut, outlining his body. He was flat on his back, staring up at the ceiling. At the sound of their footsteps, he turned his face and eyes; the rest of him he held rigid.

"Hi, Phil," Bane said as they grouped themselves around the cot. "We jus' dropped by to see how you comin'."

Lange blushed. "I'm O.K." He revolved his head and eyes to look at them all. "Where's Reilly and Polletti?" he asked. "Couldn't they come?"

"They got killed, Phil," Bane said.

Lange's voice was barely audible. "Everybody else all right?"

"Yeah," Milbank told him. "You get hurt bad, Phil?"

Lange blushed again, the bright blood flooding his pale features. "I'm O.K. now."

"Is there anything you need, anything we can get for you?"

"No, I'm fine."

Lange rolled his eyes around again to include them all. "Listen," he said in a choked voice, "I want to thank you guys for bringing me in."

"Sure, Phil."

"No, I mean it. I want to thank all of you."

He thrashed around for a moment and succeeded in bringing his right arm out from under the tightly tucked covers. He held his hand up and they saw how it trembled. "I want to shake hands."

They were still with embarrassment. Then Macchione took the proffered hand, pumped it once, and let it go. One by one the others shook hands with Lange. When they were finished they just stood there, not knowing what to do.

"Well, Ah guess we better be goin'. The nurse said you got to sleep," Bane said finally. "We'll come by to see you tomorrow."

"Don't go yet. I want to tell you something."

"Tell us tomorrow, Phil."

"No, now. I want to tell you now. Listen, when I got hit—it was in the thigh and in the hip, the doctor says it's not bad—but when I got hit I went to pieces."

Desperately he strained his eyes around until he found Milbank and then Win.

"I couldn't let you touch me, I didn't want you to know. I was afraid. I thought I was hit in the testicles. I always been afraid of that . . ."

They were silent.

"I just wanted to tell you," Lange said, his voice fading.

His eyes closed and he began to breathe deeply, evenly. Bane motioned with his head and they tiptoed away from the cot. As they filed back toward the desk, they saw the nurse motioning to someone in the corridor. A big man in a red robe, his whole head swathed in an immense white turban of bandages, peeked around at them. It was Matt Jones.

"They shaved it," he told them. "All over."

The crew edged around the desk and out into the corridor. Chicereno giggled and Macchione shot him a quieting look.

"Phil's in there," Matt said to Bane. "Ain' you goin' in to see him?"

"We jus' did. How you feel, Matt?"

"They shaved it everplace it wasn't cut."

"Now it'll look just like your bare ass," Chicereno said and laughed.

Matt grinned happily. "Where you guys headed? You goin' to town?"

"Uh-huh."

"Well, Ah'm gettin' my clothes an' comin' too."

"Ain't nothin' wrong with ol' Matt," Bane said delightedly. "You can't hurt him by hittin' him in the head."

They all laughed, and there was more than a little hysteria in it. Matt grinned at them. Motioning for them to wait, he ducked further down the corridor and disappeared into a doorway. A moment later he was back, carrying his clothes bundled under his arm. He took off his robe and let it drop to the floor, leaving him completely naked. Quickly he began to dress. The nurse looked up from her paper and saw him.

"Just what do you think you're doing, Lieutenant?" she demanded.

"Ah'm goin' with my crew," he told her, pulling up his pants. "They come to fetch me."

"You're doing nothing of the kind!"

"Aw now, Nurse—"

"Don't nurse me. Lieutenant, you take off those pants or I'll call the orderly."

"Now, honey, you don' need no one t' make me take off my pants—you jus' smile once."

"Don't get fresh, sonny." But she was caught, she was fighting back a smile. "I'm going to call for the orderly."

Matt had his shirt on and he sat down on the floor to put on his shoes. He knotted the laces and held out his hands to be helped up. Milbank and Chicereno pulled him to his feet. He kneaded the red robe into a ball and placed it on her desk.

"Now you take good care a Phil Lange," he said. "Ah'll be by in the mornin' an' bring you a bottle a cherry brandy." He turned to the crew. "Let's go, Ah'm ready."

Chicereno tooled the jeep along Cerignola's main street. In the square opposite the cathedral the army traffic thickened and finally they were halted behind a long convoy of six-by-sixes. It was darkening into evening now and the day's accumulated fatigue had begun to tell on all of them. But Matt was working on them like a catalyst. He had sustained his wound in the very beginning of the attack and passed out, not to regain consciousness until they were shaving his head in the hospital. Consequently he knew nothing about what had happened and they were telling him of the mission, all of them breaking in to add details, even Rogers, who was crouched on the floor in the back. Listening to it, Win was aware of how much of a group thing it had become, how each valued his participation in it. He did less talking than any of them and when the six-by-sixes began to roll he was the only one who noticed. They had come to the part about the parachutes and he broke in: "Listen, guys, let's not go back yet. How about getting something to eat in town?"

"Now you're talkin'!" Matt trumpeted. "Let's get something to drink too. Ah'm so dry Ah'd like to dip mah head in a barrel of vino."

"Your head?"

"Well, first mah head."

They laughed uproariously and Chicereno wheeled the jeep around in a tight circle and parked at the curb. They jumped out and were immediately surrounded by a swarm of Italian boys. These were the town's chief entrepreneurs. Under their watchful eyes Milbank lifted the jeep's hood.

"Git out! *Avanti!* you bunch a jaybirds," he yelled at them.

" 'eh, Joe, cigarette," they began.

" 'eh, *Tenente*, you wan' shine? Unita State polish, very good."

"Joe, 'eh Joe, you wan' eat?"

One of them edged up to Milbank, whose head was under the hood. " 'eh, Sarg," he said blandly, "you wan' buy rotor?"

Milbank pulled his head out and looked at him. "Let's see."

The boy dug deep into the back pocket of his patched shorts and held up a rotor.

"Ah be damned!"

The chorus laughed jeeringly. One of the biggest of the kids pushed forward.

"Two bucks, watch jeep," he offered.

"Like hell." Milbank reached back under the hood, opened the distributor cap and removed the rotor. He disconnected the spark coil, unhooked the leads from the starter and generator, slammed the hood shut, and then turned to face his audience. "See if you-all can start it now."

" 'eh, Sarg," one of the kids mimicked him, "you all wan' sleep my sister? Make fig-fig?"

They all laughed and the engineer laughed with them. "Listen, you lil pimps," he roared, but they were aware of the fondness in his voice, "we're huntin' for a good place to eat."

The kids exploded into turmoil. Macchione and Chicereno, the two Italians on the crew, took no part in the negotiations. Milbank, in the wondrous way he had of being at home anywhere, took care of it. After much bargaining he selected a boy who had been very quiet and even a little shy. The engineer gave the boy a cigarette, lit it for him, and with these two in the lead the crew set out.

The boy's home was a tiny worker's cottage at the end of one of the streets radiating out from behind the cathedral. Inside, the cottage was crowded with furniture, with too much living in too small a space, yet everything was immaculate. The woman of the house, new in her role of restaurateur, was flustered when she saw they were seven, but she recovered quickly and seated them at the round table that all but filled the main room. A moment later the boy staggered in from outside bearing two earthen wine jugs. They set them in the middle of the table while he ran to get glasses. The woman, her face tight with an anxious smile, hurried between table and kitchen. First she brought them *antipasto* of gnarled spicy sausage and anchovies and thick-sliced onions. Then a huge fire-blackened pot of minestrone, and finally spaghetti in tomato sauce and fragrant, freshly baked bread.

It was the first time since their departure from Topeka that they had all sat down to eat together. But there was no hesitancy, no embarrassment. Under the watchful eye of the woman who had posted herself in the kitchen doorway, they consumed prodigious amounts of food and grew drunk on the rich red wine. From the beginning they shouted toasts at each other. The theme, the thing they all felt and articulated, each in his own fashion, was that they were over the hump. As long as they were together they had made it; nothing could harm them. This was the mission on which they were to have died, and, having escaped, they felt themselves impervious to disaster. There was a unity among them that had never existed before. Everything everyone said was hilariously funny and they laughed until they cried. They cursed Gillespie for withholding mission credit from them, but minutes later even this bitterness was dissolved and they laughed at the group S-2 and imitated his "Cheers!" as they downed cup after cup of wine.

By ten o'clock they were all drunk, not with wine alone, but with the rich food and the good feeling and the aftereffects of tension and fatigue. They rose to go and Matt hoisted one of the wine jugs to his shoulder. In the doorway Macchione turned to the woman and spoke to her in Italian, the fluid lilting words coming easily to his lips. Beside him Chicereno stopped to listen. The tail gunner knew nothing of his mother tongue, but he cocked his head to hear and repeated the words to himself as they were spoken. They said their good-bys, and then, as they passed through the door, the woman took each one's face between her hands and kissed them and wished them well.

After they had arrived at where the jeep was parked and Milbank had replaced the rotor and reattached the wires, Win, considering himself the soberest of them all, got in behind the wheel. He drove slowly through the town, engulfed in a state of peaceful half sleep. Ahead of him the road to the base was milk-white from moonlight and embroidered with the slim tracery of the bordering poplars, and for a while he made a game of skirting the shadows. The night was still and the men dozed, their heads drooping to each other's shoulders. Then it began, at first low, muted, hesitant, but then rising and swelling toward them from the direction of the base in a wall of sound. It continued to build and the air was filled with the beating roar of airplane engines. It was the ground crews, working late into the night to repair the day's damage.

By the time they arrived back at the squadron, the noise of engines being run up had awakened all of the men except Rogers. Win drove the jeep up into the enlisted men's tent area and Milbank and Macchione picked Rogers up between them and carried him off to bed. Win turned the jeep around. As he pulled away Macchione stuck his head out of the tent and shouted after them that there was no mission scheduled for the next day.

Operations was dark, so Win drove on and parked in front of the officers' club. Matt dismounted first and hoisted the wine jug to his shoulder. He had to stoop to get through the low doorway and Win and Bane followed him in.

The entrance of the big copilot, his whole head swathed in the huge turban of bandages, the earthen jug balanced high on his shoulder, was greeted by a roar of approval. The atmosphere in the club was one of noisy, frenetic celebration not unlike a wake. Everyone was drinking, and those who were not drunk were acting like it with a desperation that Win recognized as characteristic of such nights. The usual poker game was in progress, but nobody was writing letters. Four crews from the squadron had flown in Easy box that day and only their crew had returned.

Bane began taking his own personal inventory of the sur-
vivors and Win realized that he hadn't thought of Macy once
all day, hadn't even wondered if his friend had gotten back
safely. Quickly he searched the small crowded room and almost
immediately he saw Macy smiling at him from where he sat,
still censoring mail. From the relief he felt, Win knew that
some part of his mind had not forgotten; some part of him had
not been able to relax completely until this final tension was
eliminated. As a knot of drinkers gathered around Matt and
his jug, Win started over to the corner and Bane followed.

"How's Lange?" Macy asked, pushing two chairs out for
them.

"He's O.K. He'll probably stay in the hospital awhile, but
he's O.K."

Win looked around the room again and then back at his
friend. "You hear about us?"

"Sure, everbody has." Macy turned and smiled sympathetically at Bane. "Rough, huh?"

Bane sighed. "Yeah."

"You guys like a drink, I got most of a fifth of Old Crow left."

He got up and went to the bar and returned with a bottle and
three glasses.

"Anybody get out a the others?" Bane asked.

"Yeah, there were five 'chutes out of Tilton's. The other two
blew up."

Bane sighed again. He lifted his glass to his lips and drank
it absently, in one gulp.

"Ah guess Ah'm gonna need this stuff from now on," he said
and looked straight at Macy. "You were right when you said it
was gonna be rough—all doubles."

Macy grimaced and looked down at the table. Win was
struck with Bane's peculiar honesty. He realized that in spite
of all that had happened to him this day, the pilot had been
puzzling out his stand on what Macy had said in the mess hall.

Now that he had formed an opinion he confessed it naturally and honestly.

There was a roar of laughter from the men at the bar. Turning, they saw that Matt had slung the five-gallon jug over his arm mountaineer-style and was letting a stream of wine jet into his mouth. He choked finally and the red wine flooded down the front of his shirt and some of it even stained the white bandages on his head like blood. Quieting the laughter, the copilot grounded the jug, and then resumed talking. From the way he was demonstrating with his hands, from what they could hear above the noise, Win knew that Matt was recounting the incident; blowing it up, making himself the pivot of the action, explaining how all would have been lost without him.

Win looked at Bane and the pilot giggled.

"That bugger was unconscious all the time till they shaved his head in the hospital," he said to Macy and they all three laughed.

Then someone switched the radio on, the volume turned 'way up, and the bone-dry tones of a B.B.C. announcer boomed through the room.

"Shut that limey bastard off," one of the poker players yelled.

The dial was spun and the room was filled with the second chorus of Benny Goodman's "Sing, Sing, Sing." The music built to its incredible climax, stopped, and then they heard Her voice . . .

"Do we have to listen to that bitch tonight?"

"Shut up!"

". . . a special message from the Luftwaffe to the 902nd Bomb Group——"

"That's us!"

"Well, shut up a minute!"

"—today outraged a surrender agreement. The crew lowered its landing gear as a sign of surrender. But when the pilots of the Luftwaffe, in keeping with their traditions of German gallantry, began escorting the B-24 to a safe landing, they were treacherously shot at and murdered. Murdered in cold blood by the assassins who hid behind a surrender agreement. The Luftwaffe pledges that this treachery will be wiped out in blood. Every time the 902nd crosses the borders of the Reich, revenge will be taken. The Luftwaffe gives you its solemn pledge that the 902nd Bomb Group will be wiped out, exterminated for this coward's betrayal——"

Someone switched the radio off and the club was filled with a numb, building silence. Slowly the men began looking around and Win felt the intolerable beating of his heart.

5 .The squadron lay inert under the heat of August. The day was still, with that uncanny calm found in the deep-buried eye of a hurricane. The sun-warmed, humid air combined its moisture with the sifting dust and covered everything like a blanket of invisible fur. On the flight line a ground crew was reassembling an engine cowling, the noise of their hammering muted and without definition. Sound did not carry in that atmosphere; it hung suspended and died.

Win changed his position on the bare cot and looked at his watch. Another ten or fifteen minutes, he thought. Anything longer than that would mean they had gotten hit again. He held the V-mail closer to his eyes. He had reached the last third of the letter and his sister's writing was too tiny to be easily decipherable. As he squinted at it, his head bowed, a drop of perspiration rolled down his chin and splattered on the photostat's shiny surface, dissolving half of the last three sentences. He sighed and glanced over at Bane. The pilot, naked except for his green G.I. shorts, was propped up in his corner intent on his own mail. Win turned over on his stomach and stretched out flat on his cot. He thought he felt a little cooler. The canvas walls were rolled up to allow the heat to circulate instead of storing itself, yet it was practically impossible to stand erect anyplace in the tent. Gazing out through the open sides, Win's attention focused on the three-quarters finished tent floor. Although only two weeks had elapsed since its construction, the sun had succeeded in warping some of its boards. On the other side of the brown burned grass stood Zymbrowski's easy chair. These two objects seemed related, both memorials, and looking at them deepened his sense of oppression. He sighed and picked up his V-mail again. It was no use, and he put it down on the dirt floor beside the cot and lit a cigarette. It didn't make too much difference, he reflected. All of the letters that his sister wrote were essentially similar; they all ended the same way. Without even closing his eyes he could see them together in the kitchen, his mother seated in that square heavy way so odd in a small woman, her hands folded in her lap; his sister with pen ready over paper, her face set in impatient forbearance (which by now had probably hardened into bitterness, for she was past thirty and her fiancé was away in the Pacific), sitting poised and waiting until his mother, who couldn't read or write English, looked up from the scrubbed, patternless linoleum and said, *Well, write that everything is all right.* . . . And the words minutely transcribed, for the precious space on the V-mail was all but exhausted: *Mom says take care of yourself and keep well. She says for you not to worry about how she feels. She says working in the shop with the rest of the girls is better than sitting alone in an empty house. I guess that's all for now.* . . .

Win thought he heard engines and he half rose. Bane heard the sound too. He looked up from his letter and listened intently. A moment later the far-off sound changed pitch; it was a truck on the road to Cerignola, shifting gears as it climbed out of the hollow that bordered the base. Win looked at his watch for the third time in the last five minutes.

"It's early yet," Bane said quietly. "Phil can see them before we hear 'em." He put aside the letter he had been reading and sighed.

"What's new in Jacksonville?" Win asked for something to say, anything that would speed the minutes.

"Nothin' much."

"No excitement, huh?"

Bane shook his head. "Things get kind of quiet aroun' home in the summertime."

Win waited for him to go on but he seemed to be finished. Now that the silence had been breached, its re-establishment was unbearable. He started to look at his watch again but stopped himself.

"Ah don' know if you'd exactly call it excitement," Bane said finally, "but a nigger got himself shot downtown last week."

"Shot? How?"

"On the bus. Driver tol' him to move on to the back an' this nigger wouldn't do it."

Win sat up and the sweat trickled from his armpits down his sides.

"Daddy says the driver tol' him twice," Bane explained. "Ah guess he jus' got kind of pissed off."

"And he shot him? Just like that?"

The amazement in Win's voice affected a change in Bane and he moved restlessly on his cot. It wasn't anger or even peevishness that appeared in his face, rather it was a kind of resignation, as if he had blundered into a situation that could have been avoided.

"Well, he tol' him twice," he said mildly.

Win laughed aloud. "And that makes it O.K. Christ, if the bus drivers shot everybody who wouldn't move back——"

"It's different down in Florida."

"It sure as hell must be. What did they do with this driver?"

"What d'you mean, do?"

"Nothing, I guess—nothing at all. Listen, Al, what would you have done?"

"Me? Hell, Ah wasn't even there."

"I know you weren't, but what if you had been? What if when you get home you see somebody getting lynched—what would you do?"

Bane's face closed and his voice went flat. "Ah ain' so sure of ever gettin' home, an' Ah never saw nobody get lynched."

"Never?"

"No, never. You folks up North think we ain' got nothin' better to do than go aroun' shooting niggers all day long. Hell, Ah bet there ain' been a lynchin' in Florida for five, maybe ten years."

"What d'you call this, then?"

Bane shook his head in resignation. "See, that's——"

"O.K., I suppose he would have shot a white man for sitting in the colored section."

"Now that's jus' plain silly, Win. Ain' no white man gonna sit down with niggers—least not in Jacksonville he ain'."

Bane smiled at him and Win knew he ought to drop it. It was like trying to explain purple to someone who was color blind. They had started innocently enough, wanting only to make the waiting bearable, and now they were bucking each other. The pattern seemed inevitable, endlessly repeating itself. In every attempt at communication with the other officers of the crew he had to be careful or there was conflict. The façade of unity achieved as a result of their shared anguish on the Ploesti raid had begun to crack. And all within two weeks, with each day making it increasingly difficult. Or perhaps, he reflected in a flash of personal recognition, it was because he himself had grown increasingly wary. Yet he could not let the conversation go. His shock and growing outrage at Bane's attitude was due primarily to that raid, to the fact that the men flying the fighters that had escorted their crippled bomber back to Italy had been Negroes.

"Listen, Al," he began again, the words coming slow and unsure, "can't you see what I mean? Those guys flying the P-51s that brought us home were colored too. They saved our lives."

Bane looked at him incredulously.

"Well, they did, didn't they?"

"Maybe, except we didn' see any German fighters after they picked us up. But what's that got to do with it?"

"Can't you see? They're right up there flying, same as we are." Win's voice rose as he felt it slipping away again. "That guy in Jacksonville might of been one of them."

Bane shook his head decisively. "That's crazy. Those boys all come from up North."

"How d'you know?" Win demanded, angry at himself now for his inability to make this simple thing clear. "How d'you know they all do?"

But Bane was no longer listening to him. The pilot's head was cocked, his eyes narrowed as he concentrated on something far off. Win opened his mouth to continue, but Bane raised his hand for silence. Then Win sensed it, a distant, almost imperceptible aberration in the air, subtler than sound, that he knew came from the churning of hundreds of propellers.

"Here they come!" Lange shouted from outside.

Bane rolled off his cot and in one movement ducked out of the tent. Win followed him slowly, feeling the frustration congealing within himself.

From all of the tents the men who had waited on the ground were coming out to look at the sky. There weren't more than fifteen or twenty, enlisted men and officers together. As a result of the losses suffered by the group during the past two weeks, it now took most of the flying personnel to mount eight airplanes from a squadron for a mission.

Phil Lange had a pair of binoculars, and a knot of half-naked men were clustered around him, all of them straining their eyes toward the northeast. They waited in silence, their attention divided between the still empty sky and the man with the field glasses.

"I see them now," Lange was saying quietly as Win came up. "The formation looks pretty good."

"We're in Easy and Fox," the enlisted man standing at his elbow told him.

"I know, but there's three groups. I can't tell which is ours yet."

Down on the airstrip there was a flurry of motion. Preparations were being made to receive the returning bombers. The planes would be landing toward the squadron, and the row of ambulances and fire-fighting equipment that gathered at the head of the runways was in plain sight of the waiting men. They stirred restlessly as the squadron flight surgeon dismounted from the last ambulance and carefully placed his black instrument case on the running board.

"That's how they bring babies," the enlisted man said.

"Sonofabitchin' butchers," someone else muttered.

"I can see them good now," Lange said. "Ours are the ones on the left, I think."

Win looked up and saw them too, like flyspecks on the vast blue pane of the sky, but regularly arrayed and growing steadily in size, resolving themselves finally into the whale shapes of B-24s.

"Well count 'em, for Christ's sake, will ya!"

"I was counting." Lange lowered the glasses and held them out to the impatient enlisted man. "Here, wise guy, maybe you can do it better."

"For God's sake, Lange!"

"Come on, Lieutenant, will ya!"

Lange, his face flushed with anger, raised the glasses again and focused them. Now there was complete silence. "There's six in Easy and six in Fox. I guess that means they're all here."

"What about the other boxes? Maybe some of them fell back."

"Don't be a jerk. Who'd fall back if they could move up?"

"Everybody's here," Lange repeated. "Six boxes of six. And only two feathered props that I can see."

"Then it *worked!*" The enlisted man began pounding Lange on the back. "*It worked!*"

Win felt the jubilation too, and it wiped away everything else for the moment. Now the formation was only a mile or so away, and then it was overhead, the thunder of the engines isolating each man in his own little cubicle of sound. He saw the happy faces of the men around him, saw their lips move as they screamed at each other, but he could hear nothing except the roar of the engines.

The group wheeled over the base in a wide arc and the first of the bombers peeled off prior to landing. Following it down, Win could make out the group's new insignia on its vertical fins: intersecting red squares where before there had been round white balls. The insignia change had been made after the third of the disastrous missions that the group had flown in the past two weeks since the Ploesti raid. It had been made after She had told them on the nights following each mission that they had lost so many planes and so many men. And they had waited for her each night, not even listening to the records She played, waited for what She now called her "nightly memo to the 902nd" when She gloated over their impending annihilation and reminded them of the shattered tabu. So they had changed their group insignia, and this mission, flown deep into Germany to Regensburg, had been the test. And now the planes had returned unscathed.

The first of the planes landed and taxied past the waiting line of ambulances to the revetments. They came in one after the other, thirty seconds apart. As he watched, ✕63 dipped to the ground, righted itself, and landed. When it had trundled off the runway its top hatch opened and Milbank's head popped out. The engineer made himself comfortable on top of the fuselage, and Win saw the wide grin bisecting his face. He waved to the watching men and Win raised his hand in greeting. A pickup crew was flying ✕63 with Milbank as engineer and Macy as navigator.

The men began drifting toward the S-2 hut to meet the crews. Some who were barefoot hurried over to their tents to put on shoes. The trucks would be coming up from the flight line in a matter of minutes.

They waited expectantly, and when the first of the trucks rolled up out of the hollow, they surged forward to meet it. Moving with the others, Win sensed that something was awry. The men on the truck seemed strangely subdued. His first reaction was that they only appeared that way in contrast to the exultant men who had waited for them, but as he got closer he was sure that something was wrong. All the way up from the revetments the fliers had been peeling off layers of clothing and now each man was bent to the mound of equipment at his feet. It was as if they were trying to postpone something.

Then the second truck rolled up into the squadron area and Win saw Macy and Milbank sitting together near its tail gate. He circled the knot of now hesitant men so that he was at the side of the new arrivals while their truck was still braking for a stop.

"How'd it go?" he yelled up at them.

Milbank spat carefully over the side and then grinned at him. "Like a practice mission," he said.

Win looked at Macy for corroboration and his friend smiled his slow sad smile.

"Yeah," he said. "This time *we* got two. Only they were ours."

"Ours? What d'you mean? What happened?"

Macy handed down his parachute bag without answering and climbed heavily down over the side. Win dropped the bag and reached up for Milbank's.

"You got a cigarette?" Macy asked.

Still holding the engineer's bag, he handed over his pack.

"Come on, for Christ's sake, what happened?"

Macy lit the cigarette and exhaled smoke. He shrugged, but before he could answer, one of the men still on the truck screamed: *"Look out!"* and they were on them, coming so low and so fast that they preceded their own sound, and the combined slip stream of an echelon of four hit like a breaking wave. Win stood rooted in bewilderment, still holding the engineer's bag, and as the next four bore down on them he felt himself pulled roughly to the ground. In a crazy montage he was aware of Milbank's grinning apology from beside him as he rolled over in the dust. There were sixteen P-51s in four echelons of four buzzing them. They had come in so low from across the fields that they had to pull up to clear the S-2 hut. Lying on his back, seeing everything upside down, Win watched the third echelon come straight at them, continuing low, so low that the end plane clipped the electric light wires running between the tents. Then they pulled up in a cruel, wrenching *chandelle* that had nothing of grace in it, that was only a method of rising and changing direction for another furious pass.

"Crazy sonsabitches!" he screamed. "What the hell do they think they're doing?"

"They're giving us a course in aircraft recognition," Macy answered from where he lay flat on his stomach, his chin on his hands.

Then they had to clutch the trembling earth again as the fourth echelon bore down and over, leaving the air to reverberate from the impact of their sound waves.

"Aircraft recognition!—the bastards are gonna kill somebody."

"They ought to," Macy said. "We killed two of them this morning."

Win stared at him and Macy nodded.

"On the way to the target—not a German in sight. I guess one of the gunners got nervous. Everybody opened up and before it was over we blew two of them out of the sky."

That night the noise in the club had the separate quality of loneliness. It could not hide the quiet desperation in the room. In spite of the crowd, of the many different conversations in progress, it was as if everyone was straining to hear what everyone else was saying; as if by marking every word spoken they would eventually uncover the phrase that magically dispelled guilt. And so even the full professional tones of the Armed Services' announcer booming out the nightly communiqué afforded no protection to private talk. Standing at the bar, Win could hear the muted obbligato of the poker game at the other end of the room. The *Check, check, I'll open, I'm out, I'll see you, I'll just raise you, That lets me out,* was distinctly audible. Without turning his head, he heard Jesse place the two glasses of gin and juice on the bar beside him. He picked them up and began edging his way through the crowded room to where Macy was waiting. Now that he was watching faces as he moved it seemed that not only was he able to hear their voices, but able to hear their thoughts form before the words were uttered. Looking at the glasses he was carrying, he saw how his hands shook, and he realized how irritable he felt.

"Maybe you better drink them both," Macy said when he had reached the table. "You look haunted."

"Well it's not just me, the whole joint's haunted. Any minute now somebody's gonna get up and run right through that wall."

"I know. And then run straight down to the flight line and put their head in a turning propeller. I even got the basket ready."

"You're nuts." He put Macy's drink down before him and downed his own in one swallow. "I think I'll get two more," he said.

While he leaned against the bar waiting for Jesse to mix the drinks, the door opened and Bane and Lange came in with a third man between them. It took Win a full moment to recognize Matt Jones. The big copilot had had his dirty white turban of bandages removed, revealing his head as naked as an egg. His uncovered skull was long and narrow and it made him appear foreshortened. It negated his massive shoulders and heavily muscled neck and somehow made the whole figure of the man seem puny.

Win laughed. "Hey, Samson," he called, but Matt had as yet not been initiated into the special awareness of the room and he did not hear. "Which one's Delilah, Samson?"

This time Matt heard, but before he could respond he was surrounded by the group near the door. They had finally recognized him. Win turned back to the bar to pick up the drinks and started back to the table. He was still laughing when he sat down.

"You're drunk," Macy told him. "You keep that up and one day he'll break your back."

"That pin-headed son of a bitch?"

"O.K., forget it. Have another drink."

"You know, you're right," Win said suddenly.

Macy stared at him.

"Well, not completely right. I'm high, but I ain't drunk."

Macy laughed and Win joined him. They had been drinking steadily since the bar opened. Macy had not wanted to eat, so they had stayed in the club munching salted peanuts and drinking gin and grapefruit juice.

Now Win felt that his cheek muscles were stiff. He put his hand to his face and found that his lips were bent in a smile. He'd probably been walking around with that silly grin on all evening, he realized. He looked around, but nobody was watching him. Concentrating on it, he made his face relax. When he looked up he saw Macy laughing at him and he began laughing again himself. Macy stood up and said he would get the next two drinks.

Win sat up straight. He wasn't drunk, not even a little. He had tried. First by leaving it all to the liquor, and then by urging it along, saying to himself that he was high and pretending that it had already taken hold. It had been such a wonderful idea. The endless evening had stretched ahead, and ahead of it many, many more such evenings. The long-throttled terror had stirred within him. Then Macy had said let's have another drink, let's have six more, and it had been like being helped over a high wall, like finding money in the street. But it hadn't worked.

Macy returned with the drinks and they sat in silence. The voice of the Armed Services' announcer faded away. Then it began and tonight, more than any of the nights that had gone before, it was directed at them. First She played Ellington's "Don't Get Around Much Any More" and the words, sad and fitting, littered the room like dead leaves:

> Missed a Saturday dance,
> Heard they crowded the floor,
> It's awfully different without you,
> Don't get around much any more.

Then She told them of German victories in Rumania and of Japanese victories in the Pacific. She played Jimmy Lunceford's "Blues in the Night" and Dinah Shore sang "Smoke Gets in Your Eyes." She told them that the Communists had control of Washington, that Franklin Roosevelt had suffered a relapse

and had been secretly committed to an insane asylum. That a
Negro child had been born to a white actress. That French
pilots training in America had a whore house on their field that
was staffed by the wives of men who were overseas.

It went on and on and they listened to every word. Finally
it was over. She said good night, and then, laughing, She remembered something—her nightly memo to the 902nd. Gaily
She told them to stop kidding, that they were big boys now.
She told them that She knew they had changed their group
insignia, adding coyly that she had liked the round white balls
much better than the intersecting red squares. Then, the gaiety
gone from her voice, She told them that they were going to
pay, that even if the group was dissolved and they were all
sent to different groups, the Luftwaffe would hunt them out
until each and every one of them was dead. Then she said
good night again, and it was really over.

"What a lot of crap!"

Win knew that Macy had said it, but his words were swallowed up in a crash of shattering glass. Someone had swept the
top of the bar clear of glasses and bottles.

"Now take it easy, Lieutenant," Jesse was saying. "Just take
it easy."

The scuffling set up eddies of movement throughout the
room. Win stood up and saw Jesse lying halfway across the bar
holding onto a bombardier named Keech.

"Let go of me, you sonofabitch," Keech was wailing. "*Let go
of me.*"

Jesse was a powerful man, but half off the floor in that position he was unable to apply sufficient leverage. Keech heaved
himself up and broke the bartender's hold. He lost his footing
and the men beside him held out supporting hands.

"Let go of me, all of you!" Keech yelled. He regained his
balance and stood in a little cleared circle in front of the
bar.

"Take it easy, boy," one of the men who had kept him from falling said. "She was just talking."

Keech turned to face his new tormentor. It was obvious that he wasn't drunk, that something besides alcohol was stoking his frenzy.

"Talk, huh? What about all the guys that got killed in the last two weeks? What killed them—talk?"

Jesse was moving slowly around the bar. "Now you just take it a little easy, Lieutenant," he was saying softly.

"You keep your nose out of this!" Keech roared at him. And then he began to sob. "I lost my whole crew. All my buddies . . ."

The circle began to close around him, the men murmuring their solicitude, but just as suddenly as it had started, his sobbing stopped. The bombardier whirled on Matt Jones, and as if he generated a kind of centrifugal force, everyone in the circle turned with him.

"You're responsible!" he screamed at Matt. "We're all gonna get killed on account of you!"

Matt just blinked at him.

"Well, why don't you say something? *Say something!*"

Matt shook his naked head and his lips moved, but no sound came.

Now Keech was searching the room and he saw Lange and Bane in the far corner behind the poker table. Although they were sitting motionless, they seemed to be huddling to the wall.

"Well?" Keech demanded. "What've you got to say? Why didn't you go in and land and take it like a man instead of making us pay for it?"

The room was full of waiting. Nobody spoke.

"Did we give you permission to murder us all?" Keech's voice seemed to be rising an octave with every word. "Did we? *Did we?*"

"Take it easy, Keech," Win said, the words coming of themselves, the irritation throbbing in his head so the whole room was unsteady.

"I don' take anything from you!"

The circle opened and they were facing each other across fifteen feet of breathless silence.

"*You hear me!*" Keech screamed. "I don' take anything from you! *You*—you were afraid to go in and land. They'd-a pulled your circumcised prick out of your belly!"

"Take that back." The words came automatically from across the years.

Keech laughed. "You kill my buddies and now you wan' me to take it back, huh?"

Win was moving toward him. "Take it back."

"Take it back yourself, you sneakin' little Jew bastard."

Win swung to kill him with one punch. It came so fast, out of such fury, that the bombardier had to fall back against the bar to avoid it. The bar gave behind him and he fell to the floor. In his panic to get away he swung around in a crablike motion and began to crawl. Crouched over him, off balance from the missed swing, Win felt the rage swell hot and thick within him, cauterizing guilt and fear alike. He prepared to launch himself upon the crawling man, to follow him down on the floor and beat out his life. Then he became conscious of the restraining hands on his shoulders. He shook his head to clear his vision and saw Macy and Jesse holding him.

"Let go, I'm gonna kill him."

"Take it easy, Lieutenant," Jesse whispered, jerking his head significantly, and Win saw Major Abbot standing just inside the door.

Abbot stood with his hands on his hips, looking down at Keech. "Get up," he commanded. Then he turned to Jesse. "What's going on here, Sergeant?"

"It's nothing, Major. Just a little argument."

Abbot considered him coldly and Jesse waited for some support from the others. None came.

"This one," he said miserably, pointing to Keech, "passed a remark about Lt. Helman."

"What was it?"

"It was just a remark, Major."

"What did he say?"

"Well, he called him a Jew bastard . . ."

Abbot turned on Keech. "Apologize to him," he commanded.

Keech moved his head from side to side. The other men in the room were still, waiting. Win saw their stiff, closed faces.

"Apologize," Abbot repeated automatically.

"Never mind, I don't want any apology," Win said. He walked past Abbot and out through the door.

The darkness and the uneven ground slowed him. Twenty feet outside the door he stopped. Where could he go? Then he heard Macy calling his name, and simultaneously he realized he was crying, the warm tears rolling down his cheeks.

"Gimme a cigarette," he got out when Macy was beside him.

Macy took the cigarette out of his own mouth and handed it over. They stood there in the darkness and Win wiped his face.

"You feel all right?" Macy asked.

"I should've killed him."

"Yeah, and then what? You going to kill them all?"

Win felt the tears start again. His shoulders were heaving and he couldn't control them. He needed time.

"Let's walk up to the road," Macy said.

They sat down on the stone wall that bordered the road where it dipped down into the hollow. The night was alive with insect noises. The moon wouldn't be rising for an hour yet and it was very dark.

"Listen," Win began, for it was pushing against his ribs and he had to let it out, "you remember Johnson?"

"Sure."

Win sighed. "I been carrying one of his dog tags on every mission since the day he went down. I took it out of his tent. That son of a bitch was right."

"Right? Johnson?"

"No, Keech. I *was* afraid to go in. Even with the dog tag and a nice Christian name I was afraid."

"Was that the only reason?" Macy's voice was gentle.

"I don't know. I just don't know any more."

Macy was waiting for him to go on.

"I didn't do it alone," he burst out. "Everybody was for it then. But did you see those bastards tonight?—they just sat there!"

"And you carried the ball."

"At least I shut him up, didn't I?"

"For now you did."

They sat smoking in silence. Win still hadn't touched the core of it, the real sadness. It was harder to talk about because he still hadn't given it up. He couldn't, he had depended on it too much. Then it was as if Macy could read his thoughts.

"But you were surprised," he said. "I saw. I was watching you."

"Surprised they just sat there? The hell I was!"

Macy didn't say anything and finally it wasn't so hard.

"Yeah, I was surprised. I didn't expect to catch it here." Win laughed his bitterness. "Don't worry, it's happened to me before. I been called hebe and sheeny and kike—but I didn't expect to catch it here."

"What makes you think it's different here?"

"It's gotta be! What're we killing ourselves for?"

"You tell me," Macy said. "I don't know."

6 Venus was low on the horizon, brilliant in the last darkness. There was a half hour until sunrise. The truck from briefing stopped in front of the revetment and Win jumped from its tail gate. His flying boots cushioned the impact but still he was jarred. The gin and grapefruit juice had left him feeling fretful and sodden and not yet fully awake. Then he remembered that this was Sunday morning. He let the cigarette fall from his lips and ground it savagely under his boot.

He stumbled along in the uncertain light, cursing the heavily loaded parachute bag that banged against his leg with every step. Ahead of him loomed the vague, earthbound bulk of the strange airplane. He could see the yellow finger of Bane's searchlight probing the underside of the wing and for an instant Matt's naked head was visible in the beam as he reached up to check a supercharger. Near the edge of the revetment, where he knew the enlisted men would be sitting, there glowed a cluster of burning cigarette ends. He hesitated, and then turned straight toward the bomber.

"Who's there?" Bane's voice demanded nervously.

Win turned and the searchlight beam hit him flush in the face. He raised his arm for a shield.

"Rudolf Hess!" he shouted. "Who the hell are you expecting?"

He heard Milbank laugh and Bane muttered something about not recognizing him. The beam flicked away, leaving him in darkness, and he continued up to the plane. He ducked into the bomb bay and lifted himself to the flight deck. Feeling his way, he stowed the parachute bag under the radio table, and then straightened up. In front of him the banks of instruments on the pilot's panel glowed blue-green. He made his way forward and set the panel clock. Unable to think of anything else to do, he climbed back out of the bomber to smoke a cigarette.

Standing by himself, watching the luminescence of the eastern sky spread, Win thought about the mission. He was very nervous and he could feel himself sweating beneath his heavy clothes. They were going to bomb a railroad marshaling yard at Szeged, just across the Tisza River in Hungary. It was not a bad target and the chance of German fighters coming that far south to intercept them was remote. Yet he was as apprehensive as he could ever remember being before a mission. It was two weeks now since he had been off the ground. Milbank and Rogers had flown as members of pickup crews, but for the rest of them this was the first time up, the first time they were to function as a unit since the Ploesti raid. The nightmare of that mission returned to him and he was completely unsure of how he would behave in the air. He looked over at the seated gunners and wondered if they felt the same way and almost went to speak to them as he had every other time before take-off, but what he had experienced in the club the night before held him. He turned instead to stare bitterly at the strange bomber. He hated switching planes. There was none of the sense of security derived from things being in their long-accustomed places; rather there was a gnawing fear that something you would need desperately once you were in the air would be forgotten.

The old plane, patched and battered, had been a trusted friend. It had brought them home safely so many times. But it had been sent to salvage immediately after the Ploesti raid and the cannibalistic dismemberment of its parts to feed other B-24s had quickly reduced it to a sagging skeleton.

Win glanced at his watch. It was a few minutes before 0500. The squadron across the field began starting engines, their first uneven clamor injecting the morning with urgency. It had become light enough to see and Win was surprised to find that he had been standing quite close to the enlisted men. Now that the protective darkness was gone he had to say something.

"We start engines in a couple of minutes," he said finally. "You better get ready."

They rose and for the first time he noticed the two replacement gunners. One was just a boy with red hair and a face so pale that his freckles stood out in pink blotches. The other he recognized as a ten- or fifteen-mission veteran with the flush of newly acquired toughness still on him. Win went toward them. The redhead reminded him of Reilly.

"My name's Helman," he said. "I'm the navigator."

He stretched out his hand and the veteran took it and introduced himself, but the boy was looking distractedly across the field, and when Macchione tapped him on the shoulder he was so startled that they all laughed.

"This your first mission?" Win asked him.

"No, second." His voice was choked and they all laughed again, and this time even he managed a smile.

"Well, just take it easy," Win told him. "We'll watch out for you. What are you, waist gunner?"

He nodded and Win turned to Milbank.

"You keep an eye on him, Jack."

They were all watching him now, and he saw from their faces that they were waiting for him to go on, waiting for him to give them the ritualistic speech about vigilance and not leaving the turrets and not making any mistakes. He knew that they wanted him to, but he couldn't do it. He tried but it wouldn't come.

"Well, I guess we better get started," he said, and his voice sounded strange in his own ears. "Just remember to keep your eyes open."

They nodded eagerly, waiting for more, but he turned away from their disappointment and walked slowly toward the plane.

After take-off they mounted high into the bright translucency of the morning. The sun, invisible on the ground, lay directly ahead of them, floating on the Adriatic, turning the gray-green water blue.

It was quiet in the plane from the time they left rendezvous. The air was without turbulence and the bomber like a stable platform. Lange was up in the nose fussing with his bombsight. They were leading Charley box and he was responsible for synchronizing on the target. Bane was flying, edging his throttles forward in minute corrections as they started the long climb to nineteen thousand feet. Later Matt would take over. It was less tiring for the copilot sitting in the right-hand seat to follow the lead box that flew off to their right.

This mission was without deception. There were no feints. The German armies in southern Yugoslavia and Greece were retreating back to the fatherland to avoid being trapped by the Russian thrust through the Balkans. Szeged was important because a number of railroads that the Germans were using to move troops ran through it. So the bombers proceeded in a direct line, altering course only to skirt the plotted flak guns at Sarajevo.

It wasn't until they were over the northern slopes of Yugoslavia's central range of mountains that the crews began to really watch the sky. In the valley between the mountains and the Danube a series of cumulus clouds had formed, their anvil-shaped thunderheads glistening in the thin upper air. The sunlight funneled through the laminated tiers of rolling whiteness, tinting the outer edges coral pink. It was very beautiful and very dangerous. The group's escort of P-51s had not yet appeared. The men in the bombers alternately watched the sky and the clouds. Nobody spoke.

Win checked and rechecked their position. The escort was ten and then fifteen minutes late. Soon the bombers would have to abandon their planned course to find a way through the rank of clouds and the P-51s would be unable to locate them.

Finally it was too late.

The group leader swung to the left and they entered a new valley, a passage of clear sky with the vast billowing whiteness looming thousands of feet above them on each side. The men in the turrets searched the air with an ardor that was rapidly mounting to frenzy. Then they were clear of the clouds, with the green plain stretching unbroken ahead of them into Hungary. The blue reaches of the sky were still empty of fighters, enemy or friendly.

Their Initial Point was the town of Senta in Yugoslavia. Fifteen miles farther north and across the border was Szeged. The Tisza River bisected both places.

Still in that unreal serenity, they passed Senta and began their bomb run. Matt was flying now, holding the plane steady for the bombsight. Beneath them the railroad bridge crossing the river, then the city of Szeged, and finally the marshaling yard came into view.

Then, with unbelievable suddenness, the tranquillity was demolished. Three bursts of flak blossomed magically off the right wing. The bomber reared as if in fear and they heard the shell fragments rattle on its fuselage. Matt folded his big hands tighter on the controls. Immediately the next cluster burst, this time so close in front of them that the nose of the airplane entered the miniature black cloud and immersed the flight deck in momentary darkness. Matt let go of the controls to cover his face. He pulled his feet up off the rudders and drew his knees up to his belly. Win saw him do it and Bane saw him, but it was too late. The concussion of the spent flak flung the uncontrolled bomber violently on one wing. Bane snatched the controls to steady them while the six other B-24s in Charley box skidded crazily by. Matt brought his hands down from his face, but nobody saw him. The interphone became a shrieking confusion with Lange's voice shrill with fear and fury outscreaming the others.

"BOMBS AWAY . . . BOMBS AWAY . . . BOMBS A . . ."

Then the whole morning exploded into chaos and the air was filled with streamers of red and blue and yellow flame. Rockets hissed through the black-bursting flak in lunatic arcs. Shells burst and parachute flares hung suspended, changing sunlight and blue sky into blinding incandescence. A stick of bombs laddered serenely past them. It was like some mad, monstrous Fourth of July.

Win added his voice to the idiot babble on the interphone.

"Get off, you bastards!" he screamed. "GET OFF THE INTERPHONE!"

Finally it was his own voice he was hearing. He looked out the side window. They seemed to be all alone. The plane was flying level.

"Turn to a hundred and ninety-five degrees, Al," he said in a normal voice. "We're supposed to rally right."

The plane heeled over in a co-ordinated turn. Tilted over, they all saw the ground for the first time. The marshaling yard was like an erupting volcano seething with flame and smoke. An occasional rocket arched up and burst. But they were well past it now and it was only a spectacle, without danger for them.

"We must've hit a ammunition train," Bane said.

"Not us!" Lange began to scream again. "We didn't! We threw our goddamned bombs all over hell and gone. What the hell do you guys think you were doing up there? What the hell kind of——"

"O.K., O.K.," Win cut in. "Let's knock it off until we catch up with the group. Let's keep our eyes open instead."

And as suddenly as it had begun it was over. Calm was restored. The interphone grew silent. In a matter of minutes they were up with the group and Bane attached himself to one of the end boxes. Everyone began to breathe normally again.

When they got to the mountains they found that the threatening clouds had blown away and they were able to fly a straight course back over Yugoslavia. They saw no fighters. The atmosphere in the bomber grew quiet and relaxed. The men removed their oxygen masks and lit cigarettes. But Matt just sat there in numb silence, not moving, staring straight ahead out of unseeing eyes. While they were letting down over the Adriatic he turned and offered to take the controls. Bane refused and he went back to his staring. Twenty minutes later they were back over the base.

When they had landed they quit the plane with impersonal speed. Once the base had been sighted, their ability to identify themselves with the bomber had ended, and now as its propellers stopped turning they stripped it of their belongings, leaving it an empty machine. By the time Win had lowered himself to the ground, half of the men were already out and standing at the mouth of the revetment waiting for a truck. Bane climbed down behind him, closely followed by Phil Lange. Matt came out more slowly, as if reluctant to leave the plane.

"Hold it a second," Lange said as soon as he was on the ground. "I want to know what the hell happened."

Bane rubbed his face wearily. Win was watching Matt. He had the feeling that the copilot was going to cry.

"Well, let's have it. I wasn't going to say anything in the air, but now I want to know."

Before Bane could answer the ground-crew chief came running up, yelling: "Hey, Lieutenant, come on an' take a look at this!"

He was very agitated and they followed him around the plane. The men who had been waiting for the truck saw them and came drifting back. The crew chief pointed triumphantly up at the right wing. There was a gash almost a foot long ripped clean through it.

"Take a look at it from this side, will ya?" he urged them. "You can see the gas tank. It missed it by inches!"

They stood in a circle and nodded solemnly. They were moved, but there was nothing to say. Then Rogers walked right by them. They hadn't seen him lower himself from the plane.

"That's what must've happened over the target," Milbank said finally. "Me an' Red here about bailed out."

"Not just you!" Chic exclaimed. "I was out of my turret."

But Bane wasn't listening. He was watching Rogers. The nose gunner didn't stop when he came to the perimeter strip; he kept right on going.

"Damn, Ah figured somethin' was wrong," Bane said as he watched him.

"Wrong? I'll say something was wrong! A little more an' you'd-a been tryin' to fly on one wing," the crew chief said.

"Ah didn't mean that. Ah mean him."

"Who?"

"Never mind. Hey, Rogers!" Bane called. "You wait a minute, Ah want to talk to you."

The gunner stopped but didn't turn around. Bane hurried to him and the others followed.

"Were you up in the nose turret on landing?" Bane demanded.

Rogers nodded.

"Well goddamnit, man, you know better than that! Ah had her trimmed 'way back an' still we was nose heavy."

Rogers just stood there, his face placid in repose. "I forgot," he said.

"Forgot!" Bane looked at him closely. "You O.K.? You get hit or somethin'?"

Rogers shook his head. "No," he said seriously, "I'm O.K.— *now.*"

"What the hell are you talkin' about?"

"I'm quittin'."

"Quittin'? Quittin' what?"

Rogers smiled and made a vague gesture with one hand, lifting it and letting it drop. He was completely at ease.

"I finally made up my mind," he said. "I ain't flyin' any more."

"But you're not finished, Buck," Macchione said, taking his arm. "You still got missions to fly."

"I'm gonna do it anyways. I should've quit when Reilly and Polletti got killed. I can't stand it any more."

"Well, you got to," Chic said excitedly. "You only got a couple left. Hell, you think they're gonna let you quit just like that? You know what they'll do? They'll——"

"Leave him alone," Macchione broke in. "How do you know what they'll do?"

Rogers raised his hand and let it drop in the same gesture. "I don' want to argue about it," he said. "I made up my mind."

A truck had pulled up in front of the revetment. There was another crew on it and the driver goosed his motor impatiently.

Chic turned to vent his fury. "Hold your goddamned water," he shouted. "We'll come when we're good and ready!"

On the ride back to the squadron area they all watched Rogers. He looked very composed, sitting in silence, his body rocking with the uneven motion of the truck. Where the perimeter strip joined the road he was jolted from his seat and landed on the floor. Sprawled there, he began to laugh. It was all right at first but it went on and on, not building to hysteria, but coming steadily until it seemed that it would never stop. They lifted him up and still it went on. He raised his hand as if the laughter prevented him from saying something, and they all leaned forward to hear, their own smiles by now frozen on their faces. Finally he let the hand fall and the laughter stopped. It was like shutting a valve. Without any explanation he leaned back in his seat and the peace returned to his face.

When the truck came to a stop in front of the S-2 hut Rogers was the first down. Still without saying anything, he started off toward the enlisted men's tents.

"Wait, Buck!" Macchione called after him. "We got to go to interrogation."

"Let him go," Bane said. "We'll tell 'em he don' feel well. He'll be all right in the morning."

After interrogation the four officers returned to their tent. The door had been left closed and the sides down and now it was like an oven under the canvas. Once inside, Win peeled his clothes from his sweating body. Bane slumped down on his cot. Matt remained in the doorway, undecided about what to do, and Lange had to brush by him on his way outside to wash. After a moment Bane got up and Win helped him raise the tent walls. There was a slight breeze and it was pleasantly cool on their wet bodies.

In the minutes until Lange came back in it seemed that nobody moved. Matt, grotesque with naked head, was still standing in the door, and both Bane hunched on his cot and Win lying flat on his back smoking a cigarette avoided watching his dumb agony. The bombardier examined them each in turn and then slammed his towel down on his cot.

"Christ, I'm tired," Win said softly.

Bane heard him and sighed. "It's gettin' so even the easy ones are tough."

"I still want to know what happened," Lange said, controlling his voice with difficulty. "I got a right to know, haven't I?"

"Sure, Phil," Bane reassured him. "It's jus' that Ah'm awful tired."

Win rolled over on his side in order to see better. He didn't want to miss anything. This promised some reward for the pent-up bitterness he was nursing. But today it wasn't going to affect him, he told himself, as he watched Lange glaring at Bane. Today he was going to be a spectator.

"I'm tired too!" Lange was as angry as he'd been over the target. "All you got to do is answer me. What the hell's the secret, anyway?"

"Ain' no secret——"

"Then what's going on? I had that goddamned yard right in the cross hairs before we started doing slow rolls."

Win couldn't resist it. "It was the flak," he said, grinning. "Didn't you see the hole?"

"I wasn't talking to you. You keep out of this."

"O.K., excuse me. I didn't know you hated the Germans so much—or is that the first target you ever missed?"

"I said keep out of it." Lange turned back to Bane. "I want to know what happened, Al."

Bane looked at Matt, looked into the copilot's pleading eyes, and was silent. Finally Matt mumbled something inaudible.

"What was that, Matt?" Win asked brightly. "We couldn't hear you."

Fury was momentarily kindled in the copilot's eyes, but it died. His hopelessness was so naked, so poignant, that Win felt shame instead of triumph. With a half-throttled sob, Matt turned and plunged out of the tent.

"Now what the hell's eating *him?*"

"He let go of the controls over the target, that's what. You wanted to know what happened—well, now you know."

Lange turned to Bane. "Is that right?"

The pilot, looking utterly spent, nodded. "It sure looks like the ol' crew's messed up."

"Because of him?" Win's intentions had melted away. There had been no pay-off. "All of a sudden you're worried about the crew. I didn't see you getting all excited about Rogers quitting."

"That ain' true," Bane said in gentle reproach. "I been worried a long time now. But Rogers ain' really quittin'."

"He ain't, huh?"

"Naw, he'll feel different in the mornin'."

"Like hell he will! Didn't you hear him laugh? And maybe you forgot how he spilled the whisky at interrogation that time? He's quitting, all right. It's a wonder he lasted this long."

"Ah don' know. Ah jus' don' know any more."

Win snorted. "What I want to know now is what you're going to do about Matt."

"Ah don' know." Bane was very tired. "The major was askin' me again yesterday if he was ready to move up to first pilot an' take over a crew of his own."

"What you say?"

Bane looked at Lange. "Phil was there. Ah tol' him Ah'd let him know."

"Well, now you don't have to keep him waiting any more."

"That's right, Al," Lange said quietly. "Tell him he's ready."

"Tell him he's *ready!* You know I didn't mean that." Win was staring at the bombardier's blond choirboy face. "You want to let him murder nine other men?"

"What the hell are you talking about, murder? He can fly, can't he? Well, let him fly somebody else. We got enough troubles."

"Christ, and I thought I was being tough."

"Tough?"

"You know Ah couldn't do that, Phil."

"Then what *are* you going to do?"

"Ah'll jus' have to carry him, that's all. Ah won' let him do any a the flyin'." Bane's voice grew very sad and he tolled off their names like a lament: "Polletti dead, Reilly dead, Rogers quittin'—now we lose Matt an' that leaves six outa the original ten." He sighed. "Ah used to think how we'd all finish up an' go home together. Maybe even fly back in our ol' plane——"

"Yeah! And then go on a bond-selling tour like the *Memphis Belle*. That's all lovely, but it's not going to happen. I say let Matt quit. If Rogers can do it, so can he."

"And suppose he doesn't want to?" Lange said. "Are you going to make him?"

Win was silent. The alignments had shifted, leaving him alone again, and it merged his bitterness with stubborn anger. He had been sure that this was one time he and Lange were on the same side, that all the bombardier was interested in was not flying with Matt.

"It don' make no difference," Bane was saying. "We'll carry him."

"Well, it makes a difference to me." Win spoke slowly, accenting each word. "I don't like it, and maybe the rest of the guys wouldn't either if they knew what happened. Think of where we'd be if you get hit. How would we get back? Don't forget I want to live through this tour too."

"You should of thought of that before," Lange said.

Win stood up. "I'm not sure what you mean by that, but I damn well would like to be."

"You know what I mean."

"No, I'm not sure. I keep thinking we all did it together." He turned to Bane. "We did, didn't we, Al?"

After a pause the pilot nodded.

"Well, *I* didn't!" Lange's face was white and his voice unsteady. "If we'd of gone in like we were supposed to, we would've been safe!"

"Maybe, and maybe not. But don't try to tell me you didn't, because I remember. You said, 'Kill 'em, kill the bastards!' You were for it when you thought it would save your life. Now it's a little tough and you want to crawl out. Well, you can't! And while we're on it I want to know something else. I want to know why you sat on your ass in the club last night and let that bastard Keech say what he did."

Lange reached behind him and Win got ready to hit him. But it was only his cap.

"I'm going to check the mail," Lange said. "You coming, Al?"

"Not so fast, you sonofabitch. I want to know why you sat there and let him say that."

Bane had come up behind them and he put his hand on Win's shoulder. "Let's stop this," he said. "It ain' really doin' us any good."

Win tried to shrug him off. "It's time it was out in the open. Come on, you were so tough a minute ago."

"O.K., I didn't say anything *because he wasn't talking to me!*" Lange stood up and walked around them and started for the door. "You coming, Al?"

The pilot hesitated, his hand still on Win's shoulder.

"Yes or no?"

Wordlessly Bane dropped his hand and followed Lange out of the tent.

Win remained standing where they had left him, still able to feel Bane's hand on his shoulder. In spite of his resolutions against becoming involved, he had been hurt. Now that he was calmer, the anger receding, he knew he should have been able to predict the outcome. That Bane would ultimately go with Lange should not have come as a surprise. The evidence of their compatibility and of his exclusion had been too long accumulating. Why then, with only ten missions remaining to be flown, had he opened the breach? What had he gained by bringing it out into the open? Why had the sweet thought of finishing up not been enough to make him keep his mouth shut and drift? . . .

"Because home sweet home ain't that sweet," he said to the empty tent, and was not even surprised to find that he had spoken aloud.

He went over to sit on his cot and light a cigarette. Only then did the carefully nurtured bitterness and anger return. But for the first time in longer than he could remember the anger was not all directed outwards; some of it was focused on himself. Sucker, he said, and then he tried it aloud . . .

"Sucker, *shmuck*, you *putz* you. What did you expect—gold in the air?"

And then he felt his aloneness and he could have wept. *So you'll go to the airplanes and it will be a college, they'll make you there a lawyer or a doctor,* his mother had said bitterly, and he remembered how he had tried to explain to her about the things on the posters: about the Air Force spending $25,000 to train each man, about "the cream of the nation's youth" and "only the best need apply" and about the silver wings. And how all the time he had known that he was trying to convince himself too. And then that terrible time in the examination room in the Grand Central Palace when he had faced the be-winged bank of men who had commented on his unshined shoes and broken fingernails and had asked what made him think that he was qualified to be a pilot or navigator or bombardier. His uncouth tongue had filled his whole mouth, he remembered, and he had mumbled something about always having wanted to fly and about building model airplanes, for how could he tell them that theirs was the ladder that he would mount to security? This had left them unconvinced and they had said that they didn't think he was air force officer material, that he would probably be better off in some other branch. But something of the intensity of his need must have made itself apparent, for they had finally given him reluctant approval and passed him on. So now he had outraged a surrender agreement and split a crew and decimated a squadron and group and finally turned the complete circle to where he was fighting in the streets again. . . .

"They were right," he said aloud. "Some officer, some credit to the service——"

"That's a fine way to talk, Lieutenant! On your feet! Pop to when you address a superior officer!"

It was Macy, standing in the doorway and grinning, looking as if he had been there for some time. "Congratulate me," he said. "The bastards have finally discovered my true worth. I am now a captain in my country's Air Force."

They stood one on each side of the otherwise empty truck, balanced like skiers against the uneven ride while the rush of night air peeled away layer after layer of the wine's impact. Neither of them spoke, and as the road unwound itself in the moonlight their shyness increased. They were like those lovers who in the urgency of discovery lay bare for each other the essence of themselves, and then when passion is spent and morning grows light wonder if some secrets are not better kept.

The truck nosed down into the hollow that adjoined the squadron and the driver gently applied his brakes. Even so Win lost his balance and would have fallen had Macy not reached over to steady him. When they had come to a complete stop Win climbed down. His legs were fluid, retaining the truck's motion, and as he began to walk his fatigue enveloped him.

Macy led the way through the enlisted men's section to a big six-man tent that stood off by itself. It had been isolated for quiet. Macy lived in it with the officers of a crew that was training to fly the single-plane intrusion missions that the Air

Force planned for fall and winter when the bad weather would prevent the routine daytime formations from reaching their targets with any regularity.

"They flying again tonight?" Win asked.

Macy nodded and went into the tent while Win stood in the door waiting for him to strike a light. This was another of the things about Macy, he reflected. Since Zymbrowski had gone down, he had moved from tent to tent. Now he was living with four men whose lives were the reverse of his: they flew by night and slept in the daytime.

Macy located the candle, and touching its wick with a lit match, divided the darkness into half gloom. Win entered slowly, watching his foreshortened shadow follow him across the sloped canvas of the tent wall. He flopped down on the nearest cot.

"Christ, I'm tired," he moaned.

"Watch out for the fiddle!"

There was a violin case on the foot of the cot and he had been about to stretch out. He sat up and stared at it.

"Whose is it?"

"Dusak's."

Win ran his hand over the case in wonder, trying to identify it with the small gnarled-looking man who was the pilot of the crew.

"I always figured him for a farmer," he said.

"He is, but he's like you, trying to improve himself."

Win's face clouded and Macy saw it and grinned to make it all right.

"You got to admire the guy for it. He says he always wanted to play the fiddle, so he found a music teacher in Cerignola, bought this violin, and now he's taking lessons."

Macy's smile eased him and he put the case carefully aside and stretched out. He was so tired that it was an effort to keep his eyelids from closing. He didn't want to sleep yet, he wanted to think of this day that had just passed, this strange endless day in which he had flown a mission and separated himself from his crew and told Macy things about himself that he never thought he would say aloud in the presence of any other human being. It had started upon their return from Bari when the truck had deposited them in front of the cathedral in Cerignola. Standing there in the middle of the moonlight-soothed town, feeling the wine that had honed the edges from his anger, he had found himself telling Macy of another such night when he had stood in that same place during the celebration of his own promotion, telling him of the things he had *felt*, of what the promotion had *meant* to him. And while enmeshed in the sensations of that other evening, as if his memory had conjured her from the air, a woman laden with baskets had appeared. With Macy following he had rushed across the street to her, but it had been another woman, old and panic-stricken by their approach, and they had stood watching while she fled from them. Then Win had wanted to go and find the woman of his memory, but Macy had refused, saying they couldn't go back to what was Win's, that there were things to do together and things that were best done alone, and the rejection had not hurt.

"You want a drink?"

He rolled over on his side. Macy had taken an unopened bottle of Old Crow from his foot locker and was running his thumbnail under its seal. He nodded and sat up. Across the tent from him was an unused cot and the moment he saw it the desire was full grown in him.

"Who's cot is that?" he asked.

Macy looked over his shoulder. "Nobody's. Why?"

"Could I have it? Could I move in here?"

Macy splashed whisky into the two cups and added water from a canteen. He handed one cup to Win. "Taste it," he said. "I think I put in too much water."

Win raised the cup and then lowered it. "Excuse me for asking," he said. "I didn't know it was reserved."

Macy grunted and let himself down on his cot. He lay back, his hands folded behind his head. "You'd have to ask Dusak," he said. "It's really his tent."

Win drank the whisky and water without tasting it. He set the empty cup beside the violin case and stood up.

"Why don't you say what you're thinking?" Macy asked, squinting up at him.

"Why don't *you?*" He had meant it to sound harsh, but it came out almost a sob. This was the hardest of all to take.

"All right, I will," Macy said. "I'm thinking that moving in here won't solve anything."

"And I thought it didn't make any difference to you." Win started away. "Thanks for straightening me out."

Macy slid off his cot and now he was between Win and the tent door. "Sit down," he commanded. "You thought what didn't make any difference?"

"You know what I mean." It was hard to talk. Any second now he would be crying, and if he ever started he wouldn't be able to stop. Anger was the only thing that could help him, but he couldn't summon it. He was too tired and too empty and too alone. His legs were unsteady, his head whirling. It crossed his mind that he might faint. Then he felt Macy's hands tight on his shoulders, shaking him gently.

"Sit down," Macy was saying tenderly. "Sit down and listen. What did you mean you thought it didn't make any difference to me? Did you mean about being a Jew?"

Win nodded.

"Well it doesn't! And I'll tell you something else. It really doesn't make too much difference to any of the others——"

"Let go of me." Win tried to shake Macy's hands from his shoulders. "I said let go!"

"No, you're going to listen, you pigheaded sonofabitch. Sure they use it, but there's something more important. You know what you did when you shot down those fighters? You lit the fuse of a stick of dynamite that can blow up and change the goddamned war, that's what. It's already blown up for this group. Don't you know that?"

In spite of himself, Win was listening. This was a new Macy, not guarding himself, not holding anything back. He allowed himself to be forced backward and when he was sitting on Dusak's cot again Macy released him and started pacing.

"You remember Keppler, the bombardier on my crew?" Macy asked, and when Win nodded he went on: "Keppler was a mathematician. One night he sat down and figured it all out. He knew how many guns there were at Vienna and how many rounds a minute each gun fired. Then he figured out how many fragments big enough to kill you each shell exploded into. He multiplied that by the number of minutes you were in range of all the guns while on the bomb run. That times the number of missions in a tour and he had it—the chances of getting killed. When he was all finished he showed it to Zymbrowski. Big Ski went over it very carefully and then he looked at Keppler in that dead-pan way of his and told him he'd made a mistake. He'd forgotten to figure in the possibility of a wing ship getting hit and ramming you as it went down. You know what he was really saying? He was saying it took more than mathematics to fly a tour, that it had to be more than a goddamned lottery."

Nodding vehemently, Macy retrieved Win's cup and his own and poured out two more drinks. He was very agitated. His movements were without their usual precision and he spilled a little of the whisky. His voice was thick with emotion when he went on.

"Ever since that bitch started broadcasting how the Luft-waffe is going to get revenge I been thinking about Zymbrow-ski and what he would be doing about it if he was here. Instead, we got Abbot. Abbot the abbot, with precision bombing his religion. I remember once he told us precision bombing made him decide to go into the Air Force when he graduated from West Point."

Macy laughed and let the sound of it ring through the tent. "Zymbrowski said that's one of the reasons he joined the Air Force too. But after watching it for a while, he said that he still thought the best precision bombers in the world were bedbugs —yeah, bedbugs! He came from a small mining town in Pennsylvania and he said his mother was always battling the bedbugs. She'd soak the bedsprings in kerosene and then she'd get coffee cans and fill them with kerosene and stand the bed in them, one leg in each can. Bedbugs can't fly and they can't swim, still they got back in the bed. So Ski said he lay awake one night with the light on to see how they did it. You know what they did? They crawled up the wall and across the ceiling until they were directly over the bed. Then they dropped. Precision bombing!"

Macy downed his drink by tossing it into the back of his throat and swallowing.

"You get what I'm saying?" he demanded. "That's what the Air Force is—*precision bombers.* It's impersonal, like a game. You fly four miles high and drop bombs. The flak comes up and that's the enemy, not the Nazis manning the guns, just the flak. So you go through the flak so many times and you're through, you go home, the whole thing impersonal. But that's finished for this outfit; now it's personal. Now the Nazis've got to be the enemy. She comes on the radio and says that the Luftwaffe's going to hunt every one of us out and kill us. So all of a sudden the war ain't so comfortable any more—no more off we go into the wild blue yonder to fight tournaments in the sky; we ain't the Lafayette Escadrille and they ain't Baron von Richthofen, the Red Knight of Germany. That crap's finished because you broke the rules."

"Now you sound like Gillespie," Win cut in sullenly.

"I do?" Macy's eyes glittered catlike in the candlelight. "How?"

"That's practically what he said too—we broke the rules of warfare between civilized people."

"Ha!" Macy pounded him on the shoulder. "See, that old bastard realized it right away. He knows which side his bread's buttered on, he doesn't want the rules changed."

"And neither does anybody else."

"No, that's not true."

Win laughed at him. "You're making speeches." He sneered.

"Maybe, but I'm telling you shooting down those fighters like that changed something in all of us——"

"In Gillespie too? In Keech?"

"Yeah, but in a different way."

"That's some answer."

"Answer!" Macy snorted disgustedly. "You always want answers, you think it's that simple. Last time you wanted to know why we were killing ourselves if we still got guys like Keech around and everything's the same. Well, maybe that's the answer for you: we're killing ourselves to keep everything the same."

"Shit!"

"You don't like it? You got a better one?"

"Yeah, I sure as hell have. Screw the bastards, I say. Screw them all. Finish up and get out!"

"No!"

"No? Then what? You tell me, but without the speeches."

"O.K., no speeches. Remember when we were all in the mess hall, the time they changed the tour? Remember I stood up against it? But who stood up with me? *Nobody!* And you know why? Because ever since Zymbrowski went down I been living by myself, safe and apart. And that's why. Zymbrowski knew it, and now I know it, but it's too late for me. That's your answer—you can't run away."

"Who's running?"

"I am," Macy said, and the pain, self-inflicted and festering, was evident in his voice. "I am, and now you are too."

"That's a lie. I don't run from anybody."

"You don't, eh? Then what d'you want to move in here with me for? You want to convince me that you did the right thing by shooting down those fighters? Well, you don't have to, I'm already convinced. But what about the rest? What about your own crew? Are they convinced?"

Win lowered his eyes.

"You told me once that you all did it together," Macy went on. "But that's changed now, isn't it? Do you want it to stay that way, or do you want to change it back?"

"I can't change nothing," Win muttered.

"Yes, you can! Not everybody's like Keech and Gillespie. But you got to live with them and be with them. If you want to change something you got to be part of it. If you move out you'll be cutting yourself off from your own crew. Can't you see that? Can't you?"

His hands were extended to Win in supplication, and the flickering candlelight projected his shadow against the tent wall, distorting yet magnifying his entreaty. Then he straightened up and the moment was gone. Win watched him in silence, feeling that he ought to go and put his hands on his friend's shoulders, as if it were he who now needed comfort.

"Take it easy," he said instead.

"Sure." Macy sighed. "You can stay if you want, I won't blame you."

"Thanks."

Macy smiled ruefully. "I had that coming. But stay tonight, just to show you're not angry."

"O.K.," and now Win was able to grin at him. "Let's have another drink."

7

In that minute of waiting Major Abbot was able to smell himself. Every officer who was a member of the squadron was packed into the club, yet from their mass odor, generated of heat and proximity, he could pick out the spoor of his own body. He stood still, his hands hanging naturally at his sides, while the sweat gathered in his armpits and stained his freshly laundered shirt. A thin line of will divided his irritation from fury and he controlled his desire to pace. Anger was of no use to him unless it could be directed into those channels that achieved results.

"Well, Sergeant," Abbot called finally, his voice even, "I haven't got all day."

Jesse raised his head above the level of the bar. "Yes, sir. Coming, sir," he said, and immediately began edging his way through the crowd. When he reached Abbot he held up the tee shirt he was carrying. It had a figure of a striking eagle and "Army Air Corps" stenciled on it.

"It's all I could find that's dry, Major."

Abbot hesitated, searching his face and waiting for the men to laugh, but the bartender was regarding him without expression and the men were silent.

"It'll do," he said.

Jesse spread the tee shirt to protect a maximum of the green baize-topped poker table and straightened up to offer Abbot his arm. Disregarding him, the major stepped up on a chair and then mounted the table, setting his feet carefully on the tee shirt. As soon as he was standing erect he knew it was a mistake. His head had less than two feet of clearance. The normally rising warm air that stored itself under the ceiling had been further heated by the sun's baking down on the club's thin roof, and the change in temperature was like a blow.

"All right, gentlemen," he began immediately. "Let's get down to cases." Then he stopped. Jesse was still standing in front of the table, looking up at him.

"What is it, Sergeant?"

"I was wondering if you wanted a glass of cold water, sir."

"No, that's quite all right, Sergeant. You can go now. I'll want to see you in my office when this meeting is over."

"Yes, sir."

Abbot's immediate impression was that he would be saluted and his right hand jerked slightly, but Jesse turned away and started for the door. Everyone watched him until he was outside and only then returned their eyes to the major.

"All right, gentlemen, let's get this over with," he began again. "We got a few problems to discuss. Things haven't been going too well with us these last few weeks. We've lost a lot of airplanes and a lot of men. And there's a reason for it. Maybe if you think about it you'll know why."

Abbot left the sentence hanging in air. The bald dome of his head was glistening with sweat and the moisture ran unheeded down his face. But he had them now. The lassitude that had permeated the room seemed broken. He had their undivided attention.

"But even if you do know, I'm going to tell you. Sloppiness, that's the reason!" He pointed at the pile of uncensored letters that lay on the table beside him. "See those letters, they been lying there for a week. That's sloppiness. Take a look at how you're dressed and then go take a look at your tents—sloppiness. Sloppy on the ground, pretty soon you're sloppy in the air. Down here you only get dirty. Up there you get killed. Well, it's going to stop."

The men shifted uneasily and Abbot waited for them to refocus on him. He was confident now. He took a handkerchief from his pocket and mopped his head and face, doing a careful job, letting them wait. Then he went on.

"First, as far as your future conduct on the ground is concerned. Let's take proper uniform. If you're wearing fatigues, O.K. But if you're wearing khaki you'll wear it properly. No more rolled-up shirt sleeves, no more than one button unbuttoned at the neck. When you go into town, you'll wear ties. And nobody leaves the base without permission. Another thing. When I get off this table the uncensored mail is going to be piled on it. That's where it goes from now on. No more poker games until every letter is censored. And I want the tents cleaned up. Unless there's an immediate improvement, you'll stand regular Saturday inspection. Am I clear so far?

"O.K., now in the air. A regular schedule of practice missions will be posted in Operations tomorrow. We're going to learn to fly formation all over again. And from now on there will be a critique following every mission, practice as well as combat. We'll let down our hair and you can cry on my shoulder. Are there any questions?

"If not, I want to see all the first pilots. Hawkins, Bane, Darnell, Matthews, Gillmore, McDuffee, and Dusak. The rest of you are dismissed."

The men began shuffling for the door, their exit hastened by the desire to escape the pent-up heat.

"Just a minute," Abbot yelled. "There's something else. I'm going to let the radio stay in the club, but on one condition. No more tuning in Munich. If I find out that anybody's listening to any more of Her broadcasts, out it comes. That's an order."

Arrested in departure, already partially free of his authority, the men greeted Abbot's last pronouncement without stir. Standing among them, Win expected some demonstration of resistance, but none came. Someone laughed scornfully, that was all. The basic lethargy that had been present before Abbot's speech had undergone a change, but it had not been dispelled. It had absorbed the orders and by acquiescence remained whole.

"Discipline," Win said to Macy when they were outside. "Practice missions and critiques. Chicken shit!"

"Maybe, but it helps."

"Helps? To keep your sleeves rolled down?"

Macy smiled. "Sure, now it gives them something to bitch about that they understand."

"Oh shit! What I wonder is what he's telling the pilots."

"They'll say when they come out."

"You think so? Well, I'm not so sure. I'm going to hang around and find out for myself."

"Why don't you relax? Come on and have a drink. If Bane won't tell you, I'll ask Dusak."

"I'd rather find out for myself."

Macy looked at him. "O.K., I'll be in the tent."

Win nodded and sauntered over to an open window. Standing beside it, he could hear the men moving around inside the club. He lit a cigarette and turned to watch Macy walking off, conscious of the change that had taken place in their relationship. The night they had spent together in Dusak's tent, neither of them able to sleep, had awakened him to certain facts, and as the hours had passed he had gone over them in his mind until they were shaped into a course of action. He had finally, to his own satisfaction, understood why his offer to move in had been rejected. Macy had veiled it in speeches, but when the talk was stripped away the real reason had become clear. It was Macy himself who had been running, and, what's more, had succeeded in getting clean away. Why else had he moved in with Dusak? Win smiled his bitterness. So then I come along and want to duck into his safe little corner and ruin it. All the talk about Zymbrowski had been nothing but window dressing. Zymbrowski was dead and Macy knew as well as he did that in a world full of enemies the dead were of no help. But when he, Win, had asked to share the safe retreat he had been refused. Well, he would find his own. . . .

"All right, let's settle down," he heard Abbot say inside the club. There was a scraping of chairs and the next words were lost. Then he heard Abbot talking again: "It's a hell of a fix. We're down to six crews and there won't be any replacements for at least a week. I'm going to have to form two more crews out of spares and I need two copilots to take them over. How about it, Bane?—you're the oldest crew. Is Jones ready?" Win heard Bane sigh. "Ah don' think so, Major——" "Why the hell not?" "Well, it's hard to say. Ah don' think he's all over his head wound. Ah could tell better after a few more——" "All right, forget it for now. Hawkins, how about Brunner?"

Win turned away. For a moment he was tempted to walk into the club and tell Abbot the truth about Matt. He could even see the expression on their faces, but at the same time he knew it would be wrong. Look how they stuck together. Sure Matt had to be gotten rid of—it was a matter of life and death—but he wasn't the boy to do it. And that wasn't the way to do it. If he went in there and started shooting off his mouth he would only succeed in making them all turn on him. Macy could say all he wanted about what had to be done, but he remembered what had happened in the tent when he had brought the thing about Matt out in the open. Lange had been for getting rid of Matt, but when he had said it, Lange had turned on him. And then out of a buried recess of his memory he remembered the time on the subway. He had been just a boy then. It had been one of those unbearably hot days at the end of summer. The swaying, jolting car had been packed full of people returning from work, all of them made irritable by sweat and noise and their closeness to each other. There had been an argument about a seat and he had heard the old cry of *jewbastard*. A man standing beside him, far removed from the boiling center of trouble, had tightened his face into resolution and pushed forward to intercede, and Win saw again the blood on the same man's face when they had thrust him out of the car at the next station. Win had felt the crawling of his own scalp and had wanted to at least get out with the man, but finally the door had slammed shut, the station had receded, and he had been saved from doing anything except standing there and making himself as small as possible. Well, he had grown up since then; he had gotten older and bigger and tougher. He had learned to tighten himself up like a clenched fist with all five fingers tensed to present only the best striking surface. And that was the way he had lived until the Air Force. He had wanted to drop all that in the Air Force, had in fact been sure that he would be allowed to drop it. But now they had shown him that he couldn't. So he would go back into what he had learned so well. He would take care of Matt, but he would do it without sticking his neck out, and he would do it alone.

The next day they flew and their quarry was stored oil lying beneath a shield of concrete, the tanks underground in a soft fold of the Danube on the northern outskirts of Vienna, the whole target well within the protective arc of the city's three hundred guns. Against this enemy each bomber went well laden with materials of destruction. In each of their bomb bays were hung five one-thousand-pound bombs set with delayed-action fuses to insure maximum penetration. In each of their turrets there lay coiled thousands of rounds of ammunition to feed the ten .50-caliber machine guns. And they went not alone or in pairs, but in formations of hundreds, since this was the fourth month of the Air Force's ever increasing offensive against oil. And the Luftwaffe rose to meet them, consuming precious fuel in a desperate gamble to save the oil that had to be processed and refined before it would power engines. For the Reich that was to live a thousand years was caught in the emotionless equation of modern war, trapped among factors of resource and production. Still, the men in the bombers, arrayed in their strength, went forth as the hunted, not as the hunter.

The tempo of the mission remained constant until the group was abreast of Lake Balaton, pointed toward Budapest. They had reached the top of their climb and leveled off at twenty-one thousand feet, flying through cloudless blue and unbroken sunlight. Minutes later the formation swung left to pass between Graz and Wiener Neustadt. One long leg remained and then they would be approaching the target from the southwest, edging in at a tangent to the rim of Vienna's defenses.

High above the bombers, swinging about like aerial sleds in their echelons of four, the escort of P-38s kept constant patrol, their deadliness and darting speed held in abeyance, their whole purpose integrated with that of the herd. And then, from still higher up, from out of the brilliance of the sun, the Luftwaffe appeared and gave them release.

The queues of Messerschmitts came slicing in at the long train of groups, and the bombers struggled desperately to keep their interval, clinging to each other like cattle beset by harrying wolves. But the raking fusillade exacted its toll and B-24s flamed and fell, some rising crazily on a wing to gyrate ponderously away, others exploding into fragments of fire. In the squadron two were hit and the men looked up from their guns to count the blossoming parachutes.

The formations held, and the P-38s, caught off balance,

swung back to police the long line of bombers, while the Germans slipped and spun to dodge them, intent on the bigger prey. Thus, for half a hundred miles the battle raged, before the bombers succeeded in ridding themselves of their tormentors by entering the storm of flak over Vienna. Here others fell, but the battle had altered: it now had an ending, and the crews rode out their remaining minutes of travail and it was over.

North of the city they rallied, gathering themselves for the six-hundred-mile journey home. In those elements of the Air Force where the losses had been light the men speculated about whether they had hit the target. But in the main, each man was intent on his own agony, fighting to relax his trembling limbs, until the bright wonder of being alive was again rekindled and he was able to count another mission done.

Win looked absently around the club. It was a couple of hours since they had landed and the bar was already open, but the room was still practically empty. Seated at the baize-covered poker table, three men were dealing freeze-out to pass the time until more players arrived. But some of them are never coming, Win thought, some like Gillmore and Lindstrom his navigator, both of whom had been steady players. And on the other side of the room, hugged deep into the corner formed by the bar meeting the wall, sat Hawkins, staring at a three-quarters full bottle of bourbon. Yesterday Abbot had asked for those copilots who were ready to move up to airplane commanders, and Hawkins had recommended his own, Brunner. So today, First Pilot Brunner and a crew of men formed out of the remnants of other crews, among them the bombardier Keech, had gone down. Keech, Win thought, Keech whom he had wanted to kill. He sighed and scowled down at the blank V-mail form; took a sip from his can of beer and picked up his pen. *August 21*, he wrote. *Dear Mom and Sara. Your letter*

*came two days ago and I am answering it right away so you
won't worry. We flew again today, to Vienna, and that leaves
me with nine to go . . .* He raised the pen from the paper.
What could he tell them? What could he say? He took another
sip of the cool beer. *I am feeling fine,* he wrote, *and hope you
both are too . . .*

"Lieutenant."

Win looked up. Jesse was standing near his chair.

"Sergeant Macchione wants to see you," the bartender said.
"He's waiting outside."

Macchione was standing just outside the door and the first
thing Win noticed about him was that he was very carefully
dressed in clean khaki, shirt sleeves rolled down and collar open
the regulation one button. He was wearing a cap too.

"I'm sorry to disturb you," the ball gunner said formally,
looking at the can of beer Win had carried with him.

"You're not disturbing me. What's the matter?"

"Well . . ."

It was obviously very difficult for him, but Win made no
effort to ease things. Instead he drank the rest of his beer and
tossed the can away.

"It's about Buck," Macchione said finally.

"What about him?"

"Well, I was wondering if you'd help him."

"Help Rogers? What the hell can I do for him?"

"I thought maybe you'd go with me to see the flight surgeon.
Something's the matter with Buck. All he does is lay in his cot.
He won't get up."

"Well isn't that tough!"

"They're liable to shoot him unless somebody——"

"Shoot him!" Win laughed. "They'll shoot him back to the
States, that's what. We're the ones who'll probably get shot.
He'll be back there getting discharged."

"No," Macchione said stubbornly. "They got the right to

shoot him if they want. It's in the articles of war. I looked it up. Desertion in the face——"

"For Christ's sake, are you crazy?" Win looked at this solemn-faced old-young man with whom he had flown so many times and yet understood not at all.

"It's the same thing as desertion."

"O.K., I won't argue with you. But why pick on me? Get Bane, he's the pilot."

"You won't do it?"

"No!" Win said angrily. "Why should I? Nobody ever did anything for me. Anyway, it's not my job."

"It's anybody's job that'll do it."

"Well, it's not mine."

"Then I better go back and get Milbank." He hesitated and Win saw how it was for him to ask anything from anybody. "An officer would be better," he said softly. "Please."

"He lays in his cot while you fly missions and you worry about saving his ass," Win raged. "And what the hell do you expect that sonofabitchin' horse doctor to do? He's got no say in it. It's up to a court-martial."

"But if he says Buck's sick, they'll go easy on him. This way they're liable——"

"Yeah, yeah, you already told me, you looked it up."

They stood there in silence, staring at each other.

"Buck's already flown twenty-eight missions," Macchione said. "Maybe that's his tour——"

"And ours is maybe fifty-six, or a hundred and twelve, huh?"

"Maybe." His voice was gentle. "Maybe it is. But Buck's finished at twenty-eight. He ain't faking. Couldn't you tell them that he's done enough?"

"Couldn't *I* tell them? What am I supposed to do, go alone?"

"No, I'm going with you, only you can say it better than me."

"Crap!"

Macchione smiled. "But you better button up your shirt and roll down your sleeves."

"Piss on it!"

Macchione's smile broadened into a grin and they started away together. Win rolled down his sleeves but left two buttons undone at the neck.

"It's a bloody shame," Macy said to Win as they were entering the briefing hall the next morning. "Just a bloody shame. Abbot had a practice mission all planned for this afternoon and now it'll have to be postponed."

There was a lapse of a few seconds while their eyes made the adjustment from pre-dawn darkness to the light provided by dim-glowing electricity, but even in that fleeting moment of not seeing, they were already focusing on the map. Taking off from the Spur, the thick red line that marked the mission followed the 16° meridian of longitude due north over the Adriatic and across Yugoslavia. At the tricornered meeting of the boundaries of Hungary, Austria, and Yugoslavia, the line divided itself into two thinner red lines, one proceeding to Vienna, the other ending at a point on the Danube about thirty miles west of the city. The forks were labeled ⚔1 and ⚔2.

"I don't get it," Macy said. "Didn't we go to Vienna yesterday?"

"Maybe we're number two."

"You know what number two means?" Macy was in a good mood this morning. "When you were a little kid in school and you had to ask the teacher——"

"Yeah, I remember." Win grinned in spite of himself.

"Well, now that I think about it, there's no question. Of course we're number two."

The pressure behind them of those who had still to gain

entrance to discover where they might die that day carried Win and Macy away from the door. They sat down in the rear of the rapidly filling room and lit cigarettes. Major Warren Gillespie, dressed for the air, came stalking out on the small stage and Win saw that he had on a pair of beautifully fitted English flying boots. The boots were half unzipped and the group S-2's immaculate pink trousers were stuffed negligently into their tops. Around his waist was buckled a .45-caliber automatic.

"Good hunting!" Macy said happily. "Tally-ho!"

Win laughed. Macy was very good for him this morning, separating him from his thoughts and giving him respite from the conflicting emotions that were a result of his having gone with Macchione to see the flight surgeon. Despite the fact that they had achieved nothing more than the promise of a complete mental and physical examination for Rogers, the going had left him with a certain pride. But later this pride had given way to a feeling of renewed vulnerability, as if he had after long struggle succeeded in making himself wholly inviolate, and then been immediately seduced. Even the quality of his bitterness had undergone a change and he was tortured now by the thought that he had been weak and stupid.

On the stage the major had picked up his long wooden pointer. He glanced at his watch and turned slowly to face his audience. Standing there, balanced lightly on the balls of his feet, he was the picture of the man of action, the quintessence of the gray-haired wonder of the Air Force song.

"I'd like to kick him right in the balls," Win said, and was surprised at his own vehemence.

"Him?" Macy shook his head. "Not him, he's a tough baby; don't forget he only flies the rugged ones."

"Gentlemen!" Gillespie sang out. "Let's get started. We have a job to do this morning that I think you are going to enjoy. I know I am. We're going up there and rap those bastards that hit us yesterday. We're going to paste those Messerschmitt boys right where they live—on their home field."

"Number two," Macy said.

Gillespie turned to the map and raised his pointer. "This is it. The rest of the Air Force is going back up to Vienna after the oil. We go with them most of the way and then swing off and powder the airport. We'll be carrying fragmentation bombs in aimable clusters and from the I.P. on we'll open into frag formation. Be sure to stay out from under each other on the bomb run. Are there any questions so far?"

"What about escort?"

Gillespie turned, smiling pleasantly. The question had come from near the door.

"Would the gentleman mind standing when he asks a question?"

Nobody moved.

"In that case he obviously isn't too interested in an answer," Gillespie said, still smiling. "We'll proceed now with the metro briefing."

"See," Macy said to Win. "Didn't I tell you he was tough?"

The meteorology officer mounted the stage. As Gillespie relinquished the pointer to him, the group first sergeant poked his head out from behind the map. He had a slip of paper in his hand and he waited silently until the S-2 saw him. Frowning, Gillespie took the paper and read it. The meteorologist, pointer in hand, stood watching him.

"Well," Gillespie said, only half facing the men, "maybe this will make all of you feel better. It seems we won't be going to Ploesti any more—the Russians just captured it."

There was a pause of several seconds while the men separated the meaning of the message from the tone in which it was delivered, and then the roar of their cheer rang through the hall, its volume surprising even those who were still yelling.

The pulsing engines that bore the B-24 through the upper air kept its airframe in constant vibration, and this movement was transmitted into the metal-topped radio table at which Win was working. He spread his dividers and after some difficulty succeeded in anchoring them on the chart; one point on the target, the other on the spot where the group would separate itself from the mass formation to proceed alone to the airfield. The dividers measured eighty-three miles. Previously he had calculated their ground speed at 209 knots, and now he put both figures on his computer. It came out to twenty-four minutes. You could break it down even farther, Win thought. You could separate it into fifteen and nine; fifteen minutes to the I.P., nine minutes of bomb run. But any way you sliced it, you couldn't escape the fact that the group would be hanging out there all alone, without escort, nothing but their own undermanned strength of twenty-seven bombers to depend on. And to top it off, the bomb bays were loaded with fragmentation bombs, tiny missiles that exploded on contact. They were wired together in hundred-pound clusters, but more often than not these broke open on release and the miniature bombs sprayed through the air like deadly confetti. Well, he thought, maybe everything will go fine—we're due for a break. This one and then eight left to go. . . .

He sighed and stood up. Checking to be sure that his trailing web of interphone cord, oxygen hose, and heated-suit cable were clear, he made his way forward to stand between the pilot's and copilot's seats. For a moment he stared out through the windshield at the unbroken ranks of B-24s. "Turn point's coming up any minute now," he said. "We go left about twenty degrees."

Bane nodded, preoccupied as the bomber bucked in the suddenly turbulent air. Ahead of them Able box had already altered course in a gentle bank, and as their own box banked in turn, they were caught in the waves of slip stream. Slowly, almost imperceptibly at first, the gap widened between the group and the mass of the formation. A few more minutes, Win thought, and they'll be out of sight. His reaction was closer to sadness than to fear. Then he was aware of Bane pounding his gloved fist against the instrument panel.

"Something wrong?"

Bane pointed to the R.P.M. gauge. The needle for number-four engine was flickering.

"What is it?"

"We're losin' power. Ah think Ah'm gonna have to feather it."

"Oh, Christ! We got less than a half hour to target. Twenty minutes."

Bane made no comment. He reached out and punched the red button with 4 on it. Looking out the right side window, Win saw the propeller stop and present its three blades to the air at that angle that caused the least drag. Bane began readjusting his throttles and now they watched the air-speed indicator. The needle was falling slowly away from 160. At 155 it hesitated and then became stationary. Win sighed with relief and found that he had been holding his breath.

"We're goin' to have trouble keepin' formation," Matt said suddenly, speaking for the first time since take-off. "We ought to turn back."

"You shut up!" Win said with instant fury and then turned back to Bane. "Can't you pile some more power on the other three?"

The pilot shook his head. "We wouldn' have enough gas to get back. Ah'm pullin' forty inches now."

"O.K., then let's retract the ball turret."

"No," Matt said. "This is what they been waitin' for. A chance to get us all alone. Let's turn back."

"Turn back, hell!"

"Macchione," Bane said quietly, "get your turret up."

"Yes, sir."

"There's some fighters out there," Chic broke in. "High at seven o'clock."

"Whose are they?"

"See, I tol' you. You don' *listen*——"

"They coming in?"

"I can't tell for sure—they're too far."

"I tol' you——"

"Maybe they're ours."

"I tol'——"

"Shut up!" Win turned on the copilot. Only Matt's eyes were exposed, the rest of his face concealed behind helmet and oxygen mask. "*Shut up!*" he yelled at the eyes. "Just you shut up!"

"You guys better get finished screaming at each other." Phil Lange's controlled voice took over the interphone. "The I.P.'s coming up."

"Roger," Bane said quietly.

The calm exchange shamed everyone into silence. Furious at himself, Win stepped back to get the flak suits. The woven steel aprons were piled behind the pilot's seat and it was his regular practice to bring them to Matt and Bane a few minutes before they reached the Initial Point. He picked up the top one, shifting its weight so it didn't snag his oxygen hose, and edged back into the narrow space between pilot and copilot. The plane was already banked into its turn and he had to wait.

"Bomb-bay door's coming open," Lange called.

Immediately the flight deck was engulfed in frigid air. Win placed the steel apron in Bane's lap and began adjusting it.

"They're closer!" Chic's voice rang out. "I think they're comin' in!"

Win tried to concentrate on fastening Bane's flak suit. Out of the corner of his eye he was conscious of Matt trying to reach around him for the other suit that still lay on the deck behind the pilot's seat. Then he felt the first blow. Turning, he saw Matt pounding him on the arm.

"Gimme my flak suit," the copilot demanded.

Win finished buckling Bane's suit. Matt was clutching at his arm and he shook him off.

"Gimme my flak suit, please," Matt sobbed.

"Stop it, you bastard. The more you cry, the less chance you got of gettin' it!"

"Please——"

"The formation!" Lange began screaming. "They're not opening up! Tell them to open up!"

"Please, Win, please——"

"Shut up," Win said automatically, thinking, We got to open up to drop frags, we got to spread out.

"Please——"

"No!" Win said, not even looking at him, watching the open bomb bays of the planes up ahead. "Shut up, and then I'll give it to you."

"Bombs away . . . Bombs away . . . Bombs away!"

The first clusters spilled out, laddering straight down, and then one broke open and dissolved into a hail of black dots rushing at them, coming straight for the windshield. Don't, Win pleaded silently, don't hit us, and they were still flying and someone was saying over and over again: *"Jesus Christ, Jesus Holy Christ."*

"Check the bomb bay," Lange called out. "We better be sure all of ours went out O.K. One of those frags rolling around loose can blow us all to hell."

It was something to do. Win turned and started back, jerking savagely at his trailing web of cords and cables, moving swiftly until he had traversed the flight deck and stood looking down at the open bomb bay.

Two tiny bombs were lying on the catwalk. He went to his knees to be better able to lower himself into the well and then he couldn't move. Kneeling there, he no longer saw the bombs or even the catwalk, only the open void and the earth far, far below. Then, like a scurrying squirrel, Milbank appeared from out of the waist and began to crawl out on the catwalk. He reached the bombs and delicately, one by one, picked them up and let them drop. Finished, he reached out his hand and Win grabbed it and fell backwards, pulling the engineer half up on the deck with him.

"Thanks," Milbank said, grinning at him. "Bomb bay clear!"

They rose, helping each other up, and Win felt how drained he was. But everything was quiet again, calm, the bomber flying evenly. "What happened?" he asked. "Why didn't they open the formation? They know those goddamned clusters always come apart."

"Ah guess they was scared of the fighters."

"What happened to them? They never came in."

"No," Chic said. "They just hung out there."

It was silent.

"They were a little too far to be sure," Chic said finally. "I think they were ours. P-51s."

Again the silence.

"We lose any?"

"Three," Chic said. "Three back in Dog box; they caught our bombs. You should've seen it. Jesus Holy Christ, it was like they ran into a wall."

The bomber turned in its revetment, coming to rest, and Win waited for the thing to fade, just as the roar of engines now faded, just as the detail of every other mission had faded once they were safely back on the ground. He sat at the radio table stuffing charts into his map case, his mind still in the air, still on himself kneeling before the open bomb bay unable to move. Around him the men were quitting the airplane, and still he sat, until finally he saw Milbank standing at his elbow.

Win stared at him in much the same way he had looked at Macchione the day before, as if he were really seeing him for the first time.

"What's the matter?" the engineer asked, smiling.

Win shook his head, watching how Milbank's high-cheek-boned face softened in the smile, seeing again the long bisecting scar that ended in a lobeless ear. The black eyes were like cream turned jet.

"We've come all the way around," he said finally. "Now we're killing ourselves."

"That ain't new, that's what happens most of the time in the air." Milbank's smile broadened into a grin. "You're the one that told us that yourself, in those speeches you used to make before take-off."

"Yeah, I know."

"What I mean is, you were right."

"Sure, but about what happened——" he began, and knew that it was going to be hard to say, even harder than he had imagined.

"Forget it."

"No. I'm going to tell Ethridge about it at interrogation. You ought to get something for crawling out there."

"O.K." The grin was broader now. "Get me a D.F.C. I hear they let you fly home when you're finished if you got one."

"I'm serious."

"Me too."

He was going about the whole thing wrong and he flushed, hating himself for dodging. "What I'm really trying to say is thanks. I couldn't have done it. I was so scared I couldn't move."

"You didn' have to. If you did you would of."

"No——"

"Sure you would've. But I was halfway out there when you first got to the bomb bay."

Then Milbank had to step back to allow Bane to get through. Win was completely disoriented. First Macchione, he thought, now Milbank. Every time he was sure that at last he was free, needing no one, they closed the circle on him and he found himself drawn into giving and being given. It was as if they had decided among themselves to keep pushing him back into a mold he was struggling to shatter. Now he wondered if he shouldn't stop struggling. Here they were, killing themselves in the air, and the toughness he had banked so much on failing him. It was a situation where allies were needed. He shook his head but the bewilderment remained.

"I really was," Milbank was saying. "I saw you coming up just about when I got to the bombs."

"O.K." Win smiled and now it wasn't so hard. "Maybe you were, but I'm still saying thanks. I want to."

8 The group no longer flew, and the last week of August, spending itself in flawless days, became a period of hiatus with the sound of engines the essential punctuation of the men's existence. Each morning they were awakened by the massed thunder of the Air Force's departing formations and the rest of each day was exhausted to the accompaniment of engines being run up on their own flight line as the ground crews over-hauled the group's remaining airplanes. As they waited vainly for the replacements that would again bring them up to combat strength, time lost its function and became unhinged from reality. An argument during a poker game flared into sudden violence when Hawkins, accused of failing to ante, reached across the table and with one deft motion broke his bombar-dier's nose. First-aid kits were missed from inside the bombers and later found at the bottom of an abandoned latrine, intact except for morphine syrettes. Drunkenness increased in the squadron until twice in that week the bar in the club ran out of liquor. And all through the empty days rumor grew and was made credible by the logic hatched of restless nights. The war was passing them by, they said. The invasion of southern France had been spectacularly successful and the American army was now speeding up the Rhone Valley to link up with the main force in the north. The rest of the continent lay within the grip of the Russian pincers, one claw deep in the Balkans, the other pressed against Germany's eastern border. It would soon be all over in Europe, they said. But instead of it being over for them too, *they* would be sent across the world to India, to China, to the Pacific islands. Against the Japanese their tour would be lengthened to fifty, to seventy-five, even to a hundred missions. And then, as if to give substance to their wildest dreams, the ground crews began revising the interiors of the B-24s. Straight through the heat of the day the work went on, and when night fell with the job still unfinished emergency spotlights were rigged. Under the white glare that attracted myriads of fluttering insects, the sweating, half-naked men continued their labors and the whole scene took on the mood of a grotesque. The operation was performed on nine of the group's airplanes and when it was finished the delicate balance that gave the bombers their function as weapons was completely altered. In the front bomb bays two auxiliary gasoline tanks, each with a capacity of eight hundred gallons, were installed. The rear racks were hung with five-hundred-pound unfused bombs. Every available inch of the nose compartments was crammed full of steel boxes containing .50-caliber machine-gun ammunition, and as many fifty-five-gallon drums of lubricating oil as would fit were piled into the waist sections and shored up. And day and night the fliers stood by in grim huddles and watched. They were silent, asking no questions after they found out that the men doing the work knew nothing of its purpose. Subject as they were to the half world of their own fancies, they accepted this as no more unnatural than things that had already happened. But beneath this acceptance was the awareness that whatever the purpose, they would be involved in its ultimate conclusion. They knew that the airplanes would have to be flown and they noted how the huge rubber wheels of the landing gear groaned and spread under the increasing load. Finally, on toward morning, Captain Grover came speeding out to the flight line, and from the urgency of his approach they thought that their unknowing was at an end. But they were wrong. Seated behind the wheel of his idling jeep, he announced that the squadron's three re-fitted airplanes would be taking off at eight o'clock; that Bane, McDuffee, and Hawkins, each with his copilot, navigator, and engineer, was to report for briefing in one hour. Even before he was finished talking, he kicked the jeep into gear, spun it in a tight circle, and was gone.

With the first light of the new day spilling over the eastern horizon, they gathered in the Operations hut. None of them had slept, but suspense still held their fatigue in abeyance. It was only after Grover had arrived and delivered them the anticlimax of their mission that they slid over the rim into nervous exhaustion. They were going to Lyon in France, he informed them. The Germans had turned to fight in the Bel-fort Gap, and the swift-moving American invasion army had outrun its supplies. Their job was to assist in the remedying of this condition. The B-24s would perform the function of tankers. With bomb-bay tanks each airplane would carry 4600 gallons of gasoline. In Lyon, half of this load would be pumped out, leaving enough fuel to return. They would unload the rest of their cargo at the same time and then take off again. That was all. But the mission, for which they would receive credit, was not wholly without danger. Their safety would depend upon precise navigation, since the friendly fighters in the area would only be able to patrol a narrow corridor that paralleled the Rhone River. And he would accompany them to co-ordinate the operation, Grover announced. It would be easy, he said—and he repeated it as if aware that after weeks of hallucination reality possessed little power to make them be-lieve. All they had to do was fly to Lyon, land there and un-load, then return to Italy.

In the air Lyon's municipal airport had resembled a giant fruit that had split open in the sun, attracting a swarm of rabid flies. On the ground it was like a vast railroad terminal gone mad. Taxiing past the fire-blackened wreckage that had been steel and concrete hangars, skirting the main runways that were pocked with bomb craters, Win watched the frenzied stream of airplanes that wheeled in on the field from all points of the compass. He was lightheaded from lack of sleep, and through the haze of his fatigue the circling planes appeared like gulls hovering over a carcass, filling the atmosphere with the inaudible raucousness of radio as they awaited a chance to land. Their own B-24 had made half a dozen circuits through the winged mass, with Bane trying to approximate a normal traffic pattern while he screamed into his microphone for landing instructions. No one had paid them the least heed until, in desperation, they had charged straight in and landed, clearing a path by sheer bulk. Thirty minutes they had been up there, Win reflected. Thirty minutes with the four engines eating up precious gasoline that was supposed to move stalled tanks and trucks. Gasoline they had come over seven hundred miles to deliver, but which would be half consumed by what they would need for their own coming and going. It was all mad, a fitting climax to the senselessness of the past week, and the feeling came to him again, as it had with increasing frequency of late, that even time had gone awry and ceased to move.

The squadron's other two B-24s had arrived before them and parked on the edge of the main landing area near the tower. The original glass-enclosed tower had been destroyed and this structure now served as the nerve center of the field. Its general form was that of a crazily tilted oil derrick, an interlacing of wooden stilts that supported an open engine crate high above the ground. Crouched in this crate, exposed to the broiling sun, a demon wearing British captain's pips bellowed into a hand microphone. As Bane brought their B-24 to rest beside the other two, the sustained hysteria in the Britisher's voice became evident and Win looked up again at the pandemonium that this man was attempting to reduce to order. A box of cigar-shaped B-26s thundered across the field with a flight of R.A.F. Wellingtons, still daubed in desert paint, lumbering in their wake. On the long rectangle of grass that had previously been an unused area between two runways a swarm of A-20s with both British and American insignia dipped to land. From the right, ignoring the landing airplanes, a squadron of P-47s was taking off and forming into steps of four while still in the traffic pattern. Above them circled a solid phalanx of Troop Carrier Command C-46s and C-47s. A stream of tiny liaison planes, buzzing in from out of nowhere, alighted in the aisles between the parked aircraft to disgorge hurrying passengers even before coming to a full stop. And from atop his swaying perch, adding his minor irritant to this monstrous cacophony, the British captain cursed everyone and everything with terrible impartiality.

As they were descending from their airplane a tank truck drew up, with Grover clinging to its running board. The operations officer was still in full flight, as if the momentum he had generated at the base had projected itself through four and a half hours in the air and then landed intact in France. Now he was urging the coveralled driver of the truck to hurry, but the man seemed impervious to any pace but his own. Moving deliberately, he took a small vacuum pump from the seat and set it down on the ground beside his truck. He bent over it and after many tender adjustments succeeded in getting it started so that it gave out a feeble, sucking noise. Then he looked up at Grover in triumph. Grover looked from the driver to his pump, from the tank truck to the B-24s.

"And what the hell do you think you're going to do with that thing?" he demanded. "Is that all you got?"

The coveralled driver shrugged.

"I'll be a sonofabitch! Don't you know there's a war on? You got to pump seven thousand gallons of gas out of those planes. We'll be taking off in two hours."

The driver nodded sympathetically.

Stymied, Grover reconsidered the man and his machine, the tank truck and the bombers. He was about to explode. Instead he turned and strode purposefully toward the tower.

"Hey!" he shouted. "Hey, you up there! Hey, Captain!"

The man in the tower peered down over the edge of his perch.

"Listen, we got to get seven thousand gallons of gasoline pumped out of those B-24s. And there'll be more coming. We need some equipment."

"Eh?"

"Equipment. We need a couple of vacuum pumps. Big ones."

The British captain rubbed the back of his hand across his mouth and stared.

"You speak English, don't you?" Grover shouted. "Vacuum pumps! To pump the gas out!"

"And what in hell am I supposed to know about your bloody pumps?"

"Not mine!" Grover screamed. "We haven't got any—we *need* some!"

"Eh? Well go to your Department of Supply."

"That's what I'm trying to find out. Where is it?"

"How in hell would I know?" The tower operator withdrew from the edge of his crate. "Stupid beggars got so much, they can't even keep track of it. Lose their bloody arses if they weren't coupled on."

From where Grover stood looking up at the tower he could no longer see its operator, but the Britisher's hoarse bellow, its wrath again directed up into the frenzied air, was audible to all. After a moment he turned and came slowly back to the

B-24s. Two more coveralled men in a winch-equipped truck
had joined the driver, and when Grover saw that they were re-
spectfully awaiting his orders he regained some of his former
impetus. The hose from the tank truck was uncoiled and connected to McDuffee's B-24. The vacuum pump was started. The
two men with the winch truck began unloading the unfused
bombs. When this was accomplished Grover assembled the
crew members to tell them that they were to take off, as
long as enough daylight remained for the flight back to the
base. They needn't wait to hear from him, he said; he would
be going back in the last bomber, and with that he hailed a
passing lorry and was gone.

After Grover left, the men from the B-24s lay down in the
shade of their airplanes to sleep. But sleep would not come.
They were outside the main stream of urgency that flowed
around them in unceasing din, their role was one of induced
passivity, yet detachment was impossible. The goad and spirit
of the place had instilled its mood in them and made them
restless. So not knowing what else to do, they lay on their
bellies in the grass and smoked cigarette after cigarette and
watched the unending parade of airplanes.

Beside the tower a squadron of Spitfires stood quivering in
the blast of their own propellers, impatient for the air. Each
of the fighters had a mechanic standing by it like a groom at
the stirrup of a race horse. In a matter of minutes the strident
clatter of warming engines was reduced to an even rhythm and
the mechanics pulled away the wheel chocks. Then each of
these men vaulted up on the wing of an already moving fighter,
seating himself just beyond the glittering arc of the propeller.
Tilted far back on their high landing gear, the pilot was guided
while taxiing by the hand signals of his mechanic. In this
fashion, the whole squadron moving as a unit, they threaded
their way across the field and turned into the wind for take-off.
The mechanics dismounted and, eight abreast, the Spitfires

rushed away over the grass. With one motion, while it seemed they were still joined with the earth, they folded their wheels beneath them and rose whirling upward in a *chandelle* as fluid as a ballet pattern. A hundred feet off the ground they were already flying in battle formation. And as soon as one wave had passed and risen, the next followed, until the whole squadron had disappeared into the east.

The men lying under their B-24s stirred uneasily, moved by the grace of the departed fighters. Win turned away and for the first time noticed the huddle around the vacuum pump. The coveralled driver, Milbank, and a civilian he hadn't seen before were talking together. Then, although he couldn't hear their voices, he realized that it was only the driver and the civilian who were conversing. They were arguing about something and at periodic intervals they would grow silent and look at Milbank. The engineer would then consider both of them, looking from one face to the other, either nod or shake his head, and the conversation would be resumed. Finally the talk seemed to culminate in some sort of agreement. All three of them shook hands, and the driver rose and walked to his truck. Win got to his feet, stretched, and wandered leisurely back toward the tail of McDuffee's B-24. When he had circled the airplane he saw that the driver had returned, carrying a can. The civilian drew a wallet from his pocket and counted out a sheaf of bills which he handed to Milbank. The engineer wet his thumb and re-counted the money. He gave part of it to the driver and put the rest in his pocket. Then he saw Win and smiled. Both Frenchmen followed his look with alarm but he smiled at them too and they were reassured. The driver disconnected a hose from the pump and connected it to the can.

"Get this," Milbank said, studying his wrist watch.

The driver supervised the operation by placing his ear against the side of the can. At the right moment he flicked a switch on the pump, reconnected the hose, and it was finished. The can was full.

"Two minutes," Milbank said. "I wish we had your computer."

"What for?"

"The can's five gallons. It took two minutes to fill."

Win stared at him.

"If five gallons takes two minutes, what will 2300 gallons take?"

Win thought aloud. "Two and a half gallons a minute. About fifteen hours."

The civilian had the can now and was ready to go but Milbank held him. "Want to go to town?" he asked gently. "There's plenty of time. I can fix it so they pump us out last. We could have ourselves a ball."

Win looked over his shoulder at the men lounging on the grass, but nobody was paying any attention to him.

"We'll tell Bane," Milbank said. "And maybe we better tell Matt too. What d'you say?"

"O.K."

"I'll go ask them." He pointed to the civilian. "Keep your eye on this guy, he's got a car."

Lyon was being reborn, and the tiny Renault, shuddering in every joint with the unaccustomed headiness of one-hundred-octane gasoline, carried them through streets that were like a carnival in the sunshine. Every shop was open, every café overflowing, every house bedecked with flags and flowers, and wherever they passed the crowds roared *vive l'Américain! vive le liberateur!* It was utterly unlike anything they had ever experienced, and Win, sitting crushed between Matt and Bane on the narrow back seat, felt his inability to accept what was happening as reality. The hands that were thrust into the car to be shaken, the bottles of wine offered tilted and open, the occasional girl's face raised to be kissed, the whole montage was that of a dream. Deep within him there was the desire to respond, to merge himself with the welcome, but he could not. The unnatural quality of his voice when he raised it to answer a greeting reduced him to silence and he saw reflected on the faces of the men beside him the same numb smile that twisted his own lips. Only Milbank, sitting alert beside the driver, had made the transition from spectator to participant. The engineer seemed even to understand the language, and although he answered only in monosyllables, communication was established between him and the people. It was because he understood a little Cajun, Milbank explained, but watching him, Win realized that it was more an instant affinity that had attuned him to the situation. The same thing that was true in Italy, where liberation had long been dead. There too, not knowing the language, it was always Milbank who achieved rapport.

Their progress through the city, heralded by the Renault's klaxon, was finally halted by a crowd that would not part to let them through. Milbank stuck his head out of the front window and after sampling the conversation that flowed around them announced that they had better walk. As soon as they were out of the car and part of the crowd a change took place, as if proximity had inhibited the free-flowing exchange of before. There was shyness in it now, with the people standing a little aloof from the fliers and watching them politely. Directly in front of Win an old man was holding a little boy by the hand. The child's eyes were round with breathless wonder and Win found himself caught in their gaze. Unconsciously, out of long reflex, he began feeling in his pockets, but the old man understood his intention and held out a hand to ward off the gift even before it was offered. Something within Win froze at the gesture, but then the outstretched hand was gripping his shoulder. At the same time the old man said something to the boy, who put his hand out to be shaken. Win went down on his haunches to take the little hand in his. He pumped it solemnly, twice, and heard the murmur of approval run through the watching people, the sound of it causing tears to form behind his eyes. Still holding the little hand in his, he looked up and with great clarity saw all of their faces as if for the first time. Not as a montage now, but as individual faces—the expression of warmth in a woman's sun-bleached gray eyes; the way the old man's mouth stretched into a smile revealing two chipped front teeth. He was conscious of something letting go inside of him, relaxing him so completely that he lost his balance. The old man put a hand under his elbow to steady him and he rose, feeling the response he had been unable to summon coming of itself.

All along the avenue the crowd was moving, funneling itself into a queue. Win was with the other fliers again, but the people who had surrounded him while he shook the boy's hand had moved on to be replaced by others. And behind these it seemed to Win that there were still others, for as he examined them with his new perspective, seeing them real and wondering about their lives, they became interrelated in his mind with the people of Italy, like live actors against a painted backdrop. With a growing sense of shame he realized that Italy had been a vacuum for him, unpeopled and unreal. As hard as he tried he could not summon up a single individual Italian face. They were all merged together to form a symbol of sloth and filth and menial service. Yet he knew now that they were people with faces and lives, and he thought of what Macy had said about the Air Force wanting it all impersonal. Macy had meant it in relation to the actual fighting, but he suddenly saw it as part of the whole war, true of Americans in every country in which the war had been fought. True of himself too, he admitted, filled with disgust at not having seen it before. It seemed a discovery of great importance and he thought of communicating it, but in the very act of turning to his crew-mates he knew what their reaction would be and so said nothing. Then he saw the old man and the boy whose hand he had shaken. They were standing a little way back in the crowd talking to another man. This one was shabbily dressed and Win noticed how the freshly laundered shirt he wore buttoned to the neck stood out in a white triangle under the lapels of his ancient tweed coat. A small knot of people had formed around them and the man with the boy was urging the other man forward. The people parted to let him through, but he seemed reluctant to move. The fliers, becoming aware of what was happening, stopped to watch.

"I wonder what he wants," Bane said.

Matt laughed. "I don'. Hey, Joe—*quanto costo?*"

The people were urging the man forward, but he still hesitated.

"How d'you say 'How much?' in French?" Matt asked. "Come on, you ol' bastard. How much? *Quanto costo?*"

The man in the white shirt reached a decision. Removing his battered cap, he took a few steps forward. The people grew silent. Then, with a sense of deep disturbance, Win realized that he was being singled out. The man was advancing toward him, staring at him intently, and as he returned the look a flicker akin to recognition ran through him.

"What's the matter, mister" he asked.

"*Anshuldick mir, mein yunger freint, ober binst du nicht a yid?*"

"What's he sayin'?" Matt demanded. "What the hell's that *nicht?*"

Win didn't answer, unable to remove his eyes from the man's face.

"*Du redst* Yiddish?" the man asked gently.

Win nodded, trying to summon the words, a feeling like pain gripping his throat.

"Now what's goin' on? What kin' a monkey talk is that?"

"It's Jewish." Win took a step nearer the man. "*Voss is der mer?*" he said slowly, the words unfamiliar, yet feeling right when he got them out. "*Voss ken ich tun far eich?*"

The man's face contorted with gratitude. He fumbled in his pocket and produced a letter which he handed over. Examining the envelope, Win saw that it was addressed in English to a Mrs. Waldec in London.

"*Mein veib,*" the man was explaining excitedly. "*Ich doff doss schicken tzu mein veib und kinder in England. Zay denkin as ich bin todt und di post doh arbeit nicht.*"

"Maybe it's post cards," Matt said. "I always heard about French post cards."

"*Is doss geshribin* in Yiddish?"

"*Nein, nein, af Fransasish.*"

Win held the letter out to Milbank. "He wants me to mail this for him. His wife and kids are in England and they think he's dead. Can you read it?"

"Me?"

"It's in French."

"Oh." The engineer studied the letter for a long time, moving his lips as he went over it. Matt and Win crowded closer to see. Milbank finished and folded the sheets back into the envelope. He looked at the anxiously waiting man and then handed it back to Win.

"I got most of it," he said. "It all looks O.K.—just family stuff."

"Swell. I just wanted to make sure he wasn't mailing it to Axis Sally," Win said to Matt. He put the letter in his breast pocket, buttoning the flap, and tourned back to the man. "*Ich vell doss avec shicken morgen.*"

The man grabbed his hand and tears were in his eyes. Over his shoulder Win caught the eye of the man with the little boy. They smiled at each other. Then, as the fliers started away, a policeman with shiny black boots and crossed leather belts on his chest came toward them. He stopped in front of Matt, saluted smartly, and launched into voluble French that sounded like a speech. When he finished he motioned for them to follow, and from the way the people parted to let them through they knew they were being honored. Straight through the queue he led them. Up ahead they saw the concrete piers of a bridge and remembered from their coming on the city in the air that the Rhone divided it in two. When they reached the river they saw that the bombed-out roadbed of the bridge sagged down into the water and a temporary wooden footpath had been erected, accommodating only a few people at a time. With a large gesture the policeman motioned them to go first, and with him following in escort, they crossed.

On the other side of the river the spirit of liberation was slower paced. Here they found themselves in an area of wide tree-bordered boulevards where elegance had been preserved intact. The buildings, untouched by the war, were in good repair, and the shops, some of them modern with wide expanses of glass framed by sculptured marble, all had goods on display. The streets were less crowded, the people better dressed. Very few men wore parts of uniforms as they had on the other side of the river. It was a city clean and spacious in the sunlight, a city they had imagined but not expected to find outside America. And gradually they grew conscious of the young women of Lyon. Not sullen and watchful in rags and cork-soled shoes like the women of Bari and Naples, but bright and exciting, with swaying hips under vivid print dresses, with hair worn long and free, with bare tanned legs and spike-heeled pumps. There were a great many of them, and as the fliers watched them sauntering along the boulevard it seemed that they outnumbered all the rest of the people until the whole district was flavored with an essence like the articulation of desire.

"Lordy, lordy me," Matt moaned, straining like a dog on a leash. "A man could screw himself to death in this town."

"Not me!" Win said and from the tone of his voice they were all startled into laughter.

"You?" Bane asked. "What's eatin' you? Since when *you* gettin' so pure?"

"Since now, so what?"

"O.K., O.K., don' get mad."

"Maybe he's saving himself—like you," Milbank said to Bane. "You going to buy some post cards to send to Lucy?"

Bane blushed. "Ah might."

"Well, why don' you send her one a that?" Matt said, pointing to two girls across the street. "You could show her what a good boy you're bein'."

"Yeah."

Matt laughed. "Man, you jus' as good as married, except you don' get any a the fun."

"Least Ah won' get any syph, either."

"Ain' no worse than a cold."

"Yeah."

And then they heard a voice bellowing their names, the shock of it causing them to halt in confusion and look around. Two floors above them on the ornamental ironwork balcony of a hotel, naked except for a pair of green G.I. shorts, stood Captain Grover.

"What the hell do you guys think you're doing down there?" the captain roared. "Who the hell told you that you could leave the field?"

"We were lookin' for you, sir," Milbank answered instantly. "We wanted to report about pumpin' out the gas."

"Well, what about it?"

"Maybe we better come up."

Grover looked back into the room. "Well, all right," he said reluctantly. "But you wait till I say it's O.K. to come in."

Win stood in the middle of the tall-windowed chamber, marveling at the crystal chandelier that hung from the ceiling by a thin gilt chain. The warm night air coming in through the open windows stirred it to constant effervescent motion, and in the lull in the noise he heard the dagger-shaped crystals chiming their minuet. It was as delicate as a half-heard lullaby, he thought. Maybe if he closed his eyes he would sleep. But the tiredness was so deeply rubbed into his every sense that it had gone beyond the need for sleep, leaving him suspended in numbness. Then the noise started again and he looked down at the glass he was holding and saw that he had spilled the remainder of his champagne on the rug.

"Hey!" Matt was shouting. "Hey, you-all. Look. He's one a them." The big copilot was standing in the doorway with his arm encircling a short tough-looking Englishman who wore wings and sergeant's chevrons on his tunic. "He's one a them Spitfire boys."

Win went to refill his glass. A table had been set up between the windows and on it a half-dozen magnums of champagne were sweating in ice buckets. He picked up one to look at the label: "G. H. Mumm." It was a name he had always connected with the imagined luxury of famous night clubs and people in evening clothes. Here they had pooled their belongings and traded the hotel manager three pairs of sunglasses, an army issue wrist watch, and two cartons of cigarettes for a dozen magnums of the wine. Even after Hawkins's crew had arrived in the late afternoon, directed to the hotel by the people who all seemed to know where the American Air Force had taken up quarters, there had been three quarts per man. Win filled his glass and looked down into the dark street. It had been a mistake to remain in Grover's room. Out there in the night new things were happening and he felt again that he was missing something important, wasting an opportunity. He should have gone with Milbank. The engineer had left while it was still

light to recross the river. He had considered going along, but
the thought of the lush hotel's showers and beds with sheets to
sleep in had held him. Then he hadn't been able to sleep and
the drinking had started. He turned back toward the light of
the room.

Matt was describing the Spitfire take-off to Grover. He was
very drunk, reeling around and illustrating his words with wide
gestures. The English sergeant stood off to one side for safety,
a speculative look on his face. Caught by the intensity of Matt's
recital, everyone else was watching and Win was conscious of
an instant quickening in the atmosphere of the room.

"Man!" Matt was yelling. "That's the way to fly. Sittin' up
there in one a them babies jus' huntin' trouble."

The sergeant smiled tightly. "Nobody hunts trouble, mate."

"No? Shit you don'!" Matt reached out and encircled the
sergeant with an arm. "Listen, Ah was damn near in the R.A.F.
myself, you know that? A bunch of us from the team wen' on
up to Canada to enlist, but they wouldn' have us. Coach near
died when he heard about it."

"You'd-a been too big for fighters anyway." Hawkins laughed.
"They'd-a shoved you in a Lancaster."

"Uh-uh." Matt released the sergeant to regain the use of both
hands. "Ah'd-a been on fighters, all right. Not sittin' in no
fuckin' B-24 like a nigger behin' a biggety ass mule."

"It ain' so bad, Matt," Bane said.

"Shit it ain'! Maybe it wouldn'-a been if we was in a white-
man outfit."

The sergeant looked around in surprise. "You chaps got
Negroes in your squadron?"

"Sure, white ones, din' you know?" Matt laughed uproariously, the sound going up and up until its top registers were
half sob. "This ain' no place for a white man no more. Us
Joneses been in plenty a wars—my great-granddaddy was with
General Lee—but we always did our fightin' like white men.

We din' go sneakin' aroun' like no nigger with a razor. An' Ah always figured the Air Force din' neither."

The men were silent, frozen in a tableau. Matt stood on widespread legs, his chest heaving with passion. The sergeant looked in bewilderment from face to face. Then they heard the sound of women's voices in the hall.

"Quail," the sergeant said, recovering, and in two quick bounds reaching the door. *"Bon soir, douce amie. Entrez!"*

"Anglais?" There was a pause. *"Où est l'Américain?"*

With an elegant bow the sergeant turned to indicate the roomful of men. "There's five of them," he said. "And they want Americans."

"Well for Christ's sake, send 'em in!"

A woman with loose red hair spilled over one eye poked her head through the door and then fell bodily into the room as she was pushed from behind. Amid building peals of laughter the others followed, the freedom of their entrance transforming the latent violence that had choked the room into an instant lack of restraint. Under the crystal chandelier they bunched and stopped and were immediately surrounded by the men. The redhead began calling out the girls' names, pointing to each in turn.

"Valerie . . ."

A little curly-haired blonde smiled and dropped a mock curtsy.

"Pleased to meet you." Hawkins grinned. "My name's Jim."

"Denise——"

"Hi-ya, baby."

"Amelia . . . Henriette . . ."

And in the pause between each name one of the men identified himself, so that in the very act of introduction a pairing off was achieved. The radio was switched on and turned up full blast when music was located. Hawkins extended his hands to the little blonde, who kicked her shoes away in soaring arcs and advanced into his arms. Everyone stepped back to make room and he swung her into a jitterbug routine, whirling her round and round so that her dress frothed halfway up her bare white thighs.

"Wait a second, goddammit!" Grover shouted, holding the redhead by one hand while the sergeant held the other. "There ain' enough to go around. We're three short."

"No, count me out." It was Bane, blushing furiously as everyone turned to him. "Ah was jus' goin' to bed anyway."

"Man, are you nuts?"

"You can count me out too," Win said quietly. Forgotten by the others, he and Matt were still standing apart, staring at each other across the length of the room.

The redhead said something short and hard to the sergeant, who answered her in detail. When she replied, he dropped her hand and she pulled away from Grover to make her way toward the window.

"I've got to be getting along too," the sergeant said.

"What the hell is this?" Grover demanded. "I thought we were going to have a party."

The sergeant jerked his thumb at the redhead. "She's getting some more friends—they're right downstairs."

"Well, goddammit, that's different!"

Win saw that his champagne glass was empty and went to refill it. He was wet with sweat. Standing before the open window, he unbuttoned the whole front of his shirt, but the humid night air offered no relief. Outside on the balcony he could hear the redhead calling down into the darkness. A woman's voice answered, and the redhead released a staccato burst of French that ended abruptly in a squeal of surprise. Then he heard a man's braying laugh. A moment later the redhead re-entered the room with Grover following. Her eyes were bright but the smile that curved her lips was the opposite of gay.

"Let's get that thievin' manager up here again," Grover roared. "What we need is more champagne!"

Four more girls came into the room and everything seemed to pick up a beat. The music changed. It grew louder, more frenzied in pace, the dancers whirling ever faster to keep time. The manager arrived and departed only to reappear again bearing more bottles of champagne. The room became a tangle of bodies suspended in cigarette smoke and noise. And everywhere there were girls, two and three around each man, their continuous laughter, the supple bending of their bodies promising more than delight.

Win stood propped against a wall to keep from falling. The hours of steady drinking had culminated in a sudden impact that left his whole body as if wrapped in the white remoteness of novocain. Reality was fast receding into nightmare, but in the last sober recess of his mind he clung desperately to the city outside the window, to the banquet of liberation he had witnessed and wanted never to forget. He patted the breast pocket of his shirt to feel the letter. Then he became aware that the atmosphere in the room had changed again. Grover and the redhead were standing face to face and screaming at each other.

"*Money,* you goddamned whore!" Grover was roaring in pained surprise. "You want *money!*"

The redhead turned away from him and began darting about in a vain attempt to herd the girls together and head them for the door. Grover stalked her and then lunged, falling but managing to grab the hem of her skirt, so that when she struggled to get away the skirt tore completely off, revealing her suddenly naked from the waist down. In an instant Grover had pulled her to the floor with him and turned her over his lap to pound his hand up and down on her bare rump.

"I'll give you money," he shouted. "You ain' even a real redhead. Here's *one . . . two . . . three . . . four . . .*"

A circle formed, with both men and women chanting after him in French and English. And Matt was yelling: "Line up for twenty licks apiece. Ah'm next!"

A face came close to Win's, materializing slowly as out of the wrong end of a telescope and enveloping him in a charming little-girl smile. The whole room was a whirling kaleidoscope now with objects growing larger and smaller, advancing and retreating to the beat of a giant pulse that seemed to originate inside him. He shook his head to dislodge the face and found himself looking directly into the eyes of a girl who stood with her arm around Matt. As he concentrated he saw the big copilot very clearly, saw the glee-contorted face, heard the mouth emitting the metronome chant of numbers, and a wave of accumulated hatred swept over him. Gripping the champagne glass like a dagger, he willed himself to move, felt himself lurching forward. A hand was clutching his arm and he shook it off. Then, as if by magic, the girl who had been standing with her arm around Matt was before him. He tried to get by her but couldn't. She was very tall and as he labored to refocus he saw that above her black satin skirt her midriff was bare and her huge pointed breasts were scarcely contained in a short white angora sweater.

"'ello, babee. You wan' sleep wit' me?" she demanded.

"You speak English," he heard himself saying.

"Sure, my name Clair. You like me?"

He shook his head. The little girl who had first smiled at him was clutching his arm, screaming something in French. Matt was there too, reaching out for the tall girl, but she shrugged him off and when he tottered pushed him with both hands against his chest so he fell over on top of Grover and the half-naked redhead.

"*Faire le mort, ivrogne,*" she said, and turned to jerk her thumb at the little girl who still clung to Win's arm. "You sleep wit' her?"

Win stared, open-mouthed, the sequence of events too rapid for him to follow.

"She no fuckin' *bien*," the big girl told him confidentially. "Better you sleep wit' me."

Win shook his head.

"No? Why not? Me *très* fuckin' *bien!*" With a savage gesture she flipped up her white sweater and cupped her unbrassièred breasts in both hands. " 'ere, feel!"

And from far away Win felt himself dissolving into idiot laughter.

The bed was deep, so deep that he was able to sink down into it, submerging himself in soft darkness, in the full-bodied scent of musk, but still the light reached him. Then he was awake, tossing aside the pillow he had burrowed under. Bane was hanging over the bed, a new liquor-saturated Bane with flushed cheeks and unfocused eyes. Win sat up.

"Look wha' Ah foun'!"

The room had twin beds in it that should normally have been side by side but now one was across the room against the wall. Two girls stood near the door smiling patiently.

"What's that?" Win grumbled fuzzily, still enmeshed in sleep.

"Wha's *that!* Wha's it *look* like?"

Win rubbed his eyes and looked at his watch. It was gone. Searching through the bed for it, he saw the lipstick-smudged pillow he had just cast off.

"Wasn't there——"

"Yeah, yeah, but she lef'."

"Left? When did——"

"Jus' picked herself up all naked an lef' cause Ah wouldn' have nothin' t' do with 'er." Bane giggled. "Ah even moved the bed. But then Ah changed mah min'."

Win shook his head. He was going mad.

Bane pointed to the two girls standing silently near the door. "The lil chubby one's mine; you can have t'other."

"What time is it?"

Bane grunted and moved swaying across the room to the other bed. He sat down and began unlacing his shoes. "Come on in!" he yelled without looking up. "Don' jus' stan' there!"

The girls smiled patiently. Bane heaved himself to his feet and lurched back across the room to the door. Holding each girl by an arm, he pulled them over to Win's bed. One of the girls was blond, the other dark. Bane pointed to the blond one.

"This here one's mine. T'other looks lik' Lucy. O.K.?"

"*Forte bien*," drawled the dark one.

"Listen, Al——"

"O.K.!" Bane began hauling the blonde away.

At that moment the door burst open and a man catapulted into the room. Ten feet from the door he caught himself, leaning almost forty-five degrees to the floor, but magically remaining standing. Still tilted at a perilous angle, he peered around, and after locating the girls, advanced. He was a middle-aged captain of artillery.

"Gimme back my wallet," he said pleasantly.

The girls looked at each other in amazement.

Win closed his eyes and reopened them but nothing disappeared.

"Come on, jus' give it back an' I'll go. I ain' mad."

The girls began exchanging rapid French.

"None a that now. Jus' hand over my wallet."

"Lissen, you," Bane said truculently. "Those gals came wi' me."

"I'll thank you t' mind your own business, Lieutenant. Tha's an order!" The captain turned back to the girls. "You gonna give it back, yes or no?"

The girls turned incredulous faces to him.

"O.K., now I'm mad." He walked to the open window,

cupped his hands around his mouth, took a deep breath, and began yelling: *"Police!* Help, POLICE! HEY, POLICE!"

The girls started for the door, but the captain, by some intuition, divined their intention. Spinning around, he raced them for the door and won. Slamming it shut, he placed his back against it.

"Uh-uh-uh," he chortled, wagging his finger at them. "Can' get away from Bill Tomkins tha' easy. Bill Tomkins been on a road fifteen years."

Then he was thrown halfway across the room as the door was flung open to admit three M.P.s closely followed by the hotel manager.

"Arres' those girls!" the captain commanded. "They stole my wallet. I wan' 'em arrested!"

The girls rushed up to the manager, immersing him in a flood of indignation. The manager told the M.P.s that the girls had never seen the captain before, that they demanded to be searched, but the captain kept yelling: *"Arrest 'em! Arrest 'em!"* The dark-haired girl began to strip. She took off her blouse and began furiously unhooking her skirt. Bane stood swaying on the periphery of the argument, a puzzled frown on his face, and every time he tried to intercede the captain roared at him to shut up. The dark girl kicked off her shoes, stepped out of her skirt, pulled off her pants. Completely naked, she thrust out her arms to be searched.

"Bill Tomkins don' fall for no trick like that," the captain roared stubbornly. "I wan' my wallet."

"Thos' gals came wi' me," Bane explained.

"You keep outa this, Lieutenant," one of the M.P.s snapped at him.

"O.K., O.K." Shaking his head sadly, Bane walked across the room to his bed. Without removing his clothes, he tumbled in and pulled the sheets up over his head.

The manager and the M.P.s finally succeeded in getting the dark girl to put on some of her clothes. Then they herded everyone out of the room. Win got out of bed and switched out the lights and locked the door. From down the hall he could hear the captain still bellowing for the police.

There was a dim stirring that barely reached him, immersed as he was in the vague web of memory. There was also a problem that had to do with motion, but it had no urgency. This once he had time. The problem sublimated itself in remembering and became a relaxed, an agreeable thing. A Sunday morning thing, he told himself, and then motion probed at him. He remained cunningly blind to outwit light, but the motion remained. There was no escape. He opened his eyes and the knowledge of his whereabouts, of yesterday and last night, came welling up simultaneously with the receding of the other, the mnemonic thing. Milbank was bent over him, shaking him by the shoulder.

"Jesus," the engineer was saying, "nobody wants to get up this morning."

"What time is it?"

"Almost ten and the weather stinks. What the hell happened here last night?"

Win groaned. His head was like a kettledrum radiating the pulse of nausea throughout his body. The back of his throat was caked with bile. If he swallowed he would be sick. Then the lush resiliency of the bed, the smoothness of the sheets he lay between, filled him with disgust. Gathering himself for the effort, he threw off the covers and sat up.

"I got a pint of Hennessy," Milbank told him. "Here, you better have a drink."

Win took the bottle, closing his eyes again. The liquor tasted sweet and he gagged, but then he had warmth inside him and it was better. Bane was across the room, sitting on the edge of his bed and lacing his shoes. Outside the windows it was sunless gray.

"Where's Matt?" Milbank asked. "We got to get moving—there's a truck waiting downstairs."

"Let 'em wait."

"He's in the other room," Bane said dully. "Through there."

The engineer went away. Win glanced at Bane, but the pilot was looking down at his shoes. Then Milbank hissed at him from the open doorway leading to the bathroom. Win stood up, and Bane, sighing, rose too. Milbank put his finger to his lips for silence and led them through the bathroom to the adjoining bedroom. The tall girl of last night was sitting crosslegged on the bed, naked except for underpants and shoes. She was filing her nails, squinting through the smoke of the cigarette dangling from her lips. Matt lay across the bed from her, huddled to the wall and snoring.

"Ain't that a pretty picture?"

"Yeah, I'm glad they found each other again."

The girl heard them and looked up.

"Hey, Matt!" Milbank yelled. "Wake up, Matt. *Matt!*"

The snoring was punctuated by a series of grunts. Matt flung out his arm and his hand landed on the girl's bare knee. It hesitated there, as if it had separate life, and then began exploring its way up the thigh. The girl watched it dispassionately. When she was satisfied that it wouldn't stop, she reached down and jabbed the nailfile into it. The hand slowly withdrew itself, but the snoring was unabated.

Milbank laughed. Bane pushed by them, and making a careful circle around the girl, went to the bed. He began shaking Matt by the shoulder. The girl got up and stood watching. Finally Matt opened his eyes.

"Get up," Bane said. "Come on, get up. We got to be takin' off."

Matt grunted, the film of sleep returning.

Bane continued shaking him. "Come on now, Ah ain' gonna fuss with you. Get up."

"Awrigh'!" Matt struck savagely at Bane's hand. "Stop shovin'. What's the big fuckin' hurry all of a sudden?"

"You gettin' up?" Bane's face was white with fury.

"Yeah." The copilot saw the girl for the first time and smiled. "Hi-yu, pussy."

"Listen," Bane said coldly. "There's a truck waitin' downstairs. It's leavin' in about five minutes."

"Ah heard you."

Bane spun on his heel and left the room. Matt reached out and pulled the girl to him. She smiled and he looked up at Win and Milbank, who were still watching.

"What's a matter, ain' you never seen pussy before?"

Win bared his teeth in a grin. "Sure, but some like sliding in on a wet deck and some don't."

"Lil Irwin don' like you," Matt said, laughing up at the girl. "What d'you think a that?"

With Milbank following, Win turned and went back out through the bathroom. Bane was at the window, staring out at the gray day, his shoulders rigid. The bathroom door slammed but he didn't move. Win sat down on the bed and began dressing.

A few minutes later, still in silence, they started for the door. With his hand on the knob, Bane hesitated. Then he went back to the bathroom. The door was locked. For a moment they stood looking at each other and then went out into the hall. The door to Matt's room was ajar. Bane pushed it open with his foot. The room was empty. He went in and looked in the bathroom. It, too, was empty. Quickly, without talking, they searched every room on the floor. Finally they went downstairs.

The truck was at the curb in front of the hotel entrance, its motor idling.

"Let's get a move on, for Christ's sake," Grover growled at them from where he sat beside the driver. "Where the hell's Jones?"

Eight men were sitting in sodden silence on the open back of the truck, but Matt was not among them. Milbank whispered something to Bane.

"Well, where is he?" Grover pointed up at the scudding gray clouds. "That crap's coming in a mile a minute. I don't want to get locked in here another day."

"He wen' on out to the field," Bane said finally.

"Well, why didn't you say so? Come on, let's go."

"*. . . Gyros—uncaged . . . Autopilot—off . . . Superchargers —off . . .*"

Watching the torn gray mist roiling low over the field, Win was only half conscious of Bane's monotonous reading of the copilot's check list. The clock on the panel showed eleven-forty. A Troop Carrier C-47 took off from the grass strip, disappearing into the mist as soon as its wheels were retracted. The ceiling looked less than three hundred feet.

"*. . . Cowl flaps—open . . . Mixtures—idle cut-off . . . Wing flaps—up . . .*"

"Why don't we wait awhile? That stuff might burn off in an hour," Win said, but Grover, sitting in the pilot's seat, in Bane's place, gave no indication that he had heard. "We start up through it and we'll run into something for sure; they're stacked up in it like fleas."

"Who's going up through it?" Grover asked sarcastically, without turning around. "We'll stay underneath and follow the river out."

"But what about those hills I showed you on the map?"

"When I want your advice I'll ask for it. O.K.?"

"Sure, but I don't think——"

"I don't care what you think!" Now Grover turned to include

Bane and Win. "I've taken about all from this crew that I'm gonna—and so has everybody else! The whole bunch of you ought to be court-martialed, telling me that sonofabitch Jones was out at the field. Now let's go."

Bane slid his side window open and yelled *"Clear!"* at Milbank, who was posted beneath the number-three engine with a fire extinguisher. Energized and meshed, the propeller jerked erratically, then vanished in a whirling circle. In quick succession the other three engines came to thundering life. As soon as Milbank had crawled up on the flight deck, Grover began to taxi. Threading the big bomber through the aisles between parked aircraft, he cut in front of a waiting C-47 and turned into the wind. Moments later they were airborne.

"Which way's the river?" Grover growled at Win.

"It's about six miles right. You're parallel to it."

"Right is Roger." Suddenly Grover grinned. "You better get your ass up in the nose turret. If we're gonna hit something, I want to know what it is."

Win grunted.

"You say something?"

"Yeah, I said you're one hot fucking pilot!"

Grover put his head back and roared with laughter.

They flew level with the shoulder of the bluffs that the Rhone flowed between; two hundred feet of clear air above them, a hundred feet below. Everything in sight was a variant of gray: the river's surface like corrugated lead, the clay of the bluffs drenched a blend of black and silver, the running mist like absorbent cotton dipped in mercury. Vagrant tendrils of cloud, graceful as floating moss, became splintered moisture upon contact with the plexiglass of the nose turret. When the mist lowered, Grover put the nose down and it was like hurtling along through a tunnel with the bluffs looming like walls on either side. Win had stopped looking at the map propped in front of him over the gun handles. At that altitude, with the limited visibility, navigation was impossible. Then he felt cold air on his back as the turret doors were opened. He screwed his head around and saw Milbank. The engineer was holding out a yellow disk of K-ration cheese. Win took a bite and as he was chewing Milbank handed in the now almost empty pint of Hennessy. After a long swallow, he realized that the engineer was saying something he couldn't hear and he jerked off his helmet.

"What?"

"I said how we doing?"

Win shrugged and handed back the bottle. Milbank tilted it and it was empty. "Listen," he said. "You still got that letter?"

Win touched his breast pocket and nodded.

"You going to mail it?"

"Sure, why not?"

"Well"—Milbank was embarrassed—"if you mail it you got to sign it. I ain't saying anything about that little fellow, but you better make sure so you don't get in trouble."

"What're you talking about?"

"You better have somebody read it."

"Again? Didn't you . . ."

Milbank shook his head and grinned. "I can't read French, I just made out."

There was nothing to say, but as they stared at each other, the whole thing came back to Win: the people's faces open with greeting, the kinship and joy he had finally accepted, the sense that he had been radically changed by what he had seen. And looking at Milbank, he knew that the engineer's feelings must have been the same. Then the self-disgust welled up again. For him it was stained by what had happened later. In spite of all resolution he had gone down the drain with the rest. He hadn't really changed at all. For a moment an avenue of perverse absolution was opened for him by remembering that the girl in the end had chosen to go back to Matt, but he rejected it. He would have to accept both, his change and his sameness.

"I'll find someone to read it," he said.

Milbank nodded, and when Win had turned back around, he closed the turret doors. Up ahead the gray seemed to be growing lighter. The plane veered and bucked and Win saw the ruined piers of a bridge disappear beneath them. Avignon, he said automatically, we're almost out. By the time he had gotten his helmet back on and replugged his interphone to tell Grover, the mist ahead was definitely backed with pink. As the minutes passed, they flew through a rose-colored transparency with intermittent patches of brightness. Then they were in pure sunlight and suddenly over the miraculous blue of the Mediterranean, so low that they saw the swells rise to cap themselves in snow-white foam. Ahead and below them, like a painted picture, was a fishing smack with a bright maroon lateen-rigged sail.

"Watch!" Grover yelled happily. "I got an idea."

He pulled the B-24 up sharply, gained five hundred feet, then pressed its nose down in a steep glide. He cut the engines back to idling and the vibrating plane was suddenly silent but for the rushing hiss of its descent. They were sliding in downwind, converging swiftly with the lugger that was running from them before the wind. So silent was the bomber's swoop that the five men on the boat, busy with their fishing, were unaware of its approach until the winged shadow passed between them and the sun. They raised up to look, to wave gaily, and then to be frozen with fear at the nearness of the huge plane. At the exact instant that the bomber slid over the boat, not more than fifty feet above the mast, Grover gunned all four engines to maximum power and wrenched up and away. Straining sideways in the turret to look back, Win saw the sudden blast of air from their propellers hit the sail, saw the maroon cloth belly out and split asunder, saw the mast snap off like a broken matchstick. The boat capsized instantly. Two men had their arms still raised in greeting as they were flung into the sea. And then the plane's speed had carried them out of sight, erasing the whole picture.

"You gone crazy, you sonofabitch?" Win screamed into the interphone. "What you go and do a thing like that for?"

Grover's voice was choked with laughter. "It was just a gag. Did you see their faces?"

"*See their faces?* You ruined their boat."

"It ain't ruined. All they have to do is flip it back over."

"But what if they can't swim? They're over a mile out. They'll drown."

"Ah, they won't drown."

"*But what if they do, goddammit!*"

"So they do!" Grover was getting annoyed. "What the hell do you care, they're only gooks."

9

"This was taken from twenty-one thousand and it's pretty much the way it'll look to you as you come in . . ."

The diffused outlines hardened into detail as focus was achieved. In the lower right-hand corner a gridwork of streets bounded by the dark loop of a river became visible, but the center remained an overlapping of vaguely regular shapes. The white beam from the projector, veined through with cigarette smoke, showed Major Gillespie in silhouette, the shadow of his pointer preceding itself as he touched the screen.

"The edge of the town you can just see appears on your maps as Oświecim. The Germans call it Auschwitz. The river is the Vistula. Over here"—the pointer encompassed the center —"is the industrial complex. It houses operations by Krupp, Siemens, and DAW—*Deutches Aufrüstungswerk*, and produces synthetic oil, iso-octanes, and by-product chemicals like nitrogen and methanol. Over here is Blechhammer, the main hydrogenation plant. That's what most of the Air Force will be going after. Our target is here, the iso-octane plant. I want to emphasize the importance of this thing. Without iso-octanes, the oil that comes out of Blechhammer can't be turned into high-grade aviation gasoline. Now in spite of the camouflage, our target should be relatively easy to recognize. Notice these two gashes that look like parentheses—they're marshaling yards. They bracket the plant. Get your bombs any place in between and you've hit it. Is that clear?"

The men stirred, making tense, echoing sounds in the darkness.

"Now you're sure you've got it?"

"What about the flak pattern, Major?"

"You'll get all that at the regular briefing. What I'm interested in now is making sure this thing is perfectly clear. We're first group in the wing today and they'll be watching us."

"Hell," Grover drawled, "how else would they find the target?"

Laughter broke the tension. Ignoring it, Gillespie walked across the stage and clicked on the lights. With the cover of darkness removed he surveyed them steadily and the laughter soon died.

"Very, very funny." Gillespie looked directly at Grover. "Except while you were goofing off in France, I was up at Wing. *They* don't think we're very funny. In fact, they think we're pretty sad."

"What d'you mean, goofin' off?" Grover was getting angry. "We all got back yesterday, didn't we? What did you want me to do, *suck* the gas out?"

Gillespie watched him calmly.

"And they think we're pretty sad up at Wing, huh? Well, that's just too bad. They know what they can do."

"They sure do!"

"Oh relax, will you."

"Sure, why not? We can all relax. We can sit back and make believe everything's fine and wait for them to send some new people down to take over."

"Christ! I don't get it. We're the ones get the shit kicked out of us and they cry."

"Whose fault is that?"

"Ours," said Grover sarcastically. "All ours."

"You're goddamned right, ours! Whose fault is it that we've got the Luftwaffe down on our necks—theirs?"

"Well——"

"Well nothing! And I'll tell you something else. They've taken just about all they're going to from us!"

This time Grover didn't answer. He glanced at Abbot, and finding no support, shifted uncomfortably in his seat. The rest of the men seated around the stage, Lange and Bane and the two Mickey navigators, Macy and Win, Hawkins and his people, stared straight ahead, unwilling to commit themselves even to the extent of showing any interest.

"Ah, it was just a gag," Grover said finally.

"Sure." Gillespie's voice forgave him. "I know how you guys feel. That's why I thought you'd like to know that when our regular turn to lead the wing came up they didn't want us to lead, they didn't even want us to fly. Well, some of us in this room were the ones that came over together when this group was first formed, and we came to fight—not to fly cargo."

It was so quiet now that the sound of a truck approaching was audible in the room. Gillespie looked at his watch.

"The crews will start coming in any minute now. I got you in here early to let you know where we stand. You men are flying lead and deputy lead today. It's up to you. O.K.?"

There was a general grunt of assent. Grover nodded vigorously.

"O.K., then just remember that they're watching you. And as far as the lead navigator is concerned, the whole wing will be following you—Macy."

Macy shook his head.

"What's the matter?"

"Nothing, except I won't be leading."

"What are you talking about?"

"Well, sir, I thought I'd fly in the nose turret and do the pilotage."

Macy was very sincere. He stood up and pointed to Win. "I thought it would be better to assign Helman to the D.R."

"Is this your idea of a joke?"

"A joke?" Macy asked in a hurt voice. "No, sir. After what you just said about us coming over together and forming this group I figured the job comes first. Helman's a better D.R. man than me and now with this special briefing he'll be all set."

The first men began entering the briefing hall. Gillespie looked at them and then back at Macy.

"All right, we won't discuss it here," he said. "We'll go to my office."

"Now?"

"Yes, now!"

"Yes, sir."

Win waited to catch Macy's eye, to show him with some change of expression that he understood what had just happened. It was very important, but there was no opportunity. Macy, his face closed, edged his way through the aisle and followed Gillespie out of the briefing hall.

Maybe he doesn't care, Win thought; maybe it makes no difference to him if I understand what he's doing. But I've got to make him know, because I'm changed now. France changed me all the way. . . .

Or did it? Win thought. What'll I tell him happened in France?

I'll say Grover blew over a fishing boat that was miles from shore, just for a gag, you understand, but I didn't like it. Not that I did anything about it. For instance, I didn't make him circle until we were sure those guys in the water were all right, but I didn't like it. I didn't think it was funny. Or I'll tell him about Lyon. I'll say we came to this city and the people were ready to give it to us like a banquet of liberation with us the guests of honor, but we pissed all over them. All of us—me too.

So he'll say some change, and I'll say yeah, but listen, there

was also this little boy looking up at me like me and God were
partners, fifty-fifty, and we shook hands. And then there was
this man, he was a Jew, and he picked me out of all the others
to help him tell his wife and kids that he was still alive. Not
dead like they been thinking, but alive. And I did it—or at
least I'm going to as soon as I get someone to read his letter,
it's in French . . .

Oh Christ!—Win felt his empty pocket—it's in my other shirt
back in the tent. What if something should happen to us today?
How would it get mailed? They'll go on thinking he's dead.
What if this is just the time his wife decides to give him up for
good, what if . . .

"Listen"—Win turned to Abbot—"I've got to borrow your jeep
a minute. There's some maps I left in my tent that I'm going
to need."

Win was whistling as he swung the jeep back down on the
perimeter strip. It was a great blue cup of a morning and far
off to his left, up toward Melfi and Lavello, the bulked rise of
mountain that ran down the middle of the peninsula like a
ridged spine showed darker blue against the horizon. Two cans
of beer lay on the seat beside him and when he glanced at
them he smiled. They'll freeze solid on the way up, he thought,
and then on the way back, just about the time we reach the
Adriatic, they'll be thawed out and we'll have a picnic. K-ration
cheese and beer. Me and Macy and maybe we'll invite Milbank to come up in the nose and share it. But we'll exclude
Lange; we'll blackball him. And he laughed. He hadn't felt so
good before a mission for longer than he could remember.

As he approached the revetment, Win saw that the officers
had returned from briefing. The whole crew was lined up
parallel with the B-24's fuselage, listening to Abbot, who
stopped talking when the jeep drew up alongside. Win hesitated over the cans of beer and then got out of the jeep, carry-

ing only his map case. He hurried over to stand next to Chicereno.

"I can see you're not used to standing inspection before take-off," Abbot said dryly. "That's something else that better change. Discipline on the ground never hurt discipline in the air. Now I'm just going to repeat this. You're the oldest crew in the squadron. I asked for you for lead. Give me a good ride today, everyone stay on the ball, and bygones are bygones as far as I'm concerned. Now let's go—dismissed."

"Put me in, Coach," Chicereno whispered. "I'll murder 'em."

Win laughed.

"It's exactly like the time we played Scranton for the state championship. Did I ever tell you about it?"

"I thought it was Wilkes-Barre, and I got to go."

"No, Scranton. Wait a second and I'll give you the picture. It's the fourth quarter, we're losin' 13 to 6, the last closin' minutes of play. The coach comes up to me and says, 'Chic,' he says, 'it's up to you,' and I——"

"—run out on the field with the towels."

Chicereno turned to Milbank. "That's no way to talk, brother. If you can't feel the ol' spirit de corps, if you ain't ready to do or die for the ol' squadron, don't knock it."

The engineer belched.

"That's a piss poor attitude, brother Milbank. Don't you want us to have a happy ship?"

"And let bygones be bygones?"

They dissolved into idiot laughter. It had something of the quality of an exhibition and as Win watched them he realized they were playing it to him. It made anything he wanted to say unnecessary, reversing their old roles, as if now they were reassuring him.

"Listen," he said. "You bums can clown all you want but I got work to do."

Chicereno, still unable to talk, nodded.

Win clapped them each on the back and then walked to the jeep to get the beer. The crew chief passed him carrying a fire extinguisher and took up a position under the number-three engine. Win went over to him and borrowed a fountain pen. He took the letter from his pocket, and supporting it on his map case, signed his name, rank, and serial number in the lower left-hand corner of the envelope. Then, deliberately, he licked the flap and sealed it. The crew chief was watching him, his face solemn. Win gave him the pen and letter.

"Will you do me a favor?" he asked. "If anything happens to me, if we don't get back, will you mail this?"

"Sure, Lieutenant."

"It's all set to go. You don't have to say anything to anybody, just mail it."

The crew chief nodded.

"Thanks a lot." He started away and then stopped. "No, wait a minute. Forget about that. I think you better mail it anyway. Could you do it right after take-off?"

"Sure, Lieutenant, it's no trouble." The crew chief was very serious. "I'll take it up to Group."

"Good, that'll be fine." Win laughed. "It's not what you think, Sergeant. Everything's O.K. I'll be seeing you when we get back."

The man's face broke into a smile. "Good luck, sir."

"Thanks."

I must have really sounded like a nut, Win thought as he walked over to where Macy and the Mickey navigator sat on the edge of the revetment. As he approached they looked up.

"You making your will?" Macy asked.

Win shook his head, grinning. "It was just a letter."

"You guys know each other, don't you?" Macy jerked his thumb at the Mickey man. "Captain Fitts—Lt. Helman."

"Sure, hi."

The captain nodded and got to his feet. "I better be getting aboard," he said.

They watched him walk off.

"What's eating him?"

Macy laughed. "You didn't say sir. He's a very formal fellow."

"Yeah." Suddenly he was very shy and confused. He held out the two cans. "I brought us some beer for after."

"Great."

"That was a letter I got in France," Win said. "Their postal system isn't working yet and a man asked me to mail it to his wife for him."

Macy was watching him closely.

"I just wanted to make sure she got it," he ended lamely, thinking, How do you walk up to a guy and say look, I'm different? "His wife doesn't even know he's alive—the guy that wrote the letter, I mean."

Macy nodded. "How was it up there?"

"Well, good and bad. I'll tell you about it. But listen, what happened with Gillespie?"

"I told him to clear it with Helman." Macy laughed. "I didn't really, but I should have."

"What d'you mean?"

"Nothing, it's supposed to be a joke."

"I don't get it."

"Helman—Hillman. You know, Sidney Hillman, the labor leader. It's a big thing back in the States now. Some of our best people are saying Roosevelt doesn't do anything without first clearing it with Hillman."

"Oh."

"It's not really important, but Gillespie would have gotten it." Macy smiled and stood up. "Come on, lead navigator, they'll be starting engines any minute."

"I know, but I want to tell you something first. I understood why you did that in there and I appreciate it."

Macy put his hand on Win's shoulder. "You don't have to tell me," he said. "I know."

The three navigators in the lead airplane worked in concert. Macy, from his vantage point in the nose turret, monitored the airplane's path, comparing map symbols that represented city and town, railroad line and river, with the actuality of the ground below. The Mickey man seated back on the flight deck observed the sixty-mile-round relief map that appeared on his radar scope, commanding a whole area of which they were the moving center. And using them both as his eyes, Win correlated their findings with his own reading of altimeter and air-speed indicator, drift meter and compass, and by dead reckoning directed the actual course of their progress over the occupied continent. For him the mission had become an abstract problem, an exercise in controlled ground speed over a course with five changes of heading and a climb from twelve thousand to twenty-one thousand feet, the whole to be executed in such a fashion as to cover seven hundred miles in a stated number of hours and minutes and bring them to a specific crossing of latitude and longitude at precisely the appointed time. As he worked at his plywood table in the nose, reducing the problem piece by piece, never once looking out of the airplane, his only vision of the ground the tiny circle intersected by grid lines that he saw through the drift meter, a warm pride in the complicated trade he had so thoroughly mastered grew within him. His concentration on the work, which had always before suffered the inroads of fear, now engrossed him completely. The precision he had shaped, the host of mighty machines led by it, lent him a vast security. Somehow, through the very essence of their rapport, it even became a method of communicating to Macy the kinship he had been unable to articulate on the ground. And toward the last, as another level of his consciousness recorded the efficiency within the bomber, he thought of Macchione and Milbank and Chicereno and all isolation vanished. He was powerful and allied.

Four miles high over Hungary, where the farm-checked plain heaved itself up to form the foothills of the Carpathians, the first fighters were sighted. They came out of the north, a wedge of black dots flung toward the bombers. But as the gap closed, as the dots became tiny crosses and then grew into airplanes, it was seen that their course was set to bypass the bombers. In the B-24 the anxiety that had erupted into panic passed as the fighters swept by and were out of sight, leaving behind a tension that was heightened by lack of outlet.

"More," Macy said over the interphone. "Lots more."

Two black arrowheads, higher this time and farther to the left, went winging by.

"Man, they're gonna catch it back there!"

"That straggler from Fox is dropping bombs," Chicereno said. "There's two—three——"

"All right, cut it," from Abbot. "Can you get his number?"

"No, sir."

"Well, watch him. I want his number."

"Kosice coming up on the right," Macy said.

"How far right?"

"About twelve, fifteen miles, I make it."

"Ten," said the Mickey man.

"Good." Win checked his flight plan. "We'll be swinging left twenty-five degrees to a new heading of 330. I'll tell you when."

"Roger," Bane said.

"That leg will be seventeen minutes long and then we're at the I.P."

"We on time?" Abbot asked.

"About two minutes late."

I did it, Win thought. A third of an hour, twenty stinking

minutes more and it's delivered. He turned to glance at Lange crouched on his knees over the bombsight. Then it's your baby, he thought. We'll see what you do with your twenty-thousand-dollar education. We'll come to a little town named Wadowice that I don't even know how to pronounce, that I'll never even see, and it'll be your baby. And don't forget *they've* got their eyes on you.

Win returned to his computations, but the mood had been broken. The figures were suddenly meaningless. Perversely, his mind had slipped back to when the fighters had first been sighted. In spite of having refused to witness their coming, not having given it enough importance to get up from his table and look out the astrodome, he saw them now, the black swarm deadly in the distance, twice horrible in the anticipation, and he knew again the craven relief of when they had passed. The whole cocoon of invulnerability, so carefully spun during the early hours of the mission, began to dissolve. Then, gratefully, he heard Macy's calm voice.

"Kosice is right off the wing."

"O.K., navigator to pilot, give me twenty-five degrees left. New heading three three zero."

"Roger."

The bomber tilted and the compass needle swung in accompaniment. Win recorded the turn point in his log. The notation finished, he busied himself over the drift meter, comparing his findings with the Mickey navigator. He computed the wind direction, using his drift readings on the heading they had just abandoned and the new one, and gave his result to Lange for use on the bomb run. Then he looked at his watch. It had all taken less than ten minutes.

"There's something out there," Macy said. "Twelve-o'clock level. Can anybody else see it?"

Win half rose. *No*, he said to himself, *don't look.* Seven minutes left to I.P., two and a half, maybe three for the turn and lining up, and we're safe from fighters—safe in the flak.

"I see them now," Abbot said. "Let's watch them."

Win got down on the deck and crawled over beside Lange. Looking down through the bombardier's window, he saw the mountains falling away into level ground, located the road junction, and, following the right fork, identified the I.P.

"You see it?" He pointed. "On the road there."

Lange nodded.

"We'll go right over it. You can talk him through the turn and then take over."

Lange held up his gloved hand, making a circle with thumb and index finger. You can say what you want, Win thought, but that sonofabitch sure isn't scared . . .

"They're planes, all right." Macy's voice came over the interphone. "What the hell d'you make of it, wing to wing like that?"

"There's two lines, one behind the other——"

"What's that now? *Christ—rockets!*"

The B-24 lifted, borne up as by an air pocket, and Win was thrown against Lange. He struggled to his feet, and mounting the ammunition boxes that lined the nose compartment, looked out through the astrodome.

Up ahead, lined up six abreast and coming head-on toward the bombers, were the two-engined Messerschmitt 110s. The launched projectiles were dots of flame beneath their wings that grew with incredible speed into trails of fired gas and then were past. And then again, the B-24 rearing as flame lanced out, burned neon-bright, and disappeared, and the fighters themselves were rising to vault high up and over the formation.

"They're trying to open us up!" Abbot was screaming. *"Close in! Close the formation——"*

"You're not on command, Major. You're on interphone."

There was a click and Abbot's voice was gone.

"*Here comes more!*"

Win stood transfixed, watching the new six swing into line, saw the red eyes under their wings wink again and grow and grow and pass.

"Get ready to start your turn, Al," said Lange's calm voice. "P.D.I. centered?"

"Roger."

"All right, start rolling left . . . more . . . more . . . more. Now roll out. O.K., watch the air speed now . . . O.K. . . . I got her, bomb-bay doors coming open . . ."

"*Fighters high at ten o'clock!*"

Win turned in reflex and saw the first flak blossom up and at the same time saw the V wheel and split and come swinging down into the pursuit curve that would rake the whole formation.

"*Here they come!*"

"*Let 'em!*" It was Macy's voice, deep and glad as an organ chord. "Come on, you bastards—closer. That's right . . ."

The B-24 trembled under the hammering answer of her gunners and in that moment Win hated Macy, hated him with a fierce envy of the pouring, pile-driving fifties in the nose turret.

Now the sky was pockmarked all over its face with black puff clouds of flak and still the fighters came, twisting back for another pass and still another. Inside the B-24 the interphone was a constant roar, with Macy's tones ringing through all the others like the exhortation of a bugle. And then Win was flung from his feet as the bomber rocked and settled and regained course and all other sound died before the piercing horror of a drawn-out yell.

"It's O.K.," Lange's voice sobbed. "It's O.K. . . . a few seconds more . . . bombs away . . ."

"*Rally off left to two-fifteen!*" Win heard his own voice cutting through the other sound that was already blood-throttled. "*Rally off!*"

They were out of it in placid air, the plane flying smoothly, before Win was able to turn and see Lange sunk back against the ammunition box, blood running out of his helmet and streaming down over his oxygen mask. Win moved toward him, reached him before realizing that Lange was pointing up at the nose turret.

"Macy?" Win called. "Macy, you all right?"

"Get me out . . . I'm hit . . ."

The turret was turned all the way to the left, its duralumin doors concealed within itself, its armored side now filling more than half of the opening in the fuselage.

"Straighten it out. I can't open the doors."

". . . can't . . . guns crushed down on me . . . can't move . . ."

Win pounded with his fists, tearing his hands on the turret that now enclosed Macy in a circlet of steel.

"HELP ME!" he screamed. "HELP ME, SOMEBODY!"

". . . got blood in my mouth . . . choking me . . ."

Then Lange and Milbank were beside him, struggling with the jammed turret, not able to move it, and all sound from within had ceased.

10   All of his outward perceptions were diffused, as if the normal morning life of the squadron that flowed around him was partitioned off by a wall of glass. He stood with his body still bent to see, but his attention had come unfixed from the sliver of mirror that gave him back a truncated version of his lathered face, and the razor was forgotten in his hand. His features were strained, like those of a man leaning into the wind and listening for a sound that has long since been blown away. In reality he heard nothing. I must be in shock, he thought, they ought to wrap me in blankets and give me mild stimulants to drink.

"Ain' you through yet?" Bane had come out of the tent. "You know that's the general's car out there."

Win turned to the voice, needing his whole body to hear with.

"What?"

"Ah said—— Christ, man, what you been shavin' with, an ax?"

"What's the matter?"

"Your face—look at it, it's all bloody." Bane came over. "You sure you're feelin' all right?"

"Sure, why shouldn't I be?"

Bane shrugged. "Well, hurry up then."

Win turned to find his face in the mirror again and saw the red lines raked down his cheek.

"I didn't even feel it," he said, but Bane had gone back into the tent.

He resumed shaving, careful now to pull the skin taut for the passage of the razor and when he was done he went to the water tank and stooped so his head was beneath the spout. He turned the tap on full force and the water gushed out over his face and head, running cold down his chest and back. It roused him, but by the time he had gone into the tent and started dressing, the effect had worn off and the stupor returned. Bane had to remind him twice about wearing a tie and then lend him a cap after he had searched long and uselessly for his own. Finally he was ready and they walked over to Operations, where the staff car with its red-starred shield was parked. The driver, a staff sergeant, was watching for them and they heard him call to Abbot that they were coming. The major, immaculate in his faded khaki, came out of Operations. Even he was inhibited by the general's car and personal driver and his tentative smile of greeting faded into a gruff hello. The sergeant held the door open for him and he got into the back seat. Bane and Win sat in front.

"I talked to the hospital a few minutes ago," Abbot said formally when they were under way. "Lange's all right. A mild concussion and some cuts, nothing serious."

"Are we pickin' him up?" Bane asked.

"No, he'll be better off getting some rest. They said he didn't have too good a night."

"Yes, sir, Ah know."

Driving along the perimeter strip, Win realized that they were approaching the B-24 in which yesterday's mission had been flown. His momentary impulse to look away brought a twinge of guilt, and then the desire to see and test himself was strong within him. But as they drew even with the revetment it was as he had feared. There was the bomber with the repair stands clustered around it, with its smashed nose turret removed and lying on the ground, and he felt nothing. Like a man so unhinged by the constant throbbing of a toothache that he seeks reassurance in the greater pain derived from probing the abscessed center with his tongue, he turned to keep it in sight for as long as possible. He saw the shattered plexiglass, the cams and gears and handles of the gun mounts all awry, and remembered how it had looked right after landing when the whole interior had been caked with the bloody froth that Macy had coughed up before dying. He remembered the exact angle of Macy's head leaning forward on the twisted gunmounts, the oxygen mask torn half off and part of the cheek and jaw laid open. He heard the flight surgeon explaining that it would have made no difference if they had been able to get Macy out of the turret. He saw it all again, experienced it, and felt absolutely nothing. And feeling nothing, the panic returned. The emptiness was what he couldn't bear. It had established itself during the night just finished, when, alone in the tent after Bane had gone to the hospital to see Lange, he had prepared himself for grief. But nothing had come, not even tears. So, like a flagellant fingering the strands of his whip, he had summoned and enumerated his guilt. He had reminded himself that before the attack he had envied Macy the guns in the nose turret. He had screamed at himself that he had no right to be alive, that *he,* not Macy, should have been in the turret. He had tried to feel the hot steel piercing *his* face, had torn his lip between his teeth in order to taste the blood that Macy had choked on. But none of it had moved him, and in the end, still dry-eyed, he had fallen into a dreamless sleep. And when Bane had awakened him in the morning to tell him that they had been ordered to Wing, the hollowness had awakened with him.

They were well past the revetment, the B-24 out of sight,

before Win straightened up in the seat, afraid that his face had given evidence of what he felt. He lit a cigarette and glanced at Bane and then around at Abbot, but they were both looking straight ahead.

A few minutes later they paused in front of Group Operations to pick up Major Gillespie and Captain Fitts, the Mickey navigator. After a brief exchange of greetings, they too were quiet and the silence held until they were through Cerignola and out onto the main road that led north to Foggia. Here the driver brought their speed up to fifty, and something of the authority of the big car's smooth motion, of the respectful way in which the slower traffic pulled over to let them pass, worked itself into them and they relaxed. Gillespie produced a pigskin cigar case and offered it around. Everyone helped themselves with the exception of Win, the sergeant dividing his attention from the road to select his with care. They all lit up, filling the car with the cozy confidence of aromatic plumes of smoke and then Gillespie noticed that the driver wasn't smoking.

"Need a light, Sergeant?" he asked, leaning forward.

"No thanks, sir. I thought I'd save mine if you didn't mind."

"Sure, go right ahead. Here"—Gillespie extended the case—"have another. Glad of a chance to show we appreciate being picked up like this."

"It was the general's orders, sir."

"Hell, I know that, but we still appreciate it. Go ahead, take one."

The sergeant glanced at the case and picked a cigar. "Thank you, sir," he said.

"Forget it." Gillespie closed the case and leaned back comfortably. "I got a hunch things are finally beginning to come our way. What d'you think, Sergeant?"

"Sir?"

Gillespie laughed heartily. "You don't have to give me that, I've seen you enlisted men operate around headquarters. Most of the time you know a hell of a lot more about what's going on than the brass does."

The sergeant was silent.

"Relax, man, you can level with us. Let us in on the poop. What've they been saying about us?"

"I wouldn't know, sir."

"In a pig's eye, you wouldn't. Weren't yesterday's bomb-strike photos in when you left?"

"Well——"

"Oh, for Christ's sake!"

"Well, sir, I saw the general had them on his desk when he told me to drive over and pick you up."

"That's what I thought. What he say?"

"Just said to have you there by 1100 hours, sir."

This time the laugh was general but Gillespie's boomed out over the others.

"He's too slick for you, Major," the Mickey man said.

"He sure is. I know when I'm beat. But I still think if the general sends his personal car and driver down for us it means something—eh, Abbot?"

Abbot nodded judiciously.

"And I don't think he'd have done it unless we had clobbered that target yesterday."

"No, you're probably right about that."

"You bet I'm right. We ought to get a presidential citation out of this."

"Take it easy." Abbot laughed.

"Like hell I will!" Gillespie was warming to it and his enthusiasm was irresistible. "The drought's over, I tell you, and you're the guys that turned the trick. This is one time I see to it that we get credit where credit is due."

"Well, I'd like to see Macy get something," Abbot said.

"You're goddamned right! And that bombardier too. What's his name?"

"Lange."

"That's right. By God, if we don't toot our own horn nobody will do it for us. Let's go, driver. Let's step it up. We don't want to keep the general waiting."

And Win sat huddled deep in the corner of the seat, his arms hugged tight to his sides in an attempt to keep aloof while he concentrated on noting the number-marked kilometer stones as they flashed by.

The room was the man's natural habitat. Containing nothing more than a field desk and iron folding chair, a multicolored map of western and central Europe on one wall, it provided an ideal setting for the wing commander, Brigadier General Eliot Hartshorn, U.S.A. Everything about the man was stripped down to bare essentials. His close-cropped hair that showed a glint of gray, the pared nails of his narrow and surprisingly elegant hands, his exact-fitting khaki uniform that was bleached almost white were all like the abrupt functionalism of a freshly sharpened pencil. Sitting bolt upright behind his desk after the informal exchange of greetings, he watched chairs being carried in and unfolded for the still standing men. Then, cueing himself on the click of the closing door, he leaned back a few inches and by that slight change in posture succeeded in endowing his words with a casual quality.

"I know you're wondering what this is all about," he said. "We'll come to that later. First I'd like to hear your impressions of yesterday's raid."

The semicircle of men facing him was silent.

"Who wants to start it off? Abbot, how about you? Be as informal as you like."

"Yes, sir." Abbot cleared his throat. "Is there any particular phase——"

"Anything at all you feel is significant. What would you say, over-all? Was it easy or rough?"

"Yes, sir. Well, I'd say it was kind of rough."

"Kind of!" Gillespie snorted. "Excuse me, but I think Major Abbot is being too modest."

"Yes?" The general turned politely and the flicker of a smile bent his lips. "What do you think, Major Gillespie?"

"I think it was goddamned rough!"

"Did you fly it, Major?"

"No, but I read every single crew report. And I've flown a few rough ones in my time."

"I know that." The general's smile was wider. "Weren't we together on the low-level job to Ploesti last August?"

"That we were!" Gillespie's laugh boomed out, and remaining seated became intolerable for him. He arose and strode to the wall, shifting the room's focus to himself, his unleashed energy re-establishing the optimism that had marked the ride up from Group. "That we were," he repeated. "And from the crew reports I'd say that yesterday's was pretty near as rough."

"Then that's settled." The general had lost interest in Gillespie. "You're missing some people, aren't you? I only count four of the lead crew here."

"Yes, sir," said Abbot, happy to be on safe ground. "Our bombardier was hit. And we lost Captain Macy."

"Macy—your squadron navigator? Was he leading?"

"No, sir, he was in the turret. Lieutenant Helman led."

The general's eyes began a check of insignia, pausing momentarily on Bane's silver bar. Out of pure reflex, as if warding off a blow, the pilot jerked his thumb at Win.

"Lieutenant Helman's the oldest navigator in the squadron," Abbot said to fill the pause.

Startled out of inattention by this second mention of his name, Win heard himself saying: "Now I am," and felt the general's eyes registering him, classifying him, and withdrawing.

"Yes," the general said. "I'd be interested in what you feel about yesterday's mission, Lieutenant."

"I don't feel anything," Win said and then he was out of it, completely back in the here and now. "I'm sorry, sir. I wasn't paying too good attention and I didn't understand your question."

"We lost thirty-nine bombers yesterday," said the general casually, leaning back in his chair. "Thirty-nine out of four hundred and fifty. That's a big bite out of a shoestring outfit like ours. This isn't the Eighth Air Force, you know. We lack the crews, the planes, the press agents—everything, including the fat beautiful tonnage figures. We can't compete. And now stuff is being siphoned off to the Pacific. It's a problem."

He stopped as casually as he had started and took a sheaf of photographs from under his desk blotter. Still looking at Win, he fanned them out like a deck of cards.

"How well d'you think your group did yesterday, Lieutenant?" he asked.

"I don't know, sir."

"Abbot?"

"Well, it's hard to say for sure, sir."

"Ask me," Gillespie said, pounding his fist into his open palm. "I say we clobbered it! I say we kicked the holy crap out of it!"

"That's right, sir!" Captain Fitts said. "The bombardier was lined up perfectly. I saw it in my scope."

"And who the hell are you?" the general asked abruptly, all warmth gone from his voice.

"The group Mickey man, sir. I——"

"But I was under the impression that the target was clear. All you had to do to see the target was to look down. Am I wrong?"

Gillespie was the quickest. "There was a rocket-launching attack, General."

"I'm not interested in details."

"Details, sir? With the bastards coming right down the bomb run through their own flak?"

"Still details. When Air Force calls for three or four maximum efforts in one week and I say no replacements have come in, it's a detail. They're just not interested and neither am I."

"But the bombardier was hit right before bombs away."

"You don't seem to be able to understand me, Major," the general said. "Where was the deputy lead? They had a bombardier aboard, didn't they? Was he hit too?"

"No, sir," Abbot said quickly, realizing that it was too late, that he should have known immediately upon entering the room that this was what it was leading to. "Deputy lead was untouched."

"I see. And what's your excuse."

"No excuse, sir. I was in command."

For an instant, although he didn't move, they had the impression that the general was about to fling the bomb-strike photos in their faces. Instead, he grunted and handed the sheaf to Abbot. Gillespie rushed over to lean across Abbot's shoulder. Captain Fitts joined them.

"By God!" Gillespie snatched the top picture out of Abbot's hand and advanced on the desk. "Look at this, they fell right into the camp."

"That they did," the general said dryly.

"But that's good! That means we wiped out a whole slew of workers. Workers are as essential to the operation of that complex as cracking towers, as the plants themselves."

"Not quite," the general said coldly. "Anyway, that isn't a workers' camp, it's a concentration camp."

With no real knowledge of what he was doing Win leaned forward and picked up the photograph that Gillespie had dropped on the general's desk.

"But the Germans use them as workers," Gillespie was insisting. "Intelligence is practically certain of it."

"Don't be ridiculous, Major. Those were Jews the bombs dropped on."

"*No!*" Win gasped.

"Yes. That's an extermination camp down there. You think it's smart to send bombers seven hundred miles in just to kill Jews? Don't you think the Germans do it efficiently enough themselves?"

"*Jesus Christ,* no." Win moaned, still staring at the photograph and seeing the massed pock of bombs concentrated in the oblong gray area that was the camp. "I'm a Jew too."

Now the general was turned to him in surprise. "Yes? What about it?"

"Did we—I mean were there a whole lot killed?"

"We can only guess, but there must have been."

"*Well, it wasn't my fault!*" His voice was trembling, the words tumbling over each other. "I split the I.P. right down the middle, two minutes late! I lined them up on the target! What more could I do?"

"I'm not blaming you, Lieutenant," the general said. "I'm only trying to answer this nonsense. If anything, you did those poor devils a favor."

Now he stood up and his remarks were directed to Abbot; everyone else was excluded. "I'm giving you one warning. If you don't start producing, I'm going to break every one of you down to second lieutenant. I'll relieve every commanding officer and send in people who can do the job."

"Yes, sir." Abbot was standing at attention.

"And I'm completely unimpressed by your morale problems. That's a detail too, and you at least should have recognized it. Cure your sloppy flying and you'll have morale. Schedule enough practice missions so you fly better formation and you'll stop being attacked. That's all. Dismissed!"

The car was parked beneath the general's open windows and they were silent getting in. The driver pulled away with a slash of tires, accelerating as he went, his turn carrying to the road so that all he had to do was straighten the wheel and they were on their way back to Group at fifty miles per hour. Then he took one of Gillespie's cigars from his breast pocket and bit off its end.

"Got a light, Major?" he asked, and spit.

"No, goddammit!" Gillespie snarled. "Keep your eyes front and both hands on the goddamned wheel."

"Yes, sir."

"Yes sir my ass. I'm wise to you."

The sergeant was silent.

In the front seat Win sat staring at the bomb-strike photo that he had taken with him from the general's office. What have you got to feel bad about? he was thinking. You did them a favor. You blew them to bits with five-hundred-pound bombs and now they don't have to wait their turn to be stoked into ovens and burned. Just think of all the suffering you saved them. Then, piece by piece, very precisely, he began tearing the shiny photograph into strips.

Behind him Abbot sighed, expelling a long-pent breath, and it was like tripping a trigger within Gillespie.

"Details," he raged. "Oh, that dirty little son of a bitch, that superior little snot-nosed bastard."

"He was right," Abbot said.

"Right? *Right?* Are you as stupid as he is? Do you think practice missions and better formation will change anything? Do you think it's an accident they followed this group down the bomb run? Like hell it was! They'll do it again. And the reason is right there!"

Win turned around and saw Gillespie's outthrust hand pointed at him. He saw that beside him Bane had turned too, saw the numbed shrinking look on the pilot's face, and at last felt the glad stirrings of fury.

"*It wasn't my fault*," Gillespie moaned. "Please, mister, it wasn't my fault. Well, here's something to really cry about— *it was nobody's fault but yours!*"

"You mean me?"

"Yes, I mean you! You and all the other sneaking little bastards on that crew!"

"Why, you're just full of shit!"

The words set Gillespie back like a blow in the chest, but then he was leaning forward again and Win was rising to climb over the front seat to meet him, impatient of restraining hands. Win jerked his arm loose and spun on Bane.

"Take your hands off me, I'm about to put you in the clear." Then he turned again and saw Gillespie's gray hair and bloodshot eyes and quivering lips, and almost laughed aloud. "You old shmuck," he said joyously. "You think they followed us in because we shot down those fighters? You think they stopped to see what our insignia was? You're crazy, that's what you are. You ought to be put away in a crazy house——"

"Take it easy, Helman," Abbot said.

"Why? What's he going to do? Court-martial me? Drum me out of the Air Force? See to it that my name is never again mentioned in the Corps of Aviation Cadets? Don't make me laugh, sir!"

"Why, you young——"

Win's laugh, high and piercing, drowned him out. "And I'll tell you something else you been just coming in your pants to know. *I* shot those fighters down! Not Lange or Bane or Jones, but *me!* It was all my idea. And you know something else? You know why it was really my fault? Because I was the one that missed. I missed and that German bastard of a pilot bailed out. If it wasn't for me nobody'd ever have known about it!"

He turned to Bane. "Even you didn't know that, did you? Well, now you're really in the clear. Now you can——"

But the expression on the pilot's face stopped him. It wasn't what he had expected. It was true that there was relief in the face, but the relief was stained with fear and pain and loneliness, and he turned away not to have to see it.

Gillespie was still leaning forward in his seat, but the threat of physical violence was gone. He was smiling now, and the smile had the power to frighten, where the roaring had been impotent.

"Tell me something, Helman," he said softly. "How would you feel if you ever had to bail out and a German fighter followed you down to machine-gun you? It's the same thing, isn't it?"

Win shrugged. "I'll take my chances."

"I see."

"Yeah, in a pig's ass you see." The gentle tone was beginning to make him afraid and he fought to hold his anger from draining away. "I'll take my chances on getting killed in a sloppy war the same as one of your nice neat ones."

"Sure. But you know that practically every man in the group that's dead is your fault, don't you?"

"I don't know anything. They've got to take their chances too."

"I see, and that gets rid of the responsibility. Tell me something else. We might as well understand each other. Would you do the same thing again?"

"You're damned right I would!" Now the anger was back, arming him, and he thrust the wadded bits of the torn photograph under Gillespie's nose. "I'm not making any gentlemen's agreements with bastards that treat people this way. You can do it, if that's the way you want it—but not me!"

"I see," Gillespie said, nodding pleasantly.

11 The storm began that evening. The sky was feathered over with ice-bearing tendrils of circus cloud; in its western reaches it was colored like blood by the setting sun. During the night massed ranks of cumulo nimbi rolled down from the north and at dawn released lightning, thunder, wind, and rain in a savage overture to the season's end. All that day the air was gray with slanted rain as the land beneath the Spur quenched its long summer's thirst, but when night changed gray into black and the rain continued to fall, the earth grew glutted and caked with mud. The second morning there was no dawn, no visible demarkation between night and day. The pelting rain thinned to a floating mist and merged itself with the steam rising from the still uncooled earth. The sun rose, and although it could not be seen, its heat permeated all of the wetness, and everything was clammy to the touch.

Inside the tent the bulb suspended from the ridge pole glowed with sudden light and Win awoke. He brought his left hand up before his face to look at his watch and saw that the second hand was motionless. He had forgotten to wind it. Frowning up at the light, he tried to figure the day. He remembered that the bulb had gone out without warning during the night just past, the second night of the storm, when he had already been alone for more than thirty-six hours. Slowly he became aware that the metronome drumming of rain on canvas had stopped and at the same time noticed that the pillow of his sleeping bag was wet. He moved his eyes to the tent roof above his head, searching for a leak, and finding none, realized that it was his own tears that had wet the pillow. Then he saw the melted-down stub of candle beside his cot and his memory was complete.

He had entered the tent, not to leave it, immediately after the general's car had returned them to the squadron area. There he had fretted impatiently until Bane had gone to the hospital in Cerignola to visit Lange, and, alone at last, he had lain down to think, to think or go mad. But in the end he had won no decision, achieved no acceptable rationale. He had tried again and again to convince himself that considered within the mad context of war he had done the slave laborers of Auschwitz a favor in tearing the life from their flesh with bombs. It was cleaner, he had told himself; they themselves would have chosen it against waiting to be stoked into a crematorium oven. They would have thanked him for saving them additional pain. But this argument had had no power to convince him, and the stubborn core of guilt had remained. So he had tried next to excuse himself of the whole thing, raging at the Nazis who juxtaposed a plant, a legitimate target, with a camp for the living, breathing dead and so trapped *him* into making the decision. None of the others who had flown with him in the same airplane and then sat together before the general would make the decision for him or even *with* him. They might not go all the way with Gillespie, but if it hurt them they would be able to dismiss it as an unfortunate accident. He had to resolve it alone, for after throwing the thing of the fighters in Gillespie's face he was truly alone. And lying there in darkness during the second night of the storm, impaled between the horror and the guilt, his feeling

of isolation had magnified into such a void that finally he
had doubted his own existence. Panic had roiled up to fill the
emptiness and he had driven his mind to shape for him the
immediate bodily limits of his consciousness. He had tried to
visualize the dark tent in which he lay prisoner, tried to decide
on which side of him was wall and which was empty space,
which end of him was head and which was feet. But touching
himself, reaching out a hand to feel the sodden canvas of the
tent wall, had not quieted the insane hammering of his heart.
So in abject terror he had crawled from his cot to find light with
which to reassure himself of his own being. Then, with the
candle found and lit and forming a pool of warmth, his thinking
had lost all direction, his mind had shied away from any further
prodding, and he had found himself suddenly mourning for
Macy. All of what he had been unable to feel after Macy's death
had welled up, overwhelming him, and he had wept and,
weeping, passed into unconscious sleep.

Now he lay still in the sleeping bag, listening to the day,
but no sounds came to him that gave a hint of the hour. The
normal tempo of life in the squadron area seemed to have
ceased. After unzipping the outside of the bag he sat up on
the edge of the cot and thrust his bare feet into his flying
boots. He got up and went to the tent flap, untied it, and looked
out. The whole area was mud and moving mist; the tents
drooped, every curve of canvas concave, cradling water. Three
men dressed in green G.I. raincoats were crossing the area in
single file. They were too distant for identification and he
watched them plodding along, circling puddles they could have
jumped, their progress dull as mourners returning from a fresh
grave. Then he recognized them and stepped back. Wondering
if they had seen him, he debated retying the flap, but he was
still undecided when he heard them outside on the wooden
foot walk. They hesitated there—he heard them, and then Milbank came in followed by Macchione and Chicereno.

"Hi," they said, standing bunched in the entrance, their wet raincoats glinting dull green as sea water in the electric light. Macchione took off his cap and banged it against his leg to release a shower. Chic, who was hatless, wore a halo of mist on his cropped black hair.

"Bane gone to the hospital?" Milbank asked.

"Yeah, day before yesterday," Win said. "I haven't seen him since."

"Oh." They didn't move.

"What time is it now?"

"Three-thirty," two of them said at once.

Win turned away from them and went to sit down on his cot. He set his watch and began winding it. "Well, sit down, or something," he said irritably.

All three of them made for Lange's cot and sat down side by side, facing him. They gazed at his bare legs and disheveled cot. "We'll go if you're trying to sleep," Milbank said. "We can come back later."

Win shrugged. "I'm not sleeping, but I don't know when Bane's coming back."

"We didn't come to see him, we came to see you."

"Yeah, well here I am. What's on your mind?"

There was a brief exchange of uneasy looks, and Milbank said: "Well, we figured we ought to have a talk, unless you'd rather not."

"Not what?"

"I mean, maybe you don't care——"

"Care?" Win furrowed his forehead in annoyance. "What the hell are you talking about?"

"Christ, I bet he don't know anything about it." Chic stood up excitedly. "You don't even know you're flying, do you?"

"Flying?"

"Yeah, tonight——"

"To*night!* What d'you mean? When tonight?"

"Sit down, Chic," Macchione said quietly, not taking his eyes from Win's face. "You're scheduled with Dusak tonight. We thought you already knew."

"I don't know nothing. Why me? What's the matter with their own navigator?"

"Don't you remember he went down? Two days ago, flying pickup with McDuffee?"

Win shook his head.

"Well, he did," Macchione said. "His name was Lt. Fullerton, I think."

Win was no longer listening. Automatically he reached to his breast for a cigarette only to rediscover that he was un-dressed. Then he saw the empty pack and heaped ash tray beside the gutted candle and stood up to find his shirt. When he had it down from where it hung, he began dressing.

"Here, I got some," Milbank said, holding out a package of Camels. "Where you going?"

"To see that sonofabitch Abbot, that's where." He finished buttoning his shirt and started searching for his pants. "He's not getting away with pulling anything like this on me."

"But it ain't just you," Milbank said. "That's why we came to talk."

"There's nothing to talk about. This is my baby; you guys are off the hook."

"How d'you figure that?"

"How? Because now all of you can stop wetting your drawers. The big secret is out. I told them that I shot down the fighters."

"*You* shot them down?"

Looking up at him in amazement, Win realized that he had never before seen the engineer really angry. "That's right," he said.

"And we had nothing to do with it, huh? You did it all by yourself."

"I was responsible——"

"Shit!" Chic broke in. "Us three got one and Rogers got the other. You missed."

"Don't worry, I told them that too."

"Why?" Milbank demanded. "Did we ask you to?"

"I saved you the trouble." He began to feel that something was wrong, terribly wrong, but now he was too deep in the hurt and he couldn't stop. "And there's a couple of other things you don't know. You know where our bombs went on the last one? The whole lead echelon's?"

"Yes," Macchione said, pulling at Chic to make him sit down. "We know."

"And maybe we feel as bad about it as you do," Milbank said.

"No, you can't——"

"Christ!" the engineer said, raising his hands to shoulder height, balling them into fists, seeking something to smash. Then he regained control and lowered them and thrust them deep into his raincoat pockets.

"You don't understand," Win said desperately.

"Shut up!" Milbank roared at him. "Just shut up for now! Who the hell d'you think you are, a little plaster saint? You think nobody can feel anything except you? Did you ever figure what *we* been catching these last months? You think it's been a goddamned picnic for us since we shot those fighters down?"

"I——"

"No, I'm not finished yet! You know why we're here now? Because they're splitting up the crew. Yeah! But that don't mean anything to you."

Win wanted to speak but he could not. There was nothing to say, absolutely nothing, and he shook his head dumbly from side to side.

"So *you're* going to run to Abbot and tell him that he can't do this to *you*. Shit!"

"O.K., Jack, now you can shut up," Macchione said quietly. "We won't get anyplace yelling at each other."

"We won't get anyplace anyway. Not here."

"No. I mean, come on, sit down." Win turned his head half away to hide his eyes that were welling tears, and held out his hand. "Come on, give me a cigarette. Please."

Milbank stood still leaning forward, staring at him. He brought his right hand slowly out of his raincoat pocket and they saw that he was holding the now crumpled package of Camels. Extracting one of the misshapen tubes, he held it up and laughed, the sound choked deep in his throat. "It's busted," he said.

"That's O.K." Win got the cigarette between his lips and lit it, cupping both trembling hands around the match. "It's O.K.," he said. "It's fine. What do you want me to do?"

They sighed in concert and Milbank said: "We got an idea. If you're with us——"

"If you still want me," Win said humbly.

"We want you, all right. We need you."

"Then tell me what I do."

Milbank unbuttoned his raincoat and peeled it off. He threw it on one of the vacant cots and turned to Macchione. "You tell him, Gene."

"Well." The ball gunner frowned, rubbing his hands hard against his thighs. "We discussed it and it seems like the best thing to do is try to keep the crew together, no matter what happens. That way we got a chance. We're experienced and we can look out for each other. Right?"

Win nodded.

"All right. But we can't do it with just us enlisted men. They've started it with you and now we got to answer them through you."

"How?"

"By you telling Major Abbot that you won't fly tonight."

"You mean quit——"

"No!" Chic was on his feet, unable to control himself. "Tell them to go screw. Either we fly together or we don't fly!"

Win looked first to Macchione. The ball gunner nodded solemnly. Then he turned slowly back to Chic and Milbank standing tense for his answer and the seed of it was born; the realization that there was a way to strike back began swelling inside his chest. "You think it would work?" he asked.

"You're goddamned right it would!" Chic exulted. "The abbot'll blow his top!"

"But Abbot's not really behind it."

"Then who is?"

"Gillespie."

"That old fart! Why——"

"It doesn't make any difference," Macchione cut in. "The important thing is not to let them split us up. If you go to Major Abbot it's natural. Like going through channels."

Win nodded, rising to his feet. It was surging through him, wiping everything else away. He was remembering how he had felt during the first part of the mission to Auschwitz when he had been secure in a powerful alliance with all of the men in all of the bombers behind him. And this was the same. He was needed. These three men, so tough and tried from being through so much, were waiting for him to lead them. Then he turned absently to rub out the stub of cigarette that was beginning to burn his hand and saw the gutted candle beside his disordered cot and it all came back, blunting everything.

"No," he said. "I don't know."

"Don't know what, for Christ's sake!"

"It's no good."

"What's no good?" It was a scream now. It came from Chic. "For Christ's sake, what're you talking about? If you're scared, say so. We'll go with you to see Abbot."

"It's not that." He spread his hands wide, entreating them to understand. "Look, what if he says O.K., then you don't fly."

"Then we don't fly!" Milbank put his hand on Win's shoulder. "We'll sit it out until hell freezes. All of us."

"No . . ."

"Why not?"

"Because then we're running away." Suddenly this part of it was clear to him. "Don't you see? That's what they want, that's why they're doing it. We stand for something now. Why'd we shoot those fighters down? Why didn't we surrender? Just so we could get home sooner? No! Not me! I did it because I'm not surrendering to any bastards that burn people and then make soap out of them, that put a camp right next door to a target——"

"And neither are we!" Milbank interrupted savagely. "So what do we do? Let these bastards over here rub our noses in shit and then ask for more?"

"No . . . I don't know . . ."

"Then what? That's what they're doing if we let them get away with it. Isn't it?"

"Let me tell you," Chic cried furiously. "I can make speeches too. They killed Polletti and Reilly, didn't they? Remember Polletti's guts all over the waist? I hate 'em too. So what am I supposed to do now? Let that bastard Abbot split us up, let him fly us with any green crew of cripples he wants? Not me!"

"He's right," Macchione said. "You used to say it yourself. Build a good crew and you won't get killed. And we're the best crew there is, the oldest."

"But what good is it if we don't fly?"

"And what good is it if we're dead?" Chic demanded. "You want to be a dead fucking hero?"

"No."

"Then what?" Macchione asked. "Tell us and we'll do it."

"Goddammit, I been telling you. I don't know!"

It echoed in silence, the violence of it forcing a pause, so that there was a beat in time in which nobody moved. Their eyes were all fixed on him. Then Macchione looked down at his hands, sighed, and stood up. "I guess we might as well go," he said. "There's nothing else to say."

They moved leadenly to the tent flap. Milbank picked up his raincoat but did not put it on. They stood shuffling their feet, bunched together, not knowing how to leave.

"Well, good luck," Macchione said finally.

"No!" Milbank crushed his raincoat into a ball and flung it from him. "You stupid stubborn sonofabitch, what d'you want to get killed for? You ain't even been in an airplane at night since we came overseas, much less flown in one. At least skip this one. Tell them to get a navigator from one of the other squadrons, tell them you're sick, tell them anything——"

Win shook his head.

"Why? Just tell me why?"

"Because I got to."

"But *why?*"

"Listen," Win implored them. "Maybe it's no answer, but what did we build a good crew for? Only to stay alive so we could finish our missions and go home? Don't you see? Even if that's why we did it at first, it's no good now. It's O.K. for Bane; he's off the hook. It's great with Lange; he's been sorry we shot those bastards down for a long time now. But it won't work for us. Can't you see it?"

"No," Milbank said. "They can win the war without us. But we were right and I ain't letting no Abbot or no Gillespie push me around. Not when I'm right."

"I'm not saying we weren't right——"

"Then why let them do it?"

"*I'm* not the one who's letting them!" Win yelled at him. "*You* are! You say we were right. Who agrees with you? Us four? But who else? *Nobody!* So let's run away and keep our little sewing circle nice and safe and closed so we can agree, eh?

Well, I'll tell you something. Maybe this is just what we need. Maybe they're really doing us a favor by splitting us up!"

"*Aaah*, you're crazy!" Milbank grated at him through closed teeth.

"Maybe," Win said flatly. "Only don't tell me that you feel the same as I do about where those last bombs fell. Because that's one of the main reasons I'm flying—that and shooting down those fighters and because of Macy and what happened in France. And when I fly, Gillespie'll know it and Abbot'll know it and after a while so will the rest of them. That's the best I can do for you."

They stared into each other's eyes. Then Milbank turned furiously away, bent to retrieve his raincoat and flung himself out of the tent. Chic and Macchione followed him slowly.

12 Win upended the parachute bag over his cot and then began refilling it, replacing the equipment one piece at a time. He was completely dressed for the air and this was his final check. While he was unclipping the inspection flap of his chest pack, a car approached the tent and he heard it stop outside. Moments later the wheels churned as it pulled away, the tent flap opened, and Bane came in followed by Lange. Win reclipped the flap, stowed the parachute in the bag, threw in his helmet and oxygen mask, and straightened up. They were both standing near Lange's cot, watching him. Lange had removed his cap and Win saw the skin-colored strip of adhesive that paralleled his hairline. In the dim light it seemed that his forehead had been doubled in height.

"How d'you feel?" he asked. "You out of the hospital already?"

Lange nodded.

"Where you goin'?" Bane asked anxiously. "There ain' no mission tomorrow."

"It's tonight."

"Tonight?"

"Yeah." Win looked at Lange. "They sure turned you out in a hurry, didn't they."

The bombardier returned his stare steadily. "I got a week in Rome," he said. "I earned it."

"Sure you did—we all did. Bane tell you where our bombs fell on that last one?"

"It wasn't my fault," Lange said.

Win laughed. "Who said it was?"

"Listen, you flyin' one of them intrusion missions?" Bane demanded.

"Yeah, with Dusak."

"How come?"

"Well, Dusak lost his navigator." Now he looked directly at Bane. "So they scheduled me."

Bane slanted his eyes away, but the pain was evident in the molding of his face. "Where's it to?" he asked.

"Munich, the West Marshaling Yard."

"Christ, why'd they wan' to pick on you?"

Win smiled. "I guess Abbot decided I was good enough to fill in. Maybe Gillespie advised him, he always liked my work. Why, you surprised?"

Bane dropped his eyes again and said nothing.

"It's O.K., I don't mind." Win looked at his watch. "Well, I got to be going."

"You're goin' to fly in the clouds all the way, ain' you?" Bane asked desperately.

"Sure." Win picked up the parachute bag. "Don't worry, nobody'll even see us."

"Who's worrying?" Lange asked.

Win put the parachute bag down very deliberately, and then picked it up again. He smiled at the bombardier. "Soon as you get back from Rome," he said pleasantly, "when you're all nice and healthy again, I'm going to put you back in the hospital. That's a promise."

He turned his back on them and started for the tent flap.

"Win . . ."

He stopped. It was Bane who had called.

"Good luck," the pilot said.

To the north the night sky was a cavern roofed to infinity with ever darker laminations of cloud. The mist had lifted, leaving the ghost of its moisture to chill the air. Often in the past he had come out to the flight line while it was still in darkness, but this time it was different. The mission was dependent upon the duration of night rather than upon its cessation.

In the revetment the crew was waiting for midnight. The outlines of the gray-daubed bomber, crouched belly to the ground with load, were only faintly discernible. Beyond where he estimated the tail to be, he saw the constellation of coal-red cigarette ends and went toward it. When he was within its orbit he let his parachute bag drop and asked for a light. Someone flicked the head of a match with a thumbnail and extended it cupped between sheltering hands. Inclining his head to the flare, he recognized Dusak and grinned. "Hi-yu," he said.

"This is Lt. Helman," Dusak announced. "He's the navigator."

"Hi," Win said and then listened carefully to the murmur of his greeting being returned. It was too dark to make out any of their faces and he tried to gauge his reception by ear alone. But the murmur told him nothing. "Is the Mickey man here yet?" he asked.

"Over here."

Win turned to the voice. "That you, Fitts?"

"Yes." It was almost a sigh. "Who'd you expect?"

"I didn't know. You didn't say anything at briefing."

"Fitts is unhappy," Dusak said. "He hates to fly at night."

This got a laugh.

"Well, he better not hate it too much," Win said. "He's going to have to be doing most of the navigating. I ain't been up at night since we left the States."

"We'll get along," Dusak said. "You been up to Munich before, haven't you?"

"Yeah, a couple of times."

"How is it?"

"Well"—he chose his words with care—"it's rough, but there's a lot worse. All alone like this we ought to be able to get in and out before they know it."

The shadowy circle was silent. Win wondered if he had sounded too smug. Far across the field an engine coughed, coming to life. Two other planes from the group, one from each of the other squadrons, were flying the mission.

Dusak sighed. "We better be getting started too," he said. "You want to say anything else?"

Again the silence, and this time Win could feel the tension. "You mean me?" he asked.

"Sure. This is our first one, you know. We figured with your experience you could give us a few tips."

"Well, you guys know a hell of a lot more about this night stuff than I do after all that training," Win said slowly. "All I know is keep your eyes open, keep the turrets turning every minute, don't let yourself get excited so you make bad mistakes. That's all it takes"—he laughed—"that and for the engines to keep on turning."

"We can do that," Dusak said, and his voice was lighter. "Well, let's get started."

The crew followed him as he moved toward the plane. Win remained where he was. He sat down on his bag to finish his cigarette. He felt good about the mission, keyed up, yet relaxed at the same time. And unafraid. Ever since he had made his decision to fly the thought of action had been like a tonic. He took a long last drag from the cigarette and then dropped it. It sputtered in the mud and went out.

"You ought to run for election," a voice said from behind him. "You're getting to be one hell of a speechmaker."

He spun around. It was Milbank. Chic and Macchione were there too.

"Oh, it weren't really rough," Chic drawled. "Why, us old-timers kin remember back in——"

Macchione laughed softly. "They're just jealous," he said.

Behind them the putt-putt rattled and a starter whined, built, then was lost in the crescendo of engine roar. Its slip stream buffeted them with a shower of mud.

"What're you talking about, you crazy bastards?" Win yelled. "What the hell are you doing here?"

"Because we're crazy," they mocked him. "Crazy. We caught it from you, speechmaker."

"Listen——"

The second engine kicked over, joining the first in raucous diphthong, obliterating the words in a flood of sound.

"Listen!" Win brought his voice up over the roar. "This is the way to do it, you hear? Every guy with the crew he flies with——"

They nodded, grinning yet solemn.

"That's why we're here," Milbank bawled.

The third engine started and the slip stream became a gale. "I got to go now!"

Chic snatched the parachute bag from his hand and raced for the plane. Win ran after him and the others followed. Beneath the wing he was the center of their circle. They gripped him hard by the arms.

"*Be careful!*" Milbank screamed. "*We'll see you in the morning!*"

Win nodded. He bent down and ducked into the bomb bay.

Motion without a point of reference lost its significance and time seemed denatured, standing still. As they climbed steadily into the utter darkness of the north, the limits of their world became mist and the bomber a platform suspended between the earthbound bottom and topmost arch of the cloud mass. Sitting at his table in the nose of the plane, all of his alertness focused on the green-glowing luminescence of the instrument faces, it seemed to Win that they were deep in an abyss. The rolling lurch of the B-24 as it breasted its way upward through the currents of turbulence obscured within each ascending layer of cloud was somehow subterranean in its blind rhythm. But as they gained height, unimpeded by formation with others, their progress continuing, the unending vibration of the engines lulled them, their senses adjusted to the night world, and its very opaqueness became security.

"Now hear this!" Dusak sang over the interphone. "The call sign of this mission is ball game—ball game. Take me out to the ball game—— Sonofa*bitch!*"

"Something the matter, Rudy?"

"My fiddle. On Friday I'm supposed to play Brahms's *Lullaby* all the way through for the first time. The professor'll blow his wig."

"Why?"

"Because I can't practice. The goddamned rain broke all the strings."

"Well that's just too bad. Will teacher——"

"Oh, cut it out, for Christ's sake," and the voice identified itself. "Mickey to navigator. What's your E.T.A. for landfall?"

Shielding the head of the searchlight with his palm, Win flicked it on and looked at his flight plan. "0140," he said. "In about twelve minutes."

"Well, I can see it now."

"How far?"

"About twenty-five miles."

"Then we're early. Our ground speed must be up around 220. Can you see Venice?"

"Not yet."

"Well, keep watching. I want to be sure we're not too far

right of it. Udine's down there." Win looked at the compass.
"Come on, Dusak, get your head out. The heading's 325."

"Yes, sir. Yes, sir."

"No kidding now, we'll be crossing the coast in a couple of
minutes. From then on in it's for keeps."

"Right," Dusak said. "No more."

Win smiled to himself. "Navigator to Mickey," he called.
"Can you give me a fix on Venice when we hit the coast? A
speed line on the coast and how many miles right."

"It's coming up."

Win shielded the flashlight and flicked it on again, waiting.
They're going to be all right, he thought; they're going to be
fine. Maybe not so good as the old crew, but good enough. And
this was the way to do it. He was sure now. The luxury of the
tested and toughened and efficient unit had been taken from
him, but this might turn out even better. By God, it had to. He
and Milbank and Chic and Macchione, each one in the new
crew he was assigned to. That way it would be spread over
four crews—maybe in time over the whole squadron. Just give
us time, he thought, and we'll have them all on our side. And
then he thought of Macy. We're not running now, he whispered, we're fighting . . .

"Mickey to navigator, you're over it. Seventeen miles right
of Venice."

"Right," Win said. "Thanks."

Now he began working in earnest, and as always when he
was really concentrated, working swiftly and well, his mind
ranged out over several levels. As he figured an accurate ground
speed and rechecked his metro data, he was seeing the terri-
tory beneath them: the beach above Venice, the coast line flat
with the flatness stretching inland maybe thirty miles, the rise
coming suddenly with the mouths of the two rivers cut into it,
and then the Alps looming abrupt and away in unending ser-
ration. He looked at the altimeter; they were at 24,000. The
compass needle was steady on 325.

"Navigator to pilot," he called into the interphone. "Give me five degrees right. We got forty-three minutes to target."

He doused the flashlight and leaned back, relaxing. The bombardier came crawling into the nose compartment and Win watched his dark bulk going forward. Moments later the faint shaded gleam of light showed and Win saw him pull his oxygen hose from the walkaround bottle and plug it into the main outlet. The light didn't reach back to the navigation table but it gave Win a feeling of warmth to be able to look up and see the man bent over his sight.

"I got Udine," Fitts's voice came through the interphone. "You need another fix?"

"No, I'm set. Just so we stay away from it."

"It's a good thirty miles over."

"Swell." He thought of the big fighter base at Udine, the German pilots sleeping, secure in the bad weather that prevented the bomber formations from coming over. Well, you got a surprise coming, he thought; maybe one of these nights we can come over for you.

He leaned forward into the tiny circle of light around the bombardier and looked at his watch. It had taken them five minutes to transverse the coastal plain. He turned back to his table, shielded and lit the flashlight, and went to work. Ahead of them and about fifteen miles to the left of course lay Innsbruck. He measured the distance with his dividers. It came to eighty-six miles. He put the figure on his computer, meshing it with the ground speed. Twenty-three minutes more.

"Navigator to Mickey," he called. "Listen, let's get a fix on Innsbruck and we'll use it as the I.P. We ought to reach it in a little over twenty minutes."

"O.K.," Fitts said.

"Navigator to bombardier——"

There was no answer. Win leaned forward and tapped the man on the back. The helmeted, goggled, oxygen-mask-covered face turned to him. Win motioned toward his interphone cable. The head nodded and then there was the click of a completed connection.

"What's up?" the voice asked.

"We're coming up on the I.P. in twenty minutes," Win said. "I'll give you a corrected wind and heading then."

"That'll be fine. Thanks."

"Dusak," Win called. Again there was no answer. He clicked the interphone switch. "Dusak, for Christ's sake, wake up."

"I'll get him," a new voice said. "I think he's on Command."

"Yeah," Dusak answered. He was excited. "What's the matter?"

"Where the hell you been?"

"Something's up, I'm not sure. There's some guys on Command that——"

"I don't care!" Win cut him off. "We'll be coming up on the I.P. soon. You better stay the hell on interphone."

"O.K., O.K., only——"

"Jesus——"

"What's the matter now? Who's that?"

"Nose gunner, sir. I think we're coming out of it."

"Out of what?"

"The clouds. My God, look!"

Win went down to the deck and crawled forward. He let himself down on his belly beside the sight and looked out through the bombardier's slanting window. Below him was a transparent curtain of mist, and then it was gone and he saw the Alps gleaming with new snow. Like a Christmas card, like a travelogue; gleaming sharp-etched in the moonlight.

He heaved himself up. Mounting the ammunition boxes, he looked out through the astrodome. Above him there were a million stars and a serene quarter of moon. Ahead, as far as he could see, the clearness stretched unbroken, cloudless, without a shred of cover.

"Dusak," he called.

No answer.

"Dusak, you sonofabitch——" Win controlled himself with difficulty. "Someone get him on interphone."

"Here I am. That's what I been tryin' to tell you. There was a guy ahead of us from one of the other groups and I heard him sayin' he ain't going to no ball game tonight."

"He turn back?"

"Yeah, it must've been almost ten minutes ago now." The fear in Dusak's voice came naked through the phones. "What're we going to do?"

"Take it easy!" Win roared, furious at them and at himself, thinking, Green goddamned cripples, first-mission bastards. "Let's try not to blow up at the first thing that comes along."

"Sure, O.K., but——"

"You want to go back?"

"Don't you?"

"You're the airplane commander, goddammit. You want a heading back I'll give you one."

"Well, it's clear all the way ahead," Dusak said defensively. "Everybody else is turning back."

Win said nothing and the interphone remained quiet. He wanted desperately to go on. It seemed to him that his whole new course of action was hanging in the balance, that it would be reduced to a mockery if they aborted the mission. Then the old doubts welled up in him. *To hell with it,* he thought; the whole thing's crazy anyway. I should have agreed with Macchione and Chic and Milbank in the first place and refused to fly. It's great making speeches on the ground, but when it comes to doing it . . .

"I don't know, but maybe it's a good idea to keep on just because everybody's turning back," a new voice was saying and Win was shocked out of his thoughts by its familiarity. Its solemn intonation sounded just like Macchione. "They won't be expecting nobody if it's clear. And at least we'll be able to see where we're going."

"Very funny," Dusak said bitterly. "Now you can shut up and tend to keeping that turret moving."

"Maybe Pete's got something, Rudy." It sounded like the bombardier. "What d'you think?"

"I don't know, goddammit! What d'you think, Win?"

"Well——"

"Come on, for Christ's sake!"

"Well, I think we can keep going for a while. We got plenty of time to turn back if we decide to."

"How much time?"

"We'll see. Why don't you get back on Command and see what they're saying."

"O.K., five more minutes. You time it."

The interphone clicked into silence. The nose compartment was flooded with the milky radiance of moonlight, so bright that Win could see his charts and log plainly. He looked over his shoulder. The doors of the nose turret were moving as the turret revolved. The bombardier was motionless in silhouette, crouched over the bombsight.

"I'm getting Innsbruck," came Fitts's even voice. "You want me to try for a bearing?"

"Not yet. Just be sure we're right of it."

"O.K."

The silence was restored and then Dusak's voice was piercing it like a lament: "Christ Almighty, the guys back of us are getting hit! They've sent up 109s, not even night fighters, it's so clear! It sounds like a massacre——"

"Then that settles it," Win cut in. "We turn back now and they'll get us too. This way we'll go on in, drop our bombs, and come home 'way the hell and gone through Yugoslavia. By then those bastards'll be back on the ground."

"You think it'll work?"

"Sure, why not? We'll make it work."

"He's right." Win recognized the bombardier's voice. "They said the only fighters are at Udine."

"By God, that's right!" Dusak's voice was gathering confidence. "We'll do it! Everybody keep their eyes open! I want those turrets turning every second!"

Win let the exhilaration sweep over him. They were all right! They were a crew, and he was part of it! He turned eagerly back to his work. Now the silence of the interphone was reassuring and it held until Fitts announced Innsbruck lying off the left wing. Win altered course slightly, made his final calculations, and after giving the bombardier his data, crawled forward so they could help each other on with their flak suits.

When he was crouched beside the kneeling bombardier, Win dragged an apron out from behind the ammunition boxes and fitted it across the man's head. He settled it deftly across the shoulders and tightened the side straps. The process was automatic, he had done it so many times before, yet this time it had an emotional content, a new significance, a kind of joint arming. He tested the side straps again and then knelt for a suit to be put on him. When the weight of canvas-covered steel was on his own shoulder, snugged against his chest as his straps were tightened, he reached out and put his hand on the bombardier's shoulder. The man's head, concealed in helmet and oxygen mask, turned toward him. Win nodded, and it seemed that the bombardier understood, bobbing his head happily in answer. He extended a gloved hand and Win gripped it, held it, and then turned to crawl back to his worktable.

Beneath them the Alps dipped gradually away to the Bavarian plain. Time flowed smoothly. The bomber vibrated to the engines' pulse of power. Every minute brought them closer to the outskirts of the city and the huge marshaling yard.

"Flak!" someone yelled. "There's flak!"

"What did you expect, roses?" another answered calmly.

Then the bombardier and the Mickey man began their correspondence of abrupt, technical phrases, co-ordinating the bombsight with readings of the radar scope.

And suddenly the first searchlight caught them, held them, and all was brightness, a blinding blue-whiteness, with the bomber rearing in reflex.

"Hold your heading!" Win roared. "You want to throw those bombs all over hell?"

Now time stood still. Win had stopped breathing, his eyes closed, blind in the burning incandescence. . . .

"O.K.," the bombardier intoned. "It's on its way . . . there they go . . . *bombsawaybombsaway——*"

"*Rally off right to ninety degrees!*" Win roared.

And they were on the border of sheltering darkness, twisting frantically away from the glare, out of it, and then Win felt it hit, smashing him, tearing into him. He screamed, but it was inside him, inside merged with the fire, and the whole world was fire and then darkness, utter blackness, and he felt his last frightful unending falling.

The vigil began a little after dawn. Hours before the rest of the squadron was awake, the engineer and the two gunners left their tent and walked down to the perimeter strip, looking over their shoulders to the north. In the empty revetment they squatted on their haunches and waited. As the sun gained height, the last mist left over from the storm turned pink and then was burned away, leaving the sky a bright washed blue. The ground crew of the awaited bomber arrived soon after, and when they saw the engineer and the two gunners pacing slowly back and forth, they too were silent and looked anxiously into the north. As the day matured and the sun climbed toward the vertical, the first of the men from the squadron began drifting down to the still empty revetment. Some of them went away again after a little while, but more remained. When the bombardier and pilot returned from a late breakfast, they hesitated before the tent, looking first to the north and then down to the flight line. The bombardier went into the tent, but the pilot turned and walked down to the revetment, where he stood with the others watching the north. Then he went away. An hour after noon the operations officer drove out to the revetment in his jeep. He spoke briefly to the waiting men and then drove away. The men looked a last time to the north before they began drifting back toward the squadron area. As they went some of them walked with the engineer and the two gunners, and although they were not the largest group, they were a goodly number.